OPERA

Kiára Árgenta

OPENING CHAPTER

First Printing, 2016

ISBN 10: 1-904958-65-6
ISBN 13: 978-1-904958-65-9

published by

Opening Chapter
Cardiff, Wales

www.openingchapter.com

Cover photo by Noel Dacey

Kiára Árgenta

Kiára Árgenta grew up in Paris before moving to Wales where she studied Russian at university. She worked as a journalist before leaving to live in Spain and then Hungary. She currently lives in Budapest and is a full-time writer.

THE ICE QUEEN

I am Natalija.

Opera star, glamour girl of the European stage, half Hungarian, quarter Welsh and the rest a turbulent blend of Icelandic and Sicilian. I am dangerous, ruthless and greedy, completely vain and a total diva. You should hate me and I would be disappointed if you didn't. I don't need to be liked. I would sooner be centre stage and hated than standing in the wings, quiet and shy. I don't need anyone and I don't need anyone's approval. I only need success. I only need my audience. They don't know me. They only see what I give them, and I give them beauty and talent and absolute devotion to my craft. They have come here to see something wonderful and to escape out of their ordinary lives and into a world of enchantment and I am responsible for providing that.

I'd always wanted success, ever since I could remember. I'd long given up the ice skating dream I had wanted for myself as a child. Despite giving everything to skating since I could walk and going on to win the National Junior Hungarian Figure Skating Championships at 13, then again the following year and then the silver medal in the Junior Europeans, I peaked too soon.

My coach was pushing me to get to senior level by the time I was 15 and I was training a triple Axel jump which I kept falling and falling on, until one day I took off next to the crash barrier and hit it head first on the way down. I ended up unconscious for 2 days. When I woke up in hospital, my father told me enough was enough, I could have been more seriously injured, I could have hit the ice with my head. I was so driven I would skate and skate and not stop until I was exhausted. It was not going to end well if I kept pushing myself to such extremes to win my ultimate goal – Olympic gold.

I was too broken to argue. My school work was suffering and I felt I hadn't any more to give to this sport; I had begun to resent it taking 30 hours a week out of my life. I hated it so much at times, and I was only driven on by the thought of winning gold, but I knew how much harder I had to work, how much more it would take, how I was getting injury after injury and now a serious one which had given me a kind of stage fright. It is hard to keep getting up from a sport which when you fall, can be so dangerous. The ice is lethal and performing a high speed jump could be literally death-defying. I lost some memory after the accident and missed 2 months of school and I knew I could not get back on the ice again. I became deeply religious and as I recuperated I would visit the cathedral every day even though my parents had not brought me up to believe in God. It wasn't that they didn't believe, they were against organised religion. So I would go alone, say my prayers and leave. I took my mother's sapphire necklace from the jewellery box which made my stepmother mad. I needed something to bring me luck and this would help.

"How come she gets to wear it and I don't? They are real sapphires," Lilla had demanded over dinner. She was jealous of everything I did and everything I got, every word of praise from my father, István.

"Lilla, it is hers. It belonged to her mother. I gave you enough jewellery," István had sighed not looking up from his plate. He was used to Lilla's constant greed and materialism, forever wanting designer clothes and diamonds, and she already had 100 pairs of Italian leather shoes. She demanded and he gave in. As long as Lilla was happy, nothing else mattered.

She'd sat there with diamonds round her throat demanding a sapphire necklace as if the world would end. She'd glared at me with hatred as her stones sparkled. She was more like a hateful big sister than a mother.

István was still handsome, but he looked tired. His hair was still jet black, his face younger than his 56 years but he was ageing due to working so hard; there were dark circles under his eyes and he always looked unhappy. He had once loved his work, but I sensed he liked it less and less and was continuing to work a punishing schedule to fund this spoilt woman's extravagant lifestyle. She had never returned to university, never bettered herself and still only worked part-time as a dental receptionist. She wasn't stupid. She was just greedy and lazy and spoilt. It didn't help that my father had met her when she was 17 years old and given her everything, as if to buy her happiness. If she was gentle and sweet then, by the time she was even 21 years old she was a princess, or so she thought.

I looked at her beautiful but bitter face and wondered how I had loved her once and when I stopped.

She was 28 years younger than my father. Her constant excuse for not working was to take care of the children and her so called poor health; liver damage due to her taking an overdose as a teenager. She didn't seem to suffer but it was her constant excuse for anything she didn't want to do. She was healthy but never drank alcohol, as she was warned it could trigger total liver failure. And as for taking care of the children, she never took care of me; or Levente, nine years old and a sweet loving boy, a copy of István, all dark curls and eyes and her own son but she didn't do much. He was just for show, a pretty doll to dress up and show off to the world, for eating out in restaurants or going to the

Opera. Lilla loved her showcase family but once back home she hardly bothered to even talk to me. She would get out Levente's toys in fake enthusiasm but after 10 minutes, she would be curled up on the sofa reading a glamour magazine while he sat alone with his dinosaurs or building sets. I would take over; he was sweet. She didn't deserve sweetness. He should have been wild and demanding too, but it just wasn't in his nature. He would sit at her feet with puppyish devotion, never complaining. It always helped her that she was beautiful. It got her everything she wanted in life. Levente would brush her hair as if she was a goddamn queen, gazing adoringly at her. I always wondered if he would suddenly change, reach age 14 and start smoking, drinking and rebelling and throwing his dinner at the wall but he never did. He remained the good boy he always was, studying hard at school and dutiful at home. I wouldn't have wanted him any other way, to be honest. However much I hated men at times during my career, my younger brother was not included in that figure. He remained as gentle and as thoughtful with a kind heart for all of us.

Lazy bitch Lilla. She had even insisted on moving us from our big II district apartment to a sprawling house in the XII because 'that is where everyone super rich in this city lives'.

We didn't need to move, we didn't need the extra space. But she got what she wanted. None of us wanted to leave our apartment except her. She was a ruthless social climber and wanted to be at the epicentre of wealth to feel even better. There were people in this city with nothing, 10,000 or more homeless on the streets. Yet Lilla wanted bigger and better every time.

The first day in our new house with its panorama overlooking the city she breathed, "All this is mine."

Then she turned to me with a look of satisfaction. *Mine, not ours. Mine.*

As I got older, she began to hate me more, she was jealous. My beauty which was acceptable as a child and enhanced her status when we were out together as a family detracted from the attention people paid her. In restaurants, in the Opera, I would hear tourists say, *Look at that beautiful girl, she is stunning.*

They meant me at 15, 16, 17 years old, not Lilla.

My brother was gorgeous too, but he was not a threat. He was Lilla's showcase boy, a toy to dress up and flaunt to the world. It helped that she was his mother whereas she was not mine. She could hate me for being beautiful and when I became successful, she would hate me even more. She constantly laughed at my dreams of success, saying I hadn't got it. Ice skating was over and I would never be a success at anything. It made me even more driven. What had she achieved in her life? Nothing. And that was the problem because she could have done and she just resented everyone else who was talented and hard-working. She could have been something and she resented everyone else's success in a way that only the bitter and lazy people who squander their talents can.

But I loved our visits to the Opera House, Lilla or no Lilla. When I first began going my ice-skating career had just ended and I needed something new to focus on. I longed to do what those opera singers did. I knew I had a good voice, the drive, the ability to learn languages. And I knew I could do it. I just knew. I had found something else to become obsessed with, something I could work towards and I needed that so badly in my life. I could be one of those divas on stage, reaching out for the chandelier with their powerful voices in their elegant world. We would all dress up as a family and sit in the best box in the house. Lilla just wanted to be seen, standing posing in her designer frocks with her handsome husband and beautiful children, although her nails would dig into me in rage whenever she heard or saw someone admire me, and only me. She was vain, she needed attention all the time from everyone and I was upstaging her beauty, making her insecure. When she had married my father she was only 18 and had been admired and adored by many people. I wanted to be noticed too but I wanted it in a different way. I wanted to be on that stage, singing for my life and soul.

Carmen was my first opera as a teenager. Levente had loved it too despite being so young. He was so taken by the beautiful leading mezzo that he named an exotic fish he got as a present after the opera. But the next day, as if by some strange kind of omen, the fish was floating on its side in its tank. I laughed when he asked me, "Is Carmen sleeping?"

He was distraught. I told him, *What did he expect, Carmen dies so would the fish.*

My stepmother said I was turning into a little bitch, laughing at my brother. I was cruel.

I wonder where I learned that, I thought. I hated her so much by then.

But to make it up to Levente who seemed so upset and didn't deserve me to laugh at him, I found the little plastic coffins which had held candy skeletons; they were a gift from Mexico from one of my father's Spanish dental patients. They were part of the *Day of the Dead* celebrations where they sold sugar skulls and candy bones and bread of the dead. The patient knew my father had children and had brought some candies especially for us. In Hungary all we did was go to cemeteries on November 1st and be miserable. Mexico sounded so enchanting. My mother had been there and danced in the streets with orange flowers in her hair. There was a photo of her laughing and everyone dressed up and having a party in the sunny streets. I wanted to go. It was hard to believe, seeing her so happy and carefree in the photo that she suffered such sadness in her life.

Such sadness that she chose to end it all.

We placed the fish in one of the plastic coffins and buried it in the garden with a tiny crucifix but Levente insisted on digging it up a few months later on the *Day of the Dead*, or *Mindenszentek*. He was convinced Carmen would be alive, brought back to earth on the day when the skin between the worlds was the thinnest.

I told him we should not disturb the dead. In Mexico they sit on the grave and share stories and give sweets. Wouldn't this be better? But the garden in November was damp and gloomy and Levente was set on digging up Carmen.

Inside the plastic coffin was nothing but a thin bone and a bit of liquid.

"We should never have dug it up, Natalija," he said. "Now we are cursed forever, it is like digging someone out of their grave."

"Don't be stupid," I told him as I placed the tiny coffin back into its earth and covered it over again. "We didn't know. Anyway I told you we shouldn't do it. You didn't listen."

But it put a morbid feeling into both of us. Is that what happens when we die? All that is left is a tiny bone and some liquid? Strange that the memory of that day was so strong for years. We had driven in silence to my mother's grave in Pécs an hour later, thinking about death – me, Levente and my father. Lilla would go to the cemetery in Budapest with her mother to lay flowers for her own father who had also ended his life in one of the most violent ways possible. Levente never wanted to go with her. He always wanted to travel to Pécs even though he had no blood ties with my mother and never knew her. Lilla never insisted he go with her instead. Maybe she didn't really care, I never knew the real reason. I guess Pécs was more of a day out, especially if the weather was kind. He always got an ice cream from one of the pretty Mediterranean type ice cream parlours in the Italianate city in the south of Hungary.

If that is what we really turned into after we died, a thin bone and just liquid, it made me more determined than ever to be a star. I had to succeed in this world because what was there beyond it? As a medical man, my father never really acknowledged his beliefs about religion or an afterlife but I knew he had them. He must have believed my mother was in some kind of special place. He would sit and look at her photos on the living room wall. There she was, beautiful and sad. The photos of Lilla next to her showed what looked like a younger version of my mother, except on closer inspection, there was no haunted look in the eyes, more of an emptiness about her in her beautiful white wedding dress at 18. An ice maiden. Lilla did not like these photos of my mother next to hers but it was the one thing she never questioned my father about. I guess she knew it was one argument she would never win. He would never take them down. She had to be content to share the limelight with someone long dead.

That was why she was there in the first place and she knew that.

She was the image of my mother. Especially as she got older and was approaching the age my mother was when she died.

I didn't know what lay beyond our lives on earth but I was not going to waste it; I would live my life hard and fast. I would live like today was my last mortal day because I had to leave a mark on this world. I had to become someone. I shunned everyone; I dropped the few friends I had because my obsession now turned to the world of Opera, no one else existed apart from those people who inhabited it.

At that time, Opera seemed so glamorous, a place of opulence and beauty and bouquets of roses for the leading singers. I never knew that once inside the glass bubble staring out at the blackness of the auditorium how ugly it was, how we lived in a world built on nepotism and lies and sore throats and endless fighting over roles. I never knew how much it would take from me, how much pressure I would be under. I saw myself as a diva, a star who would adore the attention but with it came such sacrifices, more than I ever thought possible. I have sacrificed every relationship, every friendship I ever had on the altar of my ambition.

DRIVEN

I am singing my soul out. Singing my soul for the role; I would sell it to the Devil if I could, like Faust, with no thought for the consequences. I always preferred the bad guys in Opera, they seem to have more fun. To hell with the consequences. Why anyone feels guilty about that I don't know and I don't care if I am heading towards Hell just as long as I get what I want. When I first saw *Faust* aged 15, I was in love with the baritone who performed as Méphistophélès. I insisted on going to stage door to meet him afterwards. Lilla was not happy, she said I shouldn't bother the singers. But being beautiful helped. And by 15 I was beautiful and vain. I could do anything. I asked the stage door men nicely could I wait; I had to speak to this dazzling singer. They looked at me in my red glamour dress and high heels and said, *Of course.*

I told this man who was about 40 or so, that he was the best performer I ever saw on stage. He was magnificent. I told him that I was planning to train as an opera singer too. He looked less dazzling although still handsome in the flesh; the stage makes everyone larger than life, more beautiful and powerful than ordinary humans.

He looked at me as I spoke, admiring my appearance, my dress, not at all in a rush to leave, and handed me his card, saying maybe we could meet, maybe he could help me with my career.

I was thrilled. I was so convinced this was the ticket and I didn't know he just wanted to seduce me, that he cared nothing about my ambitions. He thought I was 18 years old at least. I didn't tell my family waiting impatiently at the front of the building. I just said I had congratulated Viktor and that he was very nice and full of gratitude. Lilla looked at me critically. She knew by my glow that there was more to it than that.

"And that's it?" she said to me in the taxi in a quiet voice so my father in the front seat wouldn't hear her.

"Of course," I said dismissively. "What else would there be?"

"Liar," said Lilla her eyes looking straight into mine. "I know what you're up to. Little slut."

I looked out of the window avoiding her harsh gaze. She knew all those games. She had played them too, seducing and sleeping her way to the life she wanted. But I didn't think I was like that. I would do what it took but I never considered anything other than charm and hard work.

When I finally sit down for dinner with this Viktor, in some expensive restaurant he seems less keen to get to the reason I am there; my career. He evades many questions I have, but I think, *Well there is still time to talk. I am young, the world will not end tomorrow.* He takes me home a few times and finds out the third morning I stay there when he sees my ID card in my bag that I am only 15 years old. He screams I am jail bait, he thought I was 18 or 19. I have to leave. Now.

I am telling him, *Viktor, it doesn't matter, I won't say anything.*

I stole your virginity, or maybe I didn't, maybe you are a slut but whatever, Natalija, you have to leave right now and don't dare tell anyone about this.

He stuffs me in a taxi and I still have unanswered opera questions. I am hurt by the accusations that I am a slut. He is nasty, a real Méphistophélès enchanting me into his world and then taking what he wanted but I guess the best of us really do have aspects of the characters within us. This is how I became so successful later; that is when you play the role to the maximum, when you really feel the character is living within you; this is when you turn a performance into something magical. I don't know this at the time, it is something I will realise later.

I have also told my father I am at my friend, Elvira's house. He bought it the first couple of times but this time for some reason he was either suspicious or needed to talk to me and he has called Elvira and found out I lied. Not just once but three times.

I am not ashamed to tell him and Lilla where I was and who I was with and he goes mad saying he is disgusted that I am with a man old enough to be my father, cheapening myself like that when I have beauty and intelligence one hundred times more than most girls my age.

Lilla says, "Sleeping your way to the top will backfire on you. You haven't got what it takes to make it on your own anyway. No wonder you tried."

"Bitch," I say. "You're a fine one to say that!"

"Don't you dare talk to me like that, you little tart!" she shouts at me.

"Natalija, go to your room and stay there, you don't speak to your mother like that!" orders my father.

"She's not my mother!" I scream and throw the jug of orange juice over her. "My mother is worth a thousand of her and you know it!"

Lilla's claws are at my hair and pulling me to the ground and I grab at her blouse and tear it and put a claw mark across her face as we cat fight like schoolgirls until my father hauls us up, one in each strong arm, and pushes me out of the kitchen.

"You are not going out alone again, ever!" he shouts. "You are not to be trusted."

Lilla's eyes are black with rage as he holds her arms to stop her running at me again. She is still a girl herself. She would fight me like a girl.

I hate her so much it hurts. I do not care about Viktor. So what, I can find another. I had no heart to give him. Many girls my age would be devastated but I am more mad he didn't do as he said and help me with my career.

I have a whole day of arguments and lectures and I am grounded. Damn Méphistophélès. And I hate Lilla, I really hate her. My father says he is disappointed in us both. We both behaved badly.

When I eventually join The Royal Hungarian Opera, Viktor has moved to Germany permanently.

So what.

So by the time I am 24 years old I am starting to be noticed, but I am playing small roles in operas across Europe, scratching out a living. My best experience had been in London in spring, playing a minor mezzo role, aged 23 and fresh from opera training in Italy, I was given the role of Rosette in Massenet's *Manon*. True, I hated London; I had panic attacks on the metro every day, but absorbed in the opera, I could see my future stretching out and everything I wanted.

I audition for The Royal Hungarian Opera and am told I am too young; talented but too young. Come back next year, or in two years.

Next year? Damn them because I am ready now. I am so angry. I should be happy that they think I have what it takes, should be happy they truly think I have a great talent. But it is not enough. I need success. I need it like crack cocaine. I am in a rush, can't they see that?

I have also played the role of Mercédès in my longed for

Carmen in Prague. I hesitated when it was offered to me. I was 23 and would be just turned 24 when the opera opened in January. But to turn down this role would be stupid. I want Carmen, but Mercédès is a good supporting role; a strong gypsy girl, one of Carmen's buddies. And maybe in rehearsals I will learn more about the opera, being so absorbed in it. Of course I am frenzied and jealous. The company are nice but the digs are awful; stuck out on some post communist hellhole estate which could be anywhere in Eastern Europe. Carmen herself is not so beautiful. She is not beautiful like me but I hear the control she has over her voice. The control which comes with experience as she holds those notes and has the power in her voice to be heard over the chorus and the orchestra. But it doesn't stop me hating her. She is slightly chunky and I do not think she is physically right for this. I try to bite my jealousy and learn as much as I can, sleeping with the sheets of Bizet's music clutched in my hands in the depressing apartment. I live the opera, through rehearsals and into performances and even though I am Mercédès, I am already living the role of Carmen. I am absorbing everything I can in my time here before I get a taxi back to the gloomy apartment with its broken fridge and filthy balcony and someone has scrawled in English ***Welcome to Hell!*** on the main doors of our crumbly Soviet block which looks a bit like a crack den. I am not used to this. I have seen plenty of lousy digs but I think the ones I have in Prague are the most dismal because I am not used to it. Italy and Spain all have dark streets and gloomy apartments but I am not used to identikit communist housing estates as in Budapest they are far out of the city, flung well into the outskirts. Lilla herself grew up in one of these. No wonder she did all she could to get out at 17.

I sing in concerts all around Hungary that Summer, after Prague and London. I am not so comfortable in concerts as I cannot lose myself like I do on the opera stage. But I need to take anything to be noticed now and London is very prestigious and they have invited me back for *Manon* at the start of the opera season in September. Then in October I am back to Prague for Mercédès in *Carmen.* This time I book my own digs, staying somewhere too expensive in the centre near the Opera but I cannot bear to go through that grim apartment experience again.

My chance for Carmen proper comes by chance almost a year after I am first involved in the opera. It is December and 2 days after my 25th birthday and I have the role of Carmen in Bratislava; my first leading lady. I auditioned in April and I was offered a chorus role, not even Mercédès as I was still only 24 and what everyone saw as too young to take a major lead, same as Budapest. I refused as I had played Mercédès in Prague and that was not enough so I will not play chorus. Not now, not ever. I would go crazy. It turned out the mezzo who was set to play Carmen dropped out and in September when I was playing Rosette in *Manon* in London for the second time, Bratislava offered me the lead. I am young, too young to play solo roles in big opera houses but Bratislava gave me the opening I needed.

The part is mine. And now I am singing like I own it. Over 9 performances in December and January I will play my dream role of the careless heartbreaking gypsy girl. I am escaping my life, my real life and beginning to live only for Opera. It is true I had everything I needed materially but our home life had been far from happy when I was growing up, full of strife mainly due to Lilla.

My father is half-crazy and ill with bipolar disorder, my

stepmother is a bitch and my brother is the only one I truly feel close to in my family.

They occasionally attend my operas but I really don't care if they do or not. Sometimes they send me flowers on opening night, sometimes not. I gave up caring a long time ago. I gave up on people and Opera became my world.

I live in the same city as my parents now after Lilla exiled me to university in the South and then I completed my opera training at a prestigious training academy in Italy, but we might as well be on different planets. I have plans though. I have plans to sing for The Royal Hungarian Opera for maybe a few years and then move away to Spain or Italy, preferably La Scala in Milano. I just need more time. I can see it might not be better there, it might just be an illusion but sometimes I feel my home country is so poisonous, that anything would be better than this.

"Why are you so difficult, Natalija?" Lilla asks me. "Your father is ill. You know it; he has bipolar and it is not his fault he behaves like this. You grew up knowing it and you loved him."

We have been arguing over the meal we are eating in my father's house. I rarely visit. It is always such a place of conflict. I am busy anyway and Levente is studying in Germany.

I look at Lilla and tell her direct. "And your tarting around never helped. Don't think I don't remember. Opening your legs for everyone like a whore, taking my mother's place when you had no right to. You wanted out of your poverty and you were a scheming bitch. You always will be a whore. A few diamonds and a house in the XII district doesn't change that, Lilla," I spit the words at her like the Carmen I am.

Lilla slaps me across my face hard.

I slap her back and she holds her face and tells me to get out of the house. 'Our house', she stresses. 'Mine and your father's, not yours'.

My father sits dumbstruck at the kitchen table. He is so whacked out on his medicine, in poor health but still handsome. But he is not the same man. We don't talk as Lilla is always there, stopping me from being close to him like we were. She is so rabidly jealous, she can't allow any women near him. They don't fight like they once did; I remember the screaming. Each time she walked out, I had to pick up the pieces, comfort him as he cried and then see her just walk back in again as if nothing had ever happened. And it broke something deep inside him. And it remained broken and I hate her for that. Maybe there are two sides, maybe he was cruel to her but I remember her cruelty and not his as I would see the consequences in his tears, when I was 4, 5, 6 years old. I never saw her cry.

"Please stop," he whispers. "Please stop fighting." He doesn't get up as he once would and physically prise us apart. He just tells us to stop, he puts his head in his hands and tells us to stop, he is tired. He can't take all this hatred.

She is so jealous that I remember how she came home once to find him brushing my hair when I was 17. Nothing in that. I was sitting on the floor as he sat on the sofa and we were talking and he brushed my hair and I remember my eyes were closed as the soft brush swept through my curls and he talked gently to me and I was so relaxed, so happy to be special to him. I had always called him by his name, István, as did Levente. He wanted to be who he was and not just someone's father, he told me. I was able to talk to him so openly about my worries, about my hope for the future, about the career I planned as an opera singer and he encouraged me. He always told me, *Not to look where you are going, but at where you want to go. Follow that shooting star, Natalija, follow it with your whole soul and you will arrive there. Your mother loved opera, she would be so proud of you.*

The next moment a volcano erupted in the living room in the middle of us and this shooting star talk. I hadn't heard Lilla come back, she must have opened the door then crept along quietly, consumed by murderous and insane jealousy.

She was screaming like a demon and saying, *She knew it, she knew it all along. She knew he would want me when I was old enough, why was I sitting there in a silk dressing gown in ecstasy? Had we already been at it?*

I was snapped out of my relaxation by this woman who was shouting all kinds of foul language at me, calling me a whore and him a monster. I was just dumbstruck.

Why did she even think that? Can't I sit in a dressing gown in front of my own father?

Why would anyone sane even express these sentiments?

István loved me and there was nothing twisted in his love. Only someone seriously sick would believe that.

He was holding her back from flying at me, her nails clawing towards me, those chiselled nails polished the colour of de-oxygenated blood like one of Dracula's brides and her face just as evil; spitting rage, screaming, trying to reach me as István pinned her against the wall, telling her to calm down, to stop, she was losing it. He was angry but didn't hurt her.

"You in your silk dressing gown, you little slut, you seduced that opera singer when you were 15 and God knows who else and how can I even trust you with your own flesh and blood?!" she screamed at me as he dragged her out of the living room and I sat there staring at the carpet wondering what terrible thing I had done.

I had not seduced anyone. The opera singer had seduced me when I was 15 but apart from some lawyer I met some time ago, who also dropped me after a weekend when he found out I was 16 and not 22 there hasn't been anyone else. And my own father??? What was wrong with Lilla?

We had woken Levente up. He had come out of his room, and he was asking who was shouting. *What happened?* His black curls were wild and he was still in his child-like sleep.

I got up, took him gently back to his room and said, *Nothing it was a bad dream, it was something on the television.* He didn't see Lilla, since István had dragged her into their bedroom away from the crime scene. I heard her crying, and his voice low and angry, but too quiet to hear the words.

It was a bad dream for me too.

But after that, it was clear I was not going to be at university in Budapest. Lilla wanted me out of the house. The arguments went on and on behind closed doors and I ended up in university in Pécs, 3 hours away, where my father had once lived with my mother and he had links to find me an apartment there. I think Lilla was afraid of me even being in the same city.

I was sad in this pretty Mediterranean type city in the south. My mother's grave was there. I used to go to visit it a lot, tracing the name Kiára on the beautiful stone. She was so young to die. Occasionally on holidays and the anniversary of her death, István would visit me but he was never alone. The claws of Lilla would always be hanging on his arm. She was full of malice, "Italian degree, Natalija? What are you going to do with that? Move to Italy? And your opera singing, you really think you can make it in that competitive world?"

I didn't think – I knew. I always knew I had what it took. Even if it took everything from me.

But this was not the István I had grown up with. He always called the shots. He was the master. He always had been but Lilla had broken something in him when I was young, and she had cheated and run away and they had hurt each other but she was the one who was stronger. By the time I was 17, Lilla was Queen and István was her puppet. I was always told to make allowances for Lilla. Her father had committed suicide when she was young, her mother hated her and had refused to even see Levente until he was two years old and even then, only a couple of times a year, on birthdays or holidays. Then Lilla's mother was unpleasant, forever looking at her watch if she visited. She smoked for Hungary and in the few hours she stayed she'd be constantly going outside for the next cigarette. She never spoke to me; she just wasn't interested. I didn't exist. Not that I cared for this rough, ragged woman who was related to my hateful stepmother. It was difficult to see the resemblance apart from the fact they were both cold and selfish; physically they were worlds apart. Lilla would sit on the edge of the sofa, glamorous and gorgeous, her slim body encased in Dolce e Gabbana or Gucci, hair long and loose, every bit of her the Vogue cover girl. Her mother was overweight, lined from poor diet and smoking, in loose old clothes and looking at Levente as if she didn't know what to do or say to him. Mother and daughter had very little to say to each other.

After this confrontation where Lilla has told me to leave the house and we have both slapped the other, I glare at her and she glares at me. I look at her long hair, her beautiful but bitter face, the diamonds around her neck and her designer clothes and I hate her. She is slim, she doesn't get hungry, she doesn't stuff her face full of junk and vomit like me. She is just naturally that way and she is 39 and I am 25. Her life is so perfect. She hardly has to work. She lives off men, first my father and now his pension and soon off her own son, my half-brother Levente who is at university on his way to becoming a successful lawyer in Munich. She makes me sick. Lazy money grabbing bitch.

I may be a bitch, but I work hard at what I do. And I have all the talent I need.

So I am still scratching around for opera roles once I finish at the end of January in Bratislava, giving it all I have got. I follow those shooting stars and I follow them wherever they take me. I have performed in France, Italy, Spain, Czech Republic, Slovakia, Austria and London and provincial theatres in Hungary but I am still waiting for what I really want; The Royal Hungarian Opera. I am pushing myself to opera houses who don't pay on time, some who don't pay at all, some who give me lousy digs, who sideline me in parts when I believe I should have the lead. I am singing in operas I don't like, in German which I hate but I take everything thrown at me. Apart from Bratislava where I play the longed for role of Carmen to great reviews and much praise from the theatre, I am not getting what I want.

And I want and want and want and it just doesn't stop.

TOSCA'S CRUCIFIX

I remember when I had just auditioned for the third year in a row for The Royal Hungarian Opera in Budapest and I knew I had a chance of playing Carmen. I was fresh from already playing the role in Bratislava and I had played Mercédès twice in Prague but I wanted Carmen now in Budapest, where the 1700 seater Opera House plays every day of the year apart from the July and August dark period and is among the best in the world. They liked me at 23 and then the following year at 24, were reluctant to take me on seeing me as young and talented but relatively inexperienced at playing leads. The Royal Hungarian Opera has excelled since I first started going to operas as a teenager and is now known as *La Scala of the East* in the opera world. It has become one of the places everyone wants to perform in. The East still holds mystery, opulence and grandeur for westerners who flock in droves to watch our operas. I want it so badly I don't care who I kick to the ground.

And the directors have seen the write-ups I had from the Bratislava Opera House. They were better than I could have imagined. A critic from Vienna had praised me in his German newspaper as 'hauntingly beautiful, deadly and with a voice which commands the entire universe'. It is over-praising. He writes to excess but for me this is very good. I put the reviews on my opera website which is full of photos of me at my glamorous best. I am in love with myself when I see my own photos.

For the audition I had on the crucifix from *Tosca,* a stolen gift from London. I had watched the opera after my final performance in *Manon* since I had two nights before I flew home to Hungary. Afterwards, I had approached the lead soprano backstage She was a world famous singer in her forties renowned for being a total diva. I had a crush on her; she was an Italian with a mane of swinging jet black hair and huge eyes almost as dark. She was slim and glamorous, like an Italian film star. I had told her she was amazing, I told her my ambitions and instead of waving me away she had invited me to talk to her as she removed her make-up. Being beautiful always helped, and I spoke fluent Italian. And as a mezzo I was no threat to her, besides she was beautiful herself, hugely successful and confident. I tell her as I leave the dressing room I want Tosca's crucifix. I love it. She takes it off immediately and pushes it in my hand. She clasps her hand around mine and smiles. "Go, lovely girl. Go and make the dreams come true. You know you can, so do it."

"I can't," I say looking at the crucifix. "It is kind, but what will you tell the Opera House?"

"Take it," she says folding my hand around it again. "It is yours now and Marina does not take no for an answer. I will say I took it off in the dressing room, and now I can't find it. There we are. Take it for luck. Tosca's crucifix. Please." Her dark eyes look at me seriously. Then she smiles and kisses my face so I can smell her wonderful exotic perfume. She shuts her door and I am left dizzy with her intoxicating presence and holding the silver crucifix studded with diamanté. There is an amethyst in the centre. I go to rub the red lipstick mark off my face, then decide not to. She has branded me. I am hers, if only for a moment. I place the crucifix in my bag and leave. I almost want to knock on her door again and ask her to join me for dinner, though I know I most likely wouldn't eat. I would just toy with a starter and hope she would take me home. But I don't want to make an idiot of myself. It is just a crush after all, it will pass just like all the others. I don't want to ruin it.

And to ask for more after she has blessed me with Tosca's crucifix seems ungrateful and greedy.

So I am wearing it that day on the stage of The Royal Hungarian Opera when I audition. One director even asks me is it from *Tosca.* I hope he doesn't know it is stolen property.

I smile and say, a friend played Tosca in Italy and she finished her performances and left the country forgetting she was still wearing it round her neck. She gave it to me as a gift. The Opera House had told her not to worry, they didn't need it back. I don't say it is from London as I actually think it is a real amethyst and I do not want to get the lovely soprano into trouble in any way.

"It's very you," says one of the directors. "But you are a Carmen, not a Tosca. You smoulder and electrify and there is a touch of bad girl there. Tosca is pure; a demanding arrogant diva but pure and religious with a soft heart. You look like you came from the underworld and will drag everyone back down there with you. I like it, I think you have such an intense stage presence that everyone watching you will be hypnotised. I think you really don't even need to act so much, you are just you and that is enough. And so young as well but are you up to the big challenges with our company?"

"Yes," I say with absolute conviction. I am.

I smile. I sense I have won him over anyway. But this is all so subjective. I have heard of other people auditioning in opera houses and just not being favourably seen by one or more directors for 2 or 3 years in a row and going somewhere else and being snapped up like gold dust.

I get my chance when I am alone on the stage with Erzsébet. *W*e have been arguing already as she has taken an instant dislike to me as she knows I can steal her glory. She has heard my voice which has developed immensely in 2 years going from being merely a good Carmen to an exceptional one. I have to put a stop to her for good or we are going to be in constant conflict over roles in this company. I know exactly what to do. There is a lighting technician bent over a tangled snake of cables nearby but that is all. I know Erzsébet could well take the lead, she is older and has played Carmen before. I need to get rid of this woman who will be a threat to every role I take even if I get them in this Opera House.

Momentarily as Erzsébet turns away, I fall into the orchestra pit with a scream. Yes it fucking hurts, but I have planned it with military precision to fall in such a way I will hit the drums and not spear myself on a music stand. I know to make it realistic I risk breaking something but what the hell.

I am lucky or smart. The biggest drum breaks my fall but I burst it with my shoe and crash to the ground with the drum. The crash sends some of the crew and one of the stage managers running in.

"She pushed me," I say. I start to cry. I think of the saddest things ever. My dead mother, all I can summon up. "She pushed me in." I am crying harder now, my full acting persona on and Erzsébet is just standing with her mouth open, without even protesting. The lighting man is the first in the pit, slipping in from the edge of the stage, saying to send an ambulance. He is checking me for broken bones.

"No, no, let me try and get up," I say.

The stage manager starts shouting at Erzsébet,"What the hell did you do? You could have killed her!"

I just hear her whining, "But I didn't, I didn't".

No one saw. Only me and my conscience and a few

theatre spirits and we are not saying anything. The lighting man didn't see but he is helping me to my feet, freeing one leg from the now destroyed drum. My wrist fucking hurts and my whole left arm; and then I look at the torn drum which saved me from injury and cry more. "I am so sorry about the drum, it's ruined," I stand wobbling.

"Never mind the drum," the stage manager says. She virtually grabs Erzsébet by the arm and drags her away. Some of the company have emerged from dressing rooms to find out what all the shouting is about, but they are told to leave the stage, nothing to see.

"I'm sorry, I didn't see what happened but you were disagreeing with her, it didn't sound serious," says the lighting man as he helps me up the stairs.

"I just turned away for a second and then she shoved me from behind, without a word. What did I ever do to her? I know she wants the role, and I do too, but not that badly," I say.

Not that badly, more like I would kill for that role.

She's too young, the musical director had argued. *She is talented but she is too young for such a role.* But in the end after much debate, they let my self-assurance and talent and looks win them over. They will give me this chance.

Erzsébet doesn't return to the theatre again. I don't even have to say a word. No one in their right mind would believe that I was ruthless enough to throw myself into the orchestra pit risking serious injury just to get rid of my rival. I am lucky to just have a sprained shoulder and injured wrist for a few weeks. But the role is mine. It is confirmed a few days later on 3rd April. I am even more stunned when they ask me to perform in the summer on the stage in the open air festival in Margitsziget where *Aida* will première. They are taking a big chance with me; it is

Aida and Erzsébet was down to play Amneris. Now she is out. The directors debated a long time over choosing a far more experienced mezzo-soprano but one is convinced I am right for the role. I am told that if I stuff up, in front of this crowd of 4,000 it will affect my future roles and I will not play the part when it returns to the theatre in the autumn season. I might also lose some of my roles for the following season, including *Carmen* and although the schedule is not finalised yet, I am told to expect a good surprise, providing I don't crash in the festival. It is the deciding factor in my year long schedule. This is a huge opportunity for me and a lot of pressure. It is only 2 nights, a Friday and a Sunday but I have never performed to a crowd of this size before. I think the directors know that to place me under such pressure and in front of 4,000 people at a première is the make or break for a 25 year old. They know I could suffer from nerves so badly that I can't perform to the standard they require. They know this is the test so they are throwing me into the Colosseum willingly. Even if it means their opera will be a mess. They reason that the Summer Festival is not the Opera Theatre and if an unknown guest does mess up, it is totally different to me ruining their production in their own theatre.

I am up to the challenge. I know I can do this. I know it with every fibre of my soul. The Colosseum is waiting but I am strong. I can do it.

So when I fly to Sicily to play Maddalena in *Rigoletto* I am hopeful I can relax a little knowing I have so much to look forward to. I touch Tosca's crucifix and feel I am heading towards a lifetime of wonder. But in Sicily anyway, there is no such luck. The theatre has provided digs in the darkest, grimmest street in town and my apartment does not have any windows that aren't facing the tiny interior and then they are frosted glass. It is dark and gloomy and cold. None of my clothes dry properly. The first night I am trying to sleep in this morbid place exhausted from an early flight and then immediately into rehearsals. As I start to drift away, I hear the old man who lives in the apartment below calling out, "Angela, Angela, Angela....." at regular five minute intervals. This continues all night every night, sometimes stopping for an hour but then it begins again. I don't know if Angela ever comes. If she does, I don't hear her. He is either losing his mind or dying. But it adds to the feeling of gloom about the apartment block. When I leave in the morning and return at night, grubby Sicilian youths shout, "Ciao Bella!" as I walk down the street.

I am also not enjoying *Rigoletto*. It is not one of my favourites but I wanted to take a guest role to give me experience abroad. The money is pretty lousy, Sicily is virtually bankrupt but I do like to be surrounded by Italian as I studied it at university before my opera training.

I spend many evenings after rehearsals stuffing freshly made arancini into my mouth, I eat two as I even walk 400 metres to my apartment, such is my hunger and craving for something that I am not getting in life. Four or five of the local speciality every day. Cheap, swollen like fluffy clouds and easy to swallow and just as easy to throw up again. I am greedy for the ones which contain molten butter in the centre. They burst like puffy pillows and just slip down my throat. Those and the cornets of cream filled pastries. I binge on these as well immediately afterwards and then I purge with water and salt-water to make sure I get everything out. I eat as fast as I can, finishing a binge in 10 minutes so it doesn't get the chance to lay down on me as fat. I find out later that this purging with water is one of the most dangerous aspects of bulimia as it rids the body of all its vital nutrients. If I just threw up I would not be damaging myself to the same extent, but right now I do not care. I have no thought for that. I am like a demon unleashed. My bulimia rockets sky high those weeks I am in Sicily. I vomit every single day after rehearsals and every night after our performances. My voice feels husky but I don't need to hit any high notes for this role so I am feeling as though it doesn't matter. *I will be alright in Budapest,* is all I think. *I won't do this there.*

Then I sit down to my measured meal of one carefully carved up tomato, a piece of buffalo mozzarella and some basil leaves, maybe a few olives and prosciutto and some melon slices. I buy just enough for one day every day as I cannot allow myself to have more food in the apartment. And this is food I will not have the urge to binge on.

And then a miserable yoghurt and some fruit. Apart from coffee, milk, juice, a pot of honey and some bread in the freezer for the morning I do not dare have any food in the fridge. Everything that is a trigger I will vomit up again. In those early days, I was limiting my food intake as well but as I begin to take on bigger roles, I simply can't. I can't be weak and dizzy and after Sicily I am looking too thin. I look like a ballerina as my bones are sticking through my flesh and I don't like this look. I do not look so beautiful. In the end I have to choose sensible healthy foods like chicken and avocado and everything that is going to give me energy without wanting to stuff my face. I drink vegetable shakes. My father always loves those and he would blend up beetroot and cabbage and carrot and everything green. To drink was easier. Sitting down to plates of food is always a problem.

It is a relief to return to Hungary and the Sicilian theatre takes nearly a year to pay me, after numerous phone calls and letters. I have some meaningless flings with two of the male singers and drink too much at an after show party and return to Budapest. I will not go to Sicily again despite it being in my blood, on my mother's side of the family. I have memories of Sicily being so poor and closed, unlike Italy which was full of promise and open spaces. But it is extra experience for my repertoire. I do some concert performances in towns around Hungary, one singing the *Carmen* favourites of 'Habanera', the 'Seguidilla' and 'C'est toi, c'est moi' with an older Hungarian tenor which receives such congratulations and response from everyone in the festival I know I am ready to move into the big time for my beloved *Carmen.*

My mind is focussed on Amneris in the summer festival of *Aida* in Budapest. Two nights of my life which are absolutely crucial. For once I am throwing up with nerves before the show. I am not used to such a big audience. I am not used to this pressure. I have managed not to binge and throw up throughout the rehearsals as I know it affects my voice and strength. The knowledge that everything rides on this Friday night and Sunday night does make me want to though. Stuff up, and I will not only lose this role when it returns in the autumn, but other roles too. The rehearsals have been going well for *Aida.* Not perfection, but I am not messing anything up, I am not letting anyone down. Yet. That June, in rehearsals I give it all I have. In the Opera Theatre, they are winding down their season ready for the long dark of July and August, the maintenance period for the building and its performers. But I am winding up, spiralling into a frenzy. I decide if I stuff up I will not be so restrained and I will binge and purge 7 times a day as punishment for messing up my biggest ever chance. It is not even about trying to stay thin, it is about being stressed, unhappy, empty, lonely or whatever bad emotion I am feeling. Sure sometimes I binge because I have a hunger for sweet and starchy food but mostly it is emotional.

So amongst the fireflies and the birds and the darkening sky I give absolutely everything I have, lifting my voice to the star-studded Heavens. The 40c early July heat has faded to a gentle warmth once it is the 9pm show time. I know when I get such a reaction from the audience when I do my curtain call I will play Amneris in the Opera Theatre. Those two nights are a rarity. I feel such an adrenaline rush in the warm air, I feel superhuman. A group of women shout from the blackness of the audience, "Natalija, we love you!" on the Friday. The Sunday is just as good, maybe even better as the nerves are virtually gone and I am running on pure adrenaline. I know I can do it now. This was the ultimate test.

I am dressed like an Egyptian goddess in black and gold, my black hair framed by a gold tiara and the photos and reviews covering the event show me beautiful and elated, arms stretched heavenwards. The reviews are sparkling, praising this unknown new performer who has sung the role of Amneris with such power and passion. The soprano playing Aida has not really given me any attention, good or bad. She is out of the loop of the poisonous backstabbers in the company as she is 20 years older than me, guesting a lot in other theatres in Europe so she is totally absorbed in her role and totally professional which makes it much easier to work together. I am just there as a performer, I am not her rival off stage only in the opera itself. I am not a threat to her, being a mezzo so she doesn't care. Our on stage chemistry seems to work in a strange kind of way as we both fight for the love of Radamès. I am so obsessed with being the star, I actually forget that Radamès is a handsome British tenor I would normally have a fling with. I do not exist beyond this stage throughout the rehearsals and the weekend we play *Aida.*

Zita, the soprano leaves for a Wagner festival in Austria the day after the Sunday show and I won't see her until we play *Aida* again back in the autumn. She doesn't seem to care that I received more applause than her. It is just another show, she has bigger opera houses on her schedule and this is merely a guest role in her eyes.

I think this is the last time I am truly happy. I felt as though the world was mine that weekend. I was healthy and more importantly I was a star already with a long future ahead of me. I don't realise I will never truly feel happy or content again. I will only experience soaring highs and crashing lows. And even the soaring highs will be stripped of their wonder, as I will be exhausted and ill a lot of the time.

I have my opera schedule for Budapest for the September to the following June finalised after *Aida* although the rest of the company received theirs earlier. It is looking good, just like the directors promised. I have the part of Carmen for September, I have a number of roles for the year. The directors are very impressed with me after I gave such a brilliant performance in *Aida.* Their risk paid off for the one artistic director who absolutely believed I could play Amneris and the musical director who backed him up. He agreed I had a voice of exceptional quality and a wonderful stage presence. The opera company have marked up the opera year putting me in more productions than I could have hoped for. I know it means a lot of stress, a lot of performances but I crave it, I need it with every fibre of my soul. One thing I have made very clear is I will not play those mezzo roles which require dressing as a man like that dreadful Cherubino in *Figaro.* I hate *Figaro.* Or even worse Prince Orlofsky in *Die Fledermaus.* I have been offered these both in the past and now and I refuse. If I am on stage, I have to be beautiful. I am not going down that route. I will not allow them to do anything to my hair or face to make me older or ugly which in the near future only adds to my unpopularity and diva-like demands. The cutting out of roles like Cherubino only intensifies the pressure as the roles then become even more limited with fierce competition for the few solo mezzo roles going. I am also not so strong in German language operas, so have traditionally performed in mainly French and Italian, but I can do it. I have trained in the language but as my performances are usually French or Italian, I always end up in the operas sung in the Romance languages. I am already hated by most of the women in the company, who see me as too young to be getting leading solo roles and so many of them at that. But I am glad. I am so glad they hate me. I do not need friends as I do not trust people generally.

KRISZTA

I am at a première for a new version of *Turandot*. It will be the first opera of the autumn season and it is premièred first for two nights at an open air festival in August as part of the biggest national holiday weekend on Margitsziget and then moves to the Opera Theatre on 1st September and I am invited. It is the one soprano role I would love to play, aside from Tosca. Turandot is the ultimate ice queen but my mezzo voice prevents me from taking the role of Puccini's leading ladies. Mostly I wouldn't want the roles of Mimi, the pathetic whiner or the sad Madama Butterfly or the broken Manon Lescaut but I do love the music. So haunting, so beautiful. *Carmen* rehearsals have already started in the rehearsal studios downtown as I will be performing on alternate nights to *Turandot* once we are in the Opera Theatre. There is *Figaro* and a Wagner première as well but I have been invited to this first première to officially meet the company as many more singers are there for the after show than for *Aida* which was really just the two nights of production and with no after show event. Our première will be later in the season in the Opera Theatre. I am restless and I remember the feeling of being here, centre stage.

I look out at the empty auditorium during the speeches; I am hungry for it. I want it more than I ever wanted anything. I stand looking out into the darkness and breathe deeply, imagining myself as I was in *Aida* with the shouts of the audience and it feels so good. I am taken back to the nights I played Amneris with the applause and the screams as I held my arms to Heaven and felt the world was mine.

It will be mine again.

I know the company do not want to meet me, the singers that is. They do not want me here but I do not care. Right now, everyone could fade away and I am alone in my own world daydreaming as I ignore all the speeches and close my eyes imagining the crowd calling my name into eternity. I want, I want and I want.

There is a very beautiful woman who has played the part of Liù in *Turando*t. I actually think that the title role should have been hers as she is not anyone's slave. But her vocal range would have fallen slightly short of the heavy demands of singing *Turandot.* She shimmers and smoulders in a silver dress which is split at the knee with glittery high heels and she has such vitality which seems to float all around the stage at this champagne reception. Everyone else appears as cardboard cut-outs compared to her, even Turandot herself who once out of costume seems to lack any kind of life, despite being pretty enough with a voice which split the night sky like a jagged fork of lightning. As Liù during the opera, this silver-dressed soprano who I find out is called Kriszta, was soft, delicate, different but freed of her slave girl shackles and poured into this dress, she is smoking hot and confident as hell. I see her on the crowded stage afterwards and she stares back at me as I gaze at her. She stares at me not with the same look of jealous hatred the others are already giving me but with curiosity and interest. She wants to talk to me, it is clear. During the speeches she throws back a glass of champagne and continues to stare unashamedly at me. It doesn't take her long to approach afterwards with two glasses of champagne and this is where I pick up with Kriszta. The theatre director has been parading me around the stage proudly introducing me to everyone and anyone as *our young superstar from Aida.* I must be the most hated person on the stage tonight. Here is the première for *Turandot* and I am not in it and already I am the star. That is good, that is fine by me.

And then Kriszta is standing in front of me, even more sensual and lovely closer up and passing me one of her champagne flutes. I have already had one so a second is really my limit but I don't refuse her. My first words are, "You were the best and most beautiful on that stage tonight but you sure like the champagne. I thought most opera singers didn't drink much, Krisztyna."

She is already chugging down her fourth glass. "Please, call me Kriszta. Only if you are in love with me do I allow you to call me Krisztyna. Everyone calls me Kriszta. Are you in love with me?" she says leaning in closer and laughs coquettishly. She then hesitates, looking at me seriously, daring me to say something then continues. "I am not most opera singers. I am a bad girl," she replies with a wicked laugh and those smouldering eyes. "I like to do what I shouldn't." She stands too close, so I can smell her dusky perfume and feel the warm, damp skin of her face next to mine as she boldly takes a ringlet of my long black hair and twirls it with her fingertips.

"Don't you, Natalija? Don't you like to do what you shouldn't? And you're wrong about me being the best thing on this stage tonight. You are. You really are beautiful." She says this last bit in my ear seductively, placing her hand in mine, caressing my arm with her red nails and then looks for my reaction. She already knows my name. "And is that Tosca's crucifix?" she says holding it between her fingers, grazing a fingernail along my chest, dangerously low into my dress. She wants a sign from me.

I shiver as though in the presence of some wonderful goddess. I want Kriszta to scratch those sharp nails down my spine. I think about asking her there and then but someone breaks my thoughts as they come to congratulate her on her performance. She is polite and effusive but stands closer to me, hand ever so gently resting on my waist already taking ownership. She obviously wants me and only me this evening.

"Yes, it is Tosca's crucifix, a present from a soprano in Italy," I tell Kriszta when we are alone again.

"How wonderful, I would love to have played Tosca," she says with a touch of nostalgia.

"You still can," I say. "You would be wonderful as Tosca. I can see you now."

She looks at me and her smile fades and she quickly looks away and shakes her head. "No, not me. Not now." Then the light snaps back on and she is her enchanting self.

Why doesn't she think she can? is all I think to myself. She is confident, beautiful and maybe not the best soloist but she could still play Tosca. Her Italian pronunciation is lingering and flawless although she tells me she can only sing in Italian and not speak it outside of an opera. She has the stage presence of an absolute diva; Floria Tosca couldn't be more beautiful than Kriszta.

Kriszta is a terrible flirt, 36 years old she tells me outright and married with two teenage children but she has a recklessness about her I find enchanting and has a similar exotic dark beauty as me. Her husband is nowhere to be seen. *Why not?*

"I don't want him in my world, he is dull and I want some fun tonight, besides I don't really like him that much," she says. She seems much younger than her years as well as outspoken, dismissing her husband immediately as boring, too boring for this dazzling glamour girl who fixes me with a stare from those dark, smokily made up eyes as she tells me she wants fun. I am her fun that night, it is clear, or will be.

If I agree. She waits for my reaction and I feel if I don't flirt with her I will lose her to this swelling crowd of glitterati in the summer night. I do not want that. I want this Kriszta and I do not want to lose her. I sip the champagne, put my hand on her shoulder and say to her, "I want some fun tonight too. As long is it involves you, Kriszta." I twirl my hair and look as seductive as possible, not difficult for me.

I imagine she is Don José and sing the first lines of the Seguidilla to her quietly on this crowded noisy stage where everyone is clamouring for attention, so no one notices us. Or maybe they do.

The Seguidilla is enough and Kriszta takes my hand and we make our way off the stage. She is careless with everything and everyone including her profession. She is seductive and dramatic and she gets minor solo roles but mainly based on her looks and sex appeal and stage presence. Given the choice between Kriszta and a fairly plain singer with an exceptional voice, the directors are now opting for the looks. There is more pressure than ever to look beautiful for men and women. The audience want the Natalijas and Krisztas of this world. But I know I am not like Kriszta; I already have an exceptional voice and I have worked myself to death for it. I don't even think when I meet Kriszta that I have a single friend left in the world. And I honestly do not care. Everyone has been pushed aside by my commitment to my career and my peripatetic lifestyle although that should change now. It will be nice to be in my lovely apartment in the XIII district, near margitsziget for most of the time instead of spending odd nights there and jetting off all over Europe for roles. My father bought it for me; he thought if I moved abroad he could rent it out to tourists but I have no intention of giving it up as I love it. I have hardly been there in the past few years. It will be good, so good not to be travelling much and just to guest occasionally.

Now and then when she has the chance starting with our first meeting that evening, Kriszta will cheat on her husband with me, but I cannot get too close to her as for once she is the one calling the shots so I don't care about her beyond the times I am with her. She drinks too much champagne at receptions and makes no secret of the fact she wants me, boldly wrapping her arm round my waist in front of people telling me I am beautiful, whispering in my ear. But she rarely stays out all night. Typically she leaves my apartment late, 2am or 3am in the morning without even saying goodbye. Sometimes if she is tired she oversleeps and I hear her crashing around cursing at 7am trying to find her clothes and bag in my room. She has another life, a family home which will never involve me so I just don't allow myself to feel very much for her. She is there and then she isn't. She is married and bored with her husband and I represent freedom, danger and reckless lust. That is all she wants from me, or so I believe at first. Kriszta takes what she wants including me. She cares nothing about the other singers and their gossip. I am already hated and I also do not care what the others think of me.

That night we disappear into the trees as I am led by Kriszta who cannot wait and won't wait until we get home, pulling me by the hand as we trip over tree roots and my heels stick in the grass until we fall laughing into the earth. And with no good excuse from me as I have not even finished my second champagne although she is clearly intoxicated. We are gone longer than it feels so we totally miss the theatre buses leaving margitsziget. My hair is full of leaves and twigs and Kriszta is looking wild and dishevelled and beautiful like something from a mystical land. She leans close as we stagger back into the light thrown out from the now empty stage where the crew are gutting it in preparation for another show tomorrow night, her arm round my shoulders laughing and dizzy from the champagne and the theatre buses are gone as are the taxis which leaves only the two ambulances who are still waiting here as the crew dismantle the stage. One of the paramedics looks with surprise as he finishes his smoke and sees these two wild Wagnerian Rhinemaidens stepping into the light and Kriszta persuades him to drive us off the island since no extra taxis are likely. The other option is to wait 2 hours for the crew bus to arrive once they have finished on the stage, or walk 2 kilometres to get to the bridge. I am already corrupted by this Kriszta, I needed an early night and it is not happening. It is less than 10 minutes walk from the bridge to my apartment in the XIII district after our ambulance ride and Kriszta falls against me in the elevator in my block saying did I just come from Heaven or Hell, I am a bad girl for corrupting her like this. I see my reflection in the mirror and my hair is like a bride of Dracula, black and tangled full of the forest, my make up smeared over my face. She passes out on my bed when I am in the shower and I have to move her to get to sleep as she has greedily taken up the whole double bed, red talons stretched out over all four pillows even in sleep claiming ownership.

Kriszta takes and takes. I will discover this about her. She could be an amazing performer, but she is lazy. She is on stage again in 2 nights and she is drunkenly sprawled across my bed, no care for tomorrow. I notice some deep scratches on her back and a bruise lower down but think nothing of it. It was either in the trees this evening or looking closer, I touch the marks and see they are older and I decide it is someone else's nails and not mine. But knowing what I do, she probably likes that sort of thing. I think nothing of it then. Kriszta seems the wild type.

Where her husband thinks she is half the night I do not know because staying half the night is also cheating. An hour is cheating. The time is irrelevant. Of course, like all cheats it will implode horribly, emotions will explode like a volcano and I will be left with the fallout, but for now, it all seems so casual, so easy, so devoid of any real emotion other than danger and lust.

What divides us as well as an 11 year age gap is that Kriszta is happy to sing supporting roles. I am so cut-throat ambitious I will do anything it takes to play the lead. No one is as bad as me for recklessness and heartbreak. I always hear more gossip about me and Kriszta than anyone else despite the fact that I end up with many of the men in the company as well. Kriszta is the only resident female singer who will make my list. But then again no one can prove anything. A couple of the idiotic men will boast about having me, but generally there is an unspoken rule about not speaking about your conquests within the company. Especially amongst those who are sleeping with the directors. Everyone gossips but no one admits to being with anyone else as a general rule.

But Kriszta says she has always been happy enough with supporting roles. She lacks my ruthless and exceptional ambition. I would virtually kill for roles whereas she is happy to take small parts; she has her family she says. Her husband is wealthy but dull. She doesn't need to push herself. She is content enough to sing, it is her passion. And she lacks that elusive magic of the leading soloists which sets us apart from the others. That extra quality in the voice which turns an aria from something beautiful into something totally awe-inspiring but I know she could have had it, if she'd worked harder, if she partied less. When I am dying with loneliness through my early twenties, studying at my opera training in Italy, scratching around for small roles, pushing myself, until I join the company at 25, rehearsing and rehearsing and living out of a suitcase, Kriszta admits she was lazy and partying. She was skipping her singing rehearsals, arriving late at concerts despite being told she had talent, turning down chances when she could have hit the big time. She married her husband when she was only 20, had her two children young and became anchored in Hungary studying singing when she lived in Szeged while her older husband supported them. Then they relocated to Budapest. *He is rich and dull,* she repeats many times. *Handsome but so boring. And in the bedroom, Natalija.....well I usually just pretend to be asleep. I do not enjoy it at all. But I was stupid, Natalija. I had my children so I had to stay with someone I didn't really love. I would have left if it wasn't for them. All through my twenties I regretted being tied to him. And he never really supported me being on stage. In fact, he never ever wanted me to be successful.....*

Maybe you just don't like men, I say bluntly.

She looks at me sharply. *I never said that,* she says.

But she doesn't have to. She flirts with everyone, sure but I never hear her talk about men in the company. Occasionally she mentions some guest female singer as fresh meat. She gets her talons into the young singers she boasts to me and I never know if she just wants to prove she can seduce anyone or she is trying to make me jealous. At the time, I wonder if she will cast me aside, if I am just a passing phase. It stops me from feeling anything deep.

I had many men before my husband, she tells me defensively. *But honestly, the guest females are always hot,*

Natalija, and they are often lonely in our strange country with our strange language. I take full advantage of that.

I agree with her and say, *Guests are a safe bet. There is no fall-out, no comeback, they are here then they are gone.*

She smiles. She is greedy. She binges on passion as though it is forbidden food.

What about me though, Kriszta? I say as casually as possible. *I am here, I am not going anywhere.*

You, beautiful girl are extra special, she says with full honesty. She examines her scarlet nails and smiles at me mysteriously.

I still cannot let myself go. So I have affairs with many people. I have them to stop Kriszta becoming a focus as I sense she could be. There is something so amazing about her and I do not want to even feel this. So I don't.

When I studied at university before my serious opera training I never went out, I was so busy with my studies and my singing on top of that. I was known as stuck up and arrogant; 'The Ice Queen' since I was once a figure skater and also because I shunned everyone who tried to befriend me. I didn't care. Making it big was all I wanted so it was straight from classes in university into singing classes. I spent my year out in Italy in Firenze even though I hated the place because it meant I could study singing as part of my course. And I still really hate Firenze; those dark poky streets and damp, balmy nights and air choked with mosquitoes. I like big wide avenues of the cities such as Budapest and Roma.

Kriszta should hate me for having everything she should have had but she doesn't; she is the opposite. She admires me with absolutely no resentment or jealousy. I will realise too late that Kriszta underneath it all, is actually the most loyal person in my life, who cares very deeply for me despite her reckless attitude and would defend me to the death against anyone who hurt me. But I can never give myself to anyone, so I don't see it. When I go and get a calendar made from my opera photos, Kriszta wants one before I even start to think of anyone else. The bari-hunks do it in their swimming trunks, posing for calendars flexing muscles on Italian beaches to promote their careers. My calendar was classy; all opera shots, me as Carmen, me sitting on stages, draped over elaborate gold and gilt edged theatres in dresses just as opulent. Me, me, me. It was a gift for my father for Christmas that year, so I had a few more made in case and Kriszta unashamed, asks me for one.

Lilla said I was an arrogant little bitch when she saw my calendar on the wall but I know my stepmother is jealous as hell, not just of my looks but now my obvious success which she can't even accuse me of sleeping to the top to get.

"What are you going to do with that?" I ask Kriszta as she flicks through the months slowly admiring the beautiful pictures of me, the opera diva at 25.

"Hang it in the kitchen of course, what else?" she laughs like a wind-chime. "I need a calendar for next year and you will do. I like to think I have you every month of the year, Carmencita."

"And your husband? What will he think?"

"Oh, him. He won't. It's not as if you're an Italian bari-hunk half naked and 25 is it?" she asks.

But I am 25 although I take her point. Her husband is a very conservative man so she says, he will not think anything of it. Just a friend from the Opera, that's all. Just a calendar, that's all. Nothing to it.

Kriszta also makes no secret of the fact she throws up after eating, although sporadically. She is slender but unlike me she is an occasional bulimic. Just like I am an occasional lover to her. She can take it or leave it. I cannot take or leave anything and by the time I am immersed in The Royal Hungarian Opera Company, my bulimia has taken a stranglehold on my life.

I am washing my face in the sink after a long rehearsal for *Carmen* as I have gone into the theatre to sort out some financial details and I can hear someone throwing up quietly in the cubicles. Kriszta emerges looking sallow but unashamed. She smiles at me and rinses her mouth and hands and applies her red lipstick. "Got to do something to stay slim and pretty. I can't do it at home, my husband and children would ask me what the hell was going on," she says.

I see marks on her neck and am about to ask does she self harm too but it seems too serious and so unlike the Kriszta I know so I don't say it.

She blows me a kiss and leaves, promising to see me soon and I say, "Right," more to myself than her as she is already gone. "It's okay, other people do it too. Kriszta throws up and she seems healthy," I rationalise talking to myself in the mirror. *I am fine. We all do it.*

But I am out of control. I am in way too deep.

And so is Kriszta, but in a different way. I will find out too late her carelessness is a guise for her true feelings. That her smouldering sensuality and attention towards me the night we met was more than I initially thought. That her fun-loving persona, is just that, an artifice and it becomes clearer only much later; just as we play different roles in the opera, so Kriszta hides a lot under her mask. I wish I had listened to her more, to let her tell me that her home life was anything but pleasant but I was too self-absorbed and never asked too many questions.

FIAMMA

I am bored of this meaningless première for Wagner. I have just come along as Kriszta wanted to meet me since we are both in different operas, we haven't seen each other much. She is in *Turandot* and *Carmen* opens in 2 days and there are too many premières and distractions and I just want to be at home resting. Neither of us is in the Wagner opera and the cast are a very serious group who also don't want to be at the première, so it all feels a bit flat and I know I am trying to delay an eating binge. Kriszta is busy with other people and I do not want to watch her flirting around the stage tonight. She is doing it to get a reaction out of me as she keeps looking over and I am tired and also tired of her games and I need someone else to take home. I am not hanging around for Kriszta to finish her many champagnes and make her mind up which bed she is going home to tonight, but I don't really like any of the men here. I have either been there and done that with one or two of them, or don't want to. I am shattered and I don't want to drink more than a glass as *Carmen* is my focus and I want to really give it everything. Kriszta drinks too much. She should take her career more seriously. It is not good for the voice this alcohol.

But then neither is throwing up. That is probably worse.

I sit on the steps leading on to the stage. I know I should go home but I am restless and I want excitement. This lovely ethereal girl steps from out of the darkened wings towards me. She is dressed for the occasion in black lace and high heeled black shoes, an outfit so simple but so perfect for bringing out all her smouldering sensuality. She looks like an Italian film star without the attitude.

It is the Italian girl, Fiamma who will be performing in

Carmen as Frasquita. She has never left Italy before this, only one time to a horrible theatre in Spain she tells me and she doesn't know anyone here. They invited her to this after-show event to meet people, but it is not any good. She is too shy to talk to people and despite her lovely appearance, she is someone everyone else with their huge egos seems to look right through. Including me. This is the first time I have actually noticed this girl and for the first time I see how beautiful she is, how her green eyes, creamy skin and black hair are so striking but she has a softness about her, a fragility in her delicate features, her whole demeanour.

"Everyone is speaking Hungarian and I feel lost," she says as she sits down on the step next to me.

"I was here all night and you never even noticed me. You are so beautiful tonight I could not stop looking at you. You are so wonderful as Carmen."

It sounds pathetic but I look at her and I have a taste for fresh meat. If I don't take her home, Kriszta will get her talons into her. I am surprised she hasn't already but she is too busy taking centre stage drinking and flirting and I can hear her loud voice from over here. I am irritated by Kriszta tonight.

This Fiamma is very lovely, like a young Monica Bellucci but more fragile, shy and very quiet. It is hard to imagine how she ever had the confidence to become an opera singer but I remember her in rehearsals; lost in the opera, totally committed and commanding the stage instead of hiding in the wings as she is now. I had obviously taken notice of her in rehearsals but I was so totally immersed in my own role, that I never bothered to really talk to this shy girl. When I am the lead, no one else really matters.

She sounds so much like a schoolgirl. How old is she? She

has to be 27 or 28 but she looks younger and her childlike innocence make her seem younger still.

That's good, she is lonely, she thinks I am beautiful. It is my lucky night, or year more like. I am getting everything I want. I feel omnipotent. Especially after champagne. I shouldn't drink, it affects my vocal chords but I shouldn't be bulimic either. There are a lot of things I shouldn't do. But then again, I think back to Kriszta. She is drinking alcohol and throwing up her food. She is 36 and stunningly beautiful. It is working for her anyway.

I put down the champagne flute and take Fiamma by the arm. I am suddenly shattered. We go past the dressing rooms and into the bathroom and she sits on the sinks and looks at me as if I am the most wonderful person in the world.

I call a taxi from my cell phone as I gaze at my reflection in the mirror.

I start gathering my stuff together in my bag and Fiamma asks, "Where do you go now? I'm sorry, I don't understand Hungarian. No one has really talked to me much in rehearsals or here tonight. I am lonely." Her beautiful sad eyes have a pleading look and it makes me glad to have someone falling at my feet tonight. I deserve it.

I switch to Italian as her English is not so good either. She obviously wants to come with me wherever I am going, Hell or back, this girl will follow me.

"Home, baby," I tell her. "Come with me. I won't be able to sleep well tonight, I am stressed and I could use some company."

And you will not sleep either. I am hungry tonight and I will not take no for an answer. And I don't want an eating binge and throwing up again. I have been at it already today. I crave sweet flesh in an almost vampiric way. I don't care if it is a he or a she. People are people if they are beautiful. And she is beautiful.

She follows me willingly, her face losing its sadness as she can speak to me in her native tongue. She gabbles away, happy to connect with someone. I know our company are renowned for their quality but also for their general unfriendliness. It is a complaint I will hear from many a guest performer during my time there. For me, I do not care but I do see Hungary in much the same way; beneath our politeness and superficiality I see the mistrust of strangers and foreigners which still exists. I notice it particularly as I have travelled a lot already. Many of the opera company only really know Italian for the role, like Kriszta and rarely use it as a language, although there are some of the older singers who like me, studied in Italy and speak it fluently.

As for enticing Fiamma home, it is just too easy. I don't even speak to her as I say goodnight to the stage door keeper who gives me a knowing smile as I leave with my latest conquest. I let this girl get in the taxi first, she is still gabbling away. I look out of the window at the bright lights of the boulevard as we head to the XIII and think how Budapest always looks special at night under the cover of darkness. The avenues, bridges, castle and parliament lit up so gold, so beautiful and yet so false. Much the same as our world. The daylight brings a dead greyness to the city especially in the cold months and it is as though you had a wonderful dream which has gone and left you with nothing.

"Natalija! What is he saying?" Fiamma is shaking my arm.

I am so lost in this thought I forget we are outside my apartment and the taxi driver is asking for the fare. I pay him and lead Fiamma out.

The first thing she says is, "What a wonderful place to

live! I am in a dark apartment the theatre provided. It is so light and bright here and you can see the river and the lights on the bridges. It's beautiful, Natalija."

The next thing is, "Why is there nothing in the fridge?" She is standing looking into a different kind of bright light where again there is nothing. The shelves are virtually bare. She pulls out a tiny piece of French cheese and looks at it sadly. It is kind of mouse-sized.

There are things in my fridge. Well, some nail polish. There is coffee, milk, juice and some champagne I always keep for special nights. There is bread in the freezer and peanut butter in the cupboard, but this Sicilian beauty with her curves who must eat like a normal person and with a love of food is obviously not used to such a barren kitchen. She opens all the cupboards and apart from the peanut butter, she finds only rice cakes.

"Natalija, how can you live on so little?" she says with a concerned look.

I think about telling her that I have an eating disorder, that I dare not have anything in the house. That I have to order takeaway sushi or collect something healthy or I will stuff my face and throw it all up. That I only dare to have breakfast food of wholewheat bread and peanut butter. I don't like wholewheat bread so I will not binge. And peanut butter is not a trigger for me. Too much cheese can be which is why I only dare have a tiny piece in the fridge. Once I am inside the apartment, I will not go out to the supermarket down the road. Inside I am disciplined. But if I dare have too much in or am in a frenzy and buy the trash food I binge on, that is it.

I am studying my phone which has a text fresh from Miss Flirt herself, Kriszta. ***Where are you?***

I put the phone down and turn it to silent. So she did

notice I had left. Well pity for her.

Fiamma is obviously hungry so I pass her a menu from the dial a takeaway. There is one for an Italian place. She can't read it as it is in Hungarian. I order what she says she likes and just tomato and basil bruschetta for me. No cheese, absolutely no cheese.

"Is that all you are having?" she wants to know when the delivery arrives. "Aren't you hungry after the première ?"

I don't answer. I just dish out her generous heap of pasta in its rich sauces and put the three tiny pieces of bruschetta on a black plate for me. All my plates and bowls are black as it is better for smaller portion size. I don't want to tell this girl she is only here to stop me eating until I burst, that of course I am hungry but I cannot overeat. That if she wasn't here with me tonight and Kriszta was messing around, I would have stopped at the 24 hour Turkish takeaway on the corner of the main boulevard and brought back fatty savoury dishes and white bread and chocolate baklavas and stuffed until I made myself throw up time and time again.

She will hear me throwing my guts up soon enough if she stays around more than a night. I look at her curves and wish I didn't have to control everything in my life so much. I wish I could eat like Fiamma. She eats with enjoyment but leaves some of her pasta and I am mystified. If I had ordered that I would have stuffed it all and the dessert. She says she can't manage the tiramisu. I put it in the fridge and tell her she must take it tomorrow. I cannot have food like that around.

"Don't you want it, Natalija?" she says her green eyes concerned. "You hardly ate anything, you are so slim. Maybe you will eat it tomorrow, no?"

I want to tell her why but I don't. I suddenly feel very tired.

I will break the heart of this Sicilian soprano, Fiamma, who gives and gives and I just take and take, like the morbidly obese at an eat all you can buffet, who can't stop, who won't stop, who don't feel hunger satiated. The only thing I give her is one of my calendars I have made for Christmas; me in various opera outfits looking beautiful every month of the year, just like I gave one to Kriszta. This girl is obsessed with me and she says she will keep my calendar forever. It is the one time I actually feel bad after she has joined our company as a guest performer for *Carmen*. I was bored that Wagner night, I took the first beautiful creature I found who wanted me, man or woman and it happened to be a woman. For Fiamma, she was already in love with me since our rehearsals where I had barely even noticed her. She thought I was the most wonderful girl to exist and it just made me more vain, that this firefly was full of adoration. I thought nothing of her feelings. I was cruel and greedy. Fiamma with her curves and smoky Sicilian beauty who has all the men lusting after her but virtually handed her open heart on a plate and thought I could love her. She began to bore me with her adulation, leaving red roses in my dressing room and looking at me with adoring glances even during the curtain call for *Carmen* as she played Frasquita. She would hang around my dressing room post-show and gaze at me with those beautiful green eyes, not caring the other singers and company noticed and laughed. I didn't care they noticed. It just made me feel extra-special.

I hurt her badly when one night I am obviously with Kriszta who is also bored and restless and wants some excitement. Kriszta doesn't care about Fiamma, she finds it amusing that I disappeared at the Wagner première with this Italian beauty and wants to know more, and how come she didn't get there before I did because she sounds like a hot piece of flesh. *But is she better than me?* She wants to know. *Who is better, Natalija?*

Honestly, Kriszta, I tell her. *You make everything sound so cheap.*

Kriszta answers my phone cruelly and deliberately at midnight, when Fiamma calls me and laughs as Fiamma hangs up, stunned and hurt. She does it to hurt Fiamma because underneath her carefree act, she is deeply jealous of this beautiful young Italian girl. She has seen Fiamma in the theatre after I pointed her out, and I sense her envy rising. This girl is absolutely lovely.

Fiamma is the polar opposite of Kriszta; shy, gentle, easily hurt, tender-hearted and spends the next day at a vocal warm up for *Carmen* moping around looking at me like I broke her heart. She is 27, as I guessed but at 25 I am more dedicated and mature than singers 10 years older than me. And Fiamma seems like a 14 year old with her wide-eyed innocence. In reality it is more complicated than that. Kriszta and Fiamma seem like poles apart, when in reality they both share personality traits. Fiamma has angry fire burning deep within her and Kriszta has a vulnerability she hides so well. She is just a better performer than Fiamma, especially off stage. She has loved and lived longer to be able to do it. She hides her dark secrets so well under her smouldering vitality and mischievous personality. She confesses later that when she saw me leaving the stage with Fiamma that night, something burned deep within her; the fire of jealousy. Only she never lets on for a long, long time.

But for now I am only seeing the sad, lovelorn Fiamma. I take her aside in the bathroom and tell her to start acting like a professional, *No Fiamma I am not yours. I don't belong to anyone. Not you, not Kriszta, not any of these men I see either. No one owns me and they never will. I see who I please, and I will not change. You need to accept that. No, Fiamma you do not love me. You do not love so fast, it is pure obsession as you are lonely. Why don't you realise that? You just have an obsession with me because I am beautiful, because I am Carmen.*

"But Natalija, I do love you, I really do. I loved you from the minute I first saw you....."

I leave her standing there as I go back to the stage.

Love, what is love? Stupid girl.

She looks like a wounded animal for the rest of the afternoon. The director is running out of patience as her Frasquita is lacking the flirty, careless nature she has managed to sustain in the dress rehearsal. Instead she looks like she is going to cry.

"For God's sake, Fiamma. ACT the role, don't just sing it. You are a gypsy. You and Mercédès are reckless like Carmen. Act it, feel it, smoulder, seduce Escamillo with that voice. You are singing as though someone has died."

Zsuzsa who is playing Mercédès laughs out loud. Fiamma just looks down, way way out of her depth with this company. I smile too as I have already seduced Escamillo, or more like Andrea the Italian baritone who plays him. Andrea is a veteran at 40; he has been playing various roles with The Royal Hungarian Opera and major Italian opera houses as well as London for 10 years now.

I didn't care if people noticed as she wept and clung to my knees before she flew home to Napoli as I tried to exit stage door telling her it was best we didn't meet any longer. I was more irritated that this beautiful girl was behaving so pathetically with no dignity as she begged me to go with her, said she would help me find work in Italy. I had to prise her off my legs and tell her to stop embarrassing herself as the stage door men watched with amusement. They were used to me leaving with different lovers, but I was considerate towards the door staff and I had a rule; never sleep with the crew or the directors or management. And never admit anything to anyone. Guest performers were the best bet in that they would be gone after a month or so and I didn't need to see them again.

She is begging me to go to The Royal Hungarian Ballet Theatre to see *Swan Lake*. I do not like ballet, it is boring for me. All that endless spinning and leaping and applause every five seconds from the audience. It isn't like opera, especially showcase ballets such as *Swan Lake*. What the hell is it about anyway apart from a girl who is turned into a swan or something? There is no plot. I also do not have time in my life for anything other than opera.

She has bought me a ticket. *Please, Natalija. Please come to the ballet with me.*

I do not care, Fiamma. This is nothing personal but I told you, I do not like ballet. If Kriszta asked me to go I wouldn't. It is boring.

I leave her crumpled on the steps outside the Opera Theatre weeping against the stone with two tickets for the ballet. I don't even look back. I am heartless, reckless and totally Carmen. A couple of stage crew having a cigarette outside say something to each other along the lines of 'smoking hot, that Carmencita. Even the chicks are after her, who wouldn't be'.

She is every man's dream, said one of the musicians as I walked by the day before. *She loves and leaves like a man. Not clingy like all those women you end up with. She is every bit a Carmen. No wonder everyone chases her. I feel sorry for that Italian girl though. She seems so sweet but she is just throwing herself at Natalija. Poor girl. She might as well be throwing herself at a film star. Natalija is already a diva at 25.*

But once back home, opening the card Fiamma had given me, with her outpourings of love and swearing she couldn't live without me, she would die if she couldn't be with me, I did feel a jagged sliver of cruelty. Why was I unable to feel? In the end the affair will drag out stopping and starting and never really ending, just like I never really end with Kriszta. It is an eternity in my short-lived world. The reason it carries on so long is after *Carmen* finishes its run, Fiamma flew back twice just to see me and then I end up in Italy for work so I see her just out of sheer greed and to feel beautiful and adored. When I see her in Italy I am starting to have more of a conscience and do feel some guilt over my behaviour that cuts this poor girl in two. The pain I cause her by my careless nature and ruthless streak is cruel and each time for her is worse than the last. The only girl in the world to her. And of course she will return when *Carmen* returns to the opera stage at the end of season. In the end I will mess up any chance she has to be with anyone else, through my own selfish behaviour. Yes, I do have a conscience in the end but right now, I don't think I have a shred of one. Less of a shred than the tiny piece of cheese in my kitchen fridge.

Now as I looked at her photo on the table all I felt was lust, not anything near love. It felt good getting the girl everyone else wanted. Just like everyone else wanted to have me too.

Beautiful, exotic Fiamma with her enchanting appearance and delicate heart, too soft for the harsh world of theatreland especially our company which seems to be renowned for cut throat arrogant singers. A girl from small town Sicily who now lived in Napoli and at 27 still had the tender naivity of a 14 year old in love for the first time. I look at her photo and then thoughtfully place it in the bedside drawer. She is worth keeping for eye candy, but not in the flesh. She is easily the most beautiful girl I have seen and the fact she was obsessed with me boosted my ego no end. I felt like the conqueress, watching the opera men trying to fix dates with her but she wasn't interested.

But the 'I love you' and 'Be mine forever' are just too much and I tell her so and whenever I snapped harsh words at her, those lovely sad eyes would fill full of tears as though she really would die without me. I could treat her mean, I could hurt her as much as I wanted and she still loved me. She made my cruel, sadistic streak stronger and razor sharp, honed it even more each time she told me she loved me.

I never could understand why anyone loved anyone else. I especially couldn't understand how anyone could love a man. For me, the only purpose they served was physical and to act dramatic on stage with; they were good for that. I could act love, the singers had a good chemistry even when they didn't love or like each other. If I was cold at times towards Fiamma and Kriszta, I was even colder towards the men. I had absolutely no tenderness towards the singers I became involved with be it for one night or one week. If they tried to hold me in bed, I would push them away demanding my sleep like a child needing its rest. I hated being held tight to some muscular hairy chest. I at least allowed myself to be held by women. Men were just there because I was hungry. I never wanted to be dependent on anyone. Ever.

The postcards continue for some time from poor Fiamma, first after *Carmen* and then again each time she visits me, always with the same heartbroken sentiments in Italian, sometimes from Napoli, other times from Sicily and one time with a necklace made of burnished gold, heart-shaped. How tacky, how obvious but I like the necklace, it is pretty and I can wear it to more occasions than Tosca's crucifix which is too large for anything other than dressing up in, being stage jewellery. I finger the gold between my hands and decide to wear it anyway as it looks expensive. The letters carry on for a while but eventually they die out, although Fiamma never truly gives up on me even when she will later scream it is over forever when I fail to tell her I am guesting in Roma. She cannot let go. Fiamma who could leave a trail of weak-kneed men in Sicily lusting after her as she shimmered along in her black lace dresses while her sad eyes looked across the water to cold cruel Hungary and me, unrelenting and unresponsive. The only one she ever wanted and could never have.

Kriszta finds the whole Fiamma fiasco entertaining. She wants all the details, *Yes all of them, Natalija, you know what I mean, what was she like in bed?* she quizzes as she turns the gold heart necklace over and over in her hand. *Come on, tell me.*

You should find out for yourself, I say poking Kriszta in the ribs. *Try and seduce the girl.*

"Everyone falls in love with you, Natalija," she says eventually, with a laugh and a touch of wonder. "And I did hit on Fiamma in the backstage toilets. I stroked her hair away from her face, put my hand on her waist and said she was beautiful, was about to move in for the kill but she said she was sorry and then just walked away! Damn girl is just too in love with our leading lady."

"Well it wasn't the most romantic of pick up joints," I say. "Honestly, Kriszta. Toilets."

I am not jealous, just surprised Kriszta didn't get what she wanted. She always gets what she wants. But then Fiamma is loyal. However disloyal, mean, selfish or just plain heartless I am, Fiamma can't even look at anyone else.

I never asked Kriszta did she include herself in that figure; the list of everyone who fell in love with the heartless Natalija. I never asked her what she ever felt about me. I always mistake her lack of jealousy as lack of feeling but Kriszta just isn't a jealous person so I think, but I am totally wrong about that. She is jealous from the start which is why she takes pleasure in hurting Fiamma, answering my phone before I do and laughing when the poor girl hangs up. I know I could be a rabidly jealous person, but I channel all my energy into Opera and it leaves me with nothing left to feel for anyone once I am off the stage. And if there is anything left to feel, I fill it full of trashy food and vomit and vomit until I am cleansed of everything. Until I feel nothing and I like that feeling. As though I can throw up all my feelings with the huge cake I have just swallowed.

I wondered what it would be like to be in love. I had never felt the emotion, for a man or a woman. Never had my heart broken, there was something long in the past that stopped me from feeling, maybe what I witnessed between my father and stepmother didn't help. Maybe cut throat ambition was really the reason though; it swept aside everything and kept the focus on me but I knew there was more to it than that. I swept through lovers with a greed and hunger like one of my many food binges but it felt just like that, empty and vacant and full of fatty chocolate grease once my appetite and uncontrollable hunger were stuffed to bursting point.

My cell phone would chime with night time messages from lovers scorned or waiting longingly in the wings, usually literally on the Opera House stage. The messages were always pleading, desperate, crazy with love or lust or just plain alcohol but I didn't care. They were gone to me once I decided they were gone. They were never there at all unless they were pretty.

I would turn over in bed and sleep without a conscience. I was truly Carmen, a living breathing Carmen. Never did I play a role with such heartfelt passion. She was me with her mesmerising carelessness. Other roles felt flat and dull in comparison.

And there were plenty of people to lust over and the next day I knew I would be coldly taking one of the Hungarian tenors home with even less feeling.

IL TROVATORE

I do not like the theatre director forever putting his arm round my waist this evening but I am his new rising star, Queen of the new Opera World and I need to be nice to him. I represent everything Opera is turning into. Where beauty and youth are rivals for the best voices, where looking glamorous in an evening dress post-show is every bit as important as the show itself. I am saccharine sweet towards him. It helps when I have to stick the knife in to get rid of my rivals. One thing I will not do is sleep my way to the top. I would be just like Lilla if I started that. Sure I date whoever I want, but I am not going to go down that road. I want to get to the top with my talent and my fierce backstabbing technique. I am already on the cover of one of the upmarket Hungarian fashion magazines looking every bit the diva I am, smouldering in a shimmering gold dress and tiara sitting on the Opera House stage. The theatre director is loving this media attention, the fact that I am beautiful enough to rival any of the world's greatest opera stars in the looks department anyway. He said he has waited a long time to put Hungary at the centre of the Opera World. Our company is talented but the Western opera houses get the glory and the media attention. He thinks there is a sea change and we will get what we deserve, what we finally worked so hard for and he is counting on me to bring it here. The senior singers are talented but I take it to a different league. I am out of this world. Well, so he says. That and the East holds hidden mystery and it will be unlocked. He gives long motivational speeches at each première about this sort of thing.

Unlocking the mysteries of the East. It is a bit tedious really as the speeches go on and on and on and all everyone wants to do is socialise and drink champagne and relax. Or get completely smashed on the free drinks and take someone home for a meaningless fling.

As for me, I am becoming ruthless in every area of my existence. I date people I don't care about, I leave them, I break their hearts. I say people because men or women it doesn't matter. I just like beauty but I just cannot love, I cannot give myself to anyone for longer than a week or two maximum. Apart from Kriszta that is, she is undemanding, just around when I need her and doesn't throw herself at my feet like all the others. If she did, I would probably ditch her or actually maybe I wouldn't. Maybe I could accept it in her. The fact she doesn't seem obsessed with me makes me continue with her. I respect her carelessness and the way she can turn her passion on and off like her stage persona.

It never occurs to me that I am repressing every emotion I should be feeling. That the throwing up is to stop me caring about anyone when I should be feeling emotions, that I am lying to myself that Kriszta is just one of the many lovers who is just there, just convenient. If I allowed myself to feel I would realise I am not just having fun, that I can feel emotions like everyone else but that means to hurt like everyone else. I just see emotions as weakness and the throwing up makes me feel cleansed. I also do not want to hurt. I have seen the pain of love and felt it in my performances and that is as far as I want to take it. I am missing out big time but it seems a sacrifice worth making. My heart is closed because I have closed it to the world of love.

It is the première of *Il Trovatore*, a new version and I am centre stage throwing down the champagne. I hardly need much to feel the effects and after two glasses I am an obnoxious diva, worse than usual. It burns my throat, scratched and sore from vomiting earlier but I like the feeling. I realise I am talking louder than anyone else, *I am, I am, I am.*

I do not care people are looking at me like I am a diva, and a bitch.

And I am the youngest leading soloist in this opera company; in December I will have my 26th birthday. There was such outrage amongst the older mezzos when I got the role of Azucena. I am just fulfilling the demand that is all. I even insisted they not turn me into an old Azucena, okay I will wear the ragged gypsy clothes they want for the role, but they do not grey my hair or line my face; I am not appearing on stage as an old gypsy hag as they have in some productions I have seen. I demand and I get. They want me as Azucena and they have to accept what I want from the role too. Opera has changed since I first started watching it as a teenager. Now, the pressures to be younger and slimmer and more beautiful are reaching insane proportions. No longer can Butterfly be played by older singers. But the younger soloists can play older roles. And the men are feeling the intensity too. One of my conquests, a 40 year old baritone, Mikki, is slowly becoming anorexic. His once muscular figure getting thinner and thinner, his face chiselled. He is getting fewer roles because of it; he has got too thin but we don't talk about it. He knows, I know and he probably knows that I know what he is doing. His strength and vitality to leap around the stage as a muscular Don Giovanni have ebbed away and his voice is suffering. He looks sad all the time, broken by pressure. I want to ask him what happened, when did he suddenly turn a corner from being the leading handsome baritone of the company to a thin, anxious figure sidelined in supporting roles but I don't. A few years ago, I watched him in *Faust* and fell in love with his persona in the opera; the bad guy and so devilishly handsome and with such on stage presence spinning out those rich low notes like silk. He could reach the Heavens with that voice. We have so much in common. But as ever, we hide under the facade. I am sure other singers know I am bulimic but I never hear anything and I look slim but not dangerously thin as the anorexics do.

But Mikki is spineless. He is bossed around by his costume designer girlfriend who is forever appearing at his side at parties and premières and hates him talking to other women especially me. She even sticks nauseating photos on his Facebook page of her and him, and scrawls idiotic cartoons of them both. I am disgusted that a man of his talent allows this woman not only access to his private account but lets her put up such childish stuff. He is a serious opera singer and he is pulled along as her puppet. This is why I truly can't respect Mikki for putting up with this shit.

No wonder he cheats on her. He is also in my life occasionally because he never ever boasts about having me. He never demands. It is up to me if I want him or not. In another lifetime, we could actually be friends but in the Opera World I don't have any friends. At this stage I don't count Kriszta as one although later I do, when I realise the depth of her loyalty and discretion despite being flirt of the century. And when later I realise her feelings are also being suppressed by her behaviour. She too can't deal with heartbreak, so she does it her way by tarting around, drinking too much and forgetting everything that hurts.

As we pose for the saccharine photos, the cast of *Il Trovatore* together, I feel the nails of Zsófia the lead soprano dig into my back. I am wearing a backless flowing evening dress in red silk and we smile, the row of us together so false for the photos as the nails grip at my flesh tighter.

Maybe I outdid myself tonight. I was wearing a poison ring. Zsófia is the one who takes the poison from a ring in the opera itself as Leonora but I found this beautiful silver ring on a trip to London when I performed first as Rosette in Massenet's *Manon* in Covent Garden. It was in a witchcraft shop and I had run in to escape a panic attack, one of many I had in this sprawling crammed to the hilt city. The horrible metro was the worst; so deep underground and whatever time of day it was I could never ever get a seat. It felt like being buried alive. So as I hid in the magic shop I decided I should buy a lucky ring, something to help me through my fear. Here I was performing in Covent Garden, okay in a small role, with no fear of the audience or my ability but my fear was terrifying once I stepped out of the Opera House. It was the terrible agoraphobia of being swallowed in this metropolis. The lady working there suggested something empowering and she pulled out this ring. It is a spider made of silver but his back opens, yes it is fashioned on a genuine poison ring, the shop owner told me. *With this, all your rivals could be poisoned in one night. There is nothing to fear when you wear this ring, young lady.*

I remember putting it on for that première of *Il Trovatore* after I changed from my costume into my red dress and dropped flour I had placed in the spider's back into Zsófia's drink during one of the long speeches as she was about to take a sip. I give her a fake smile and snap the spider ring together again and draw my finger across my windpipe mockingly in a gesture of death. It freaked her out and she dropped the glass and called me a crazy bitch as I just laughed at her stupidity. Did she really think I would poison her? The glass shatters on the floor and the bar staff clean up, everyone around carries on drinking and socialising. Zsófia is rattled and I see her gesticulating wildly to a group of bitches, pointing at me and describing what I just did and I feel their hate from across the stage, all five of them. I inhale it as though it is a cloud of sweet perfume. It feels so good, so good to be bad.

So good to be hated. If I am hated it means they want to be me. They all want to be me.

I do not care Kriszta is not here for me. She promised to come along for the dress rehearsal and didn't show up but she swears she will be here for me the next performance after the première. She is rehearsing herself and she has to be at some parents' night at school for her daughter tonight. Whatever, I do not care, or more like I make myself not care. Maybe that is why I threw up today. On a performance night. I had made a rule that I would never do this, but here it is broken already. And twice in one day. No wonder I have a sore throat.

At the end of the night I look out into the auditorium and the empty seats and everyone has suddenly gone and I am alone with my champagne glass and bad throat and a bouquet of lilies lying on the stage, barely touched. Lilies are for funerals, although the opera is dark that's true, made darker by the director who loves tragedy and pain; I actually think he is a sadist. But I don't get involved with directors. Not now, not never. I gather up the lilies, maybe it is unlucky but they are too beautiful to waste. Their scent is overpowering and I feel as though I am at my own funeral.

Where the hell is everyone? This is my night and they have all disappeared. This is my glory.

To hell with them all. And Kriszta too. Although she did

have the thought to send me some roses which were waiting in my dressing room when I arrived that night. She is not entirely heartless. Not that I allow myself to really care. The roses are pretty, yellow and brighten up the gloomy dressing room.

It is round about this time that I get my first real stalker. And he isn't one of the audience but one of the senior managers, Ádám. He is obsessed with me. He has followed me home several times. He knows my schedule inside out so when I arrive at stage door he is just happening to go in or out. He watches me from the company box, he has told me this and I think nothing of it at first. Many people do this. That's why it is there, he works here. Why not?

He asks me to have dinner with him but I refuse. Not because I wouldn't want to, he is handsome and seems pleasant but I made a rule which I will never break; never ever date anyone other than the other singers. That means no directors, stage crew, management or even musicians. I stick to that. But the more I have to be curt with him as he is forever hanging around, the worse he becomes. It is starting to become annoying. He is there every evening I perform and just happens to be in the backstage area when I am there. So when I turn around, sensing someone watching me, I am thinking, *Not again.*

And I turn around as only the stage crew are here moving in the set for the next night except she is there; my devoted little Italian girl Fiamma standing in the wings too shy to speak. She has returned just to see me and I have not even noticed her all night. Why would I? She has less of a stage presence than a theatre mouse. I am almost irritated by her pathetic behaviour and the fact she was even too shy to approach me until everyone has left. I feel like just walking off, but I am still on a high from my première and I do not want to be alone tonight.

And I am pretty relieved it is not my stalker. I would not be happy tonight although I feel safe enough with all the crew around, and big stage door keepers on duty but all the same I would rather not deal with him.

As for Fiamma, I would have had more respect for her if she had boldly walked up to me and said she had come to see me and I was amazing. I would have respected her for that but not this, hiding in the wings, too shy to speak. I am irritated and feel like just walking out on her. I thought I got rid of her by my cold indifference. But there is no doubt, as she steps out of the shadow of the side of the stage, she is hauntingly beautiful. She has that hypnotic ethereal quality Kim Novak has in Hitchcock's *Vertigo,* where she shimmers as she steps along, sad and mesmerising but hardly a creature of this world. It is hard to say no to someone like that, however much I disrespect them. I take Fiamma by the arm and into my dressing room where she burbles on about having to see me, how wonderful I was tonight. How she loves me, only me. Misses me like crazy. She has no shows on for the next month but she might get the chance to play Tosca in a small theatre in southern Italy.

I shove the lilies into her arms and she takes them and still talks on and on. The heavy scent of the flowers makes me feel almost sick.

I pull on my fur coat, my beautiful midnight blue one which changes colour in the light, not really listening to her mindless chattering and take her by the hand without a word. I am tired but can't resist. I hand the dressing room key back to the stage door man and my taxi is waiting. I can't say no to Fiamma; for one thing she is just too damn pretty. And even I am not that cruel to leave her standing in the chill November air outside the theatre alone. The girl came all this way to see me, for God's sake. Who does that? I should be flattered. But I am tired.

I do tell her to shut the hell up though, I need to think after a demanding night and her constant chatter is really irritating. I say it rudely and abruptly as I check my phone for messages from Kriszta in the back of the taxi. Hurt, she obeys me. She follows still holding the lilies and the small bunch of flowers I had in my dressing room from Kriszta.

No messages. Goddamn Kriszta. I take the flowers she gave me from Fiamma's arms so I can hide the card with its kisses and leave her holding the lilies. I don't want her acting like I broke her heart over some stupid good luck card.

It is clear, however, I am not just having my passion for one night. This girl seems to have installed herself in my apartment. After three days, when I return from the theatre after a meeting, Fiamma is still there, cosy on the sofa, dinner waiting ready and the table set as if she is staying for good and I really do not need this. She didn't even tell me when she was leaving and as I was busy, I didn't think to ask, assuming it would be in a day or two. But here she is, her clothes hanging in my closet, curled up and at home. And my dinner waiting as if I am her goddamn husband. Instead of being touched by this, I am angry. I tell her she needs to go back to Napoli. I have to concentrate on this run. My next performance is tomorrow night and she is a distraction. My career comes before everything; my health, my family, my life even.

If I wanted a house-husband, I would have taken one, Fiamma.

Yes, I am an ungrateful cruel bitch but I cannot stand this clingy, needy girl right now. We eat the dinner, she is still deeply hurt and tears run down her face as she twirls her pasta.

I look at her and sigh. Even I am not so cruel. I have already snapped at her not to dish out my pasta, I like to do it myself. Because I am such a control freak, because she might heap too much on and I might overeat and feel horrible. She has even made fresh garlic ciabatta bread and I take the tiniest piece and shout at her when she tries to give me more.

I go over and wrap my arm around her, "Come on, Fiamma. Don't do this. Let's just eat now. I need my space, I told you that. And it is kind of you to make this fresh Italian food for me, really it is."

"I thought you loved me," she says putting her fork down. "I thought you loved me too."

"Fiamma, honey," I say taking her face and wiping her tears away. "I don't love. I just don't love people. I can't. It is who I am. But I do care about you. So please, just be happy tonight."

This makes her cry harder. And I am ending up looking at my watch as I comfort her.

For God's sake. But I can't be nasty to her tonight. I have said enough already.

I think she still thinks she can change my mind as the next morning she has made my goddamn breakfast. She has found all the Italian places in Budapest and bought special pastries for us. She is like a puppy who is kicked and still comes back for more. She has juiced a heap of oranges and set out the table immaculately.

But no, she is not to come to the theatre and watch me again tonight.

Please, please let me see you again. I have to see you. I love you, Natalija. Please.

I give in as I just do not want to waste my energy arguing. After all she will be on her way home soon. So she watches me from the company box and immediately after the curtains close, she is already at my dressing room before I get changed. The costume lady laughs and says in Hungarian, "Natalija your stalker is here."

I laugh too. "Let her in, she likes to watch me change."

It must be every man's dream being stalked by this girl so I revel in it. Who wouldn't mind a young version of Monica Bellucci being obsessed with them? Watching them as though they were the only person on the planet.

But I cannot deal with it every day as Fiamma sits on the sofa in the dressing room and gazes at me with such adoration. Nice now and then but she is just too child-like, too easily hurt and too demanding of love. Which I cannot do.

And the same tears as I have to put her in a taxi two days later after I book her a flight back to Napoli, the same outpourings of love and lifelong devotion. I have to virtually drag her into the elevator to the waiting taxi as she is crying so much the morning of her flight.

And then she is gone. I feel a bit guilty, a bit empty, a bit sad so I go into the kitchen and stuff as many chocolates and biscuits and our leftover Italian pastries from breakfast to stop this feeling and vomit immediately, cleansing with salt water to get everything out. Why the hell did Fiamma have to go and fill my fridge and cupboards with food? I am cleansed and ready for the next chapter. I sleep heavily and wake up feeling emptier than ever. My throat is sore and it spells the beginnings of tonsillitis, one of the many bouts I will have that year.

By the end of the run I am well and truly ill and have needed antibiotics from the company doctor to sing the final performance. He tells me I am risking damaging my voice singing in this condition, I should stand down even just for the final show and at least take a few days but I dismiss his warnings. It is the final show, what else am I going to do?

Besides, the following morning I am due to start rehearsals for *Aida*. Controversially, it will play as one of the Christmas and New Year operas but the company wants to maximise ticket sales so needs to alternate as many as possible to bring in the tourists over consecutive nights. One of the artistic directors had insisted it play a long Christmas run, he had new ideas to make Verdi's towering majestic opera on a grand scale. He wants to turn Christmas on its head, he wants some pyramids and a load of sand dumped outside the theatre, he wants and he wants and he wants. He is even demanding camels but they draw the line at this. He is actually jumping up and down demanding we have camels from the zoo. But this is the artistic director who believed in me the most. He was the one who insisted I play Amneris in *Aida* over the summer festival. He is the one who takes the biggest risks, and with it plays with fire; we could end up with a theatre only half full with the choices he makes.

The theatre director is not happy. It looks like a schizophrenic has designed our decorations. One side of the theatre is the Christmas tree and candy cane and mulled wine stall with the snow covered pavement, the other side is ancient Egypt complete with pyramids, bejewelled Egyptian Gods, the snow swept aside for a load of sand dumped on the ground. It looks like a theatre decorated by a madman or a genius, I can't decide which.

But this artistic director is demanding and intense and will not say no.

Just like me.

Just like me he gets his wish. His argument that Opera would be boring if we gave the public the same seasonal shows. *Maybe some people want exotic Egypt, maybe they don't want Christmas and New Year. Maybe some people are Jewish and don't celebrate Christmas. We have to take risks, without risk there is nothing,* he says emphatically chopping his hands through the air in a frenzy.

One of the Spanish guest soloists asks me to marry him in a restaurant two days after the end of the run of *Il Trovatore* where I had played Azucena, the gypsy. Strange in Hungary, which is a country divided with hatred for gypsies or 'cigányok', I excelled in playing them. I loved the lawlessness of the roles, for me they were the best. Even if I had been a soprano, I couldn't imagine playing Mimi or Butterfly, maybe Tosca the ultimate diva or cruel Turandot but even she is broken by the end. Tosca it would have to be. She at least has the courage to leap from the parapet to her death.

I wondered if the roles where I fizzled and snapped with energy were causing everyone to fall in love with me. But this poor Carlos who wanted to possess me, own me, marry me was so pathetic I laughed in his face. He said he had never been so humiliated in his entire life. He loved me he said. I am still on antibiotics and not feeling well at all. My throat is inflamed and not healing up. The wine has made me dizzy after one glass and I really want to just be alone right now in my apartment and in bed. I do not even want to spend the night with this man again. And he is asking for a lifetime? He must be out of his mind as he is not even drunk. And why is he still here? The run finished two days ago. *Go home, Carlos*, I think.

I am thinking about *Aida,* running through the

rehearsal in my mind and not even registering half of what he is saying. They have made changes since its appearance in the summer festival and the staging and space is allowing for maximum scene changes and I am running through the stage space in my head when I realise Carlos is looking for my answer to his idiotic question.

"You don't even know me, you've seen me in rehearsals and on the stage and we had some mindless fling from what I remember and that wasn't very memorable, but that's about it, Carlos," I say, wondering if it is rude to go and throw up in the bathroom after someone has bought me a dinner but already I feel that tiramisu settling in my stomach, the food rich and oily turning me into a fat person. I try to sit on my hands. The door to the bathrooms downstairs is a glowing light in the dark restaurant and I need to get down there.

I do not want to be here. I am already tired after the rehearsals for my demanding role of Amneris in *Aida*. I want to just go home. I look at my watch. It is 9.30pm and Carlos is going on and on and on.

"You are so cold. Hungarians are the coldest, cruellest people I ever met. You all have this facade of polite behaviour, and underneath it, none of you are nice."

Like Fiamma these Mediterranean types are so out of their depth in our strange land. They are used to warmth and openness not the guarded suspicious mindset so many of us have.

"Then you have learned something in our beloved country. It is important to learn something new every day," I say, and smile a little.

"And you are the coldest woman I ever fell in love with," he says his eyes full of pain that I don't care I've caused. He is handsome but dull. I think he must be naive too, for a man of 40 to ask someone to marry him after such a short time. I do not want to be married to anyone ever as I do not trust or love. And especially not to be owned by a man like a piece of property.

"Then stop falling in love so easily," I say.

He looks like I stabbed him. He says, "You eat so much, Natalija. I am surprised you stay so slim. Always eating."

He is being nasty. He is trying to hurt me as he knows my weakness. But I do not see it like that.

I am full of rage, "I eat less than 2000 calories a day. I hardly eat. One starter and a bit of your pasta and some dessert."

"You eat so much," he says his eyes cold.

"Go fuck yourself!" I scream and dump his espresso onto his white shirt. "I do not eat and I would never want another night with you and you wanted a lifetime of me! You stupid idiot! Go back to Spain with your idiotic ideas of love, you are just a boy!"

Everyone around us is looking but I don't care, I have lost it. He has hit my raw nerve with the nastiness that a man scorned will do. But I do not see that. I just think, *My God I have to cut back if people are noticing I am eating too much. I must be. I must be.*

I grab my coat and bag and get up and I go downstairs to the bathroom. It is rude to throw up an expensive dinner but I can't hold it in. I will worry all night. And now after what he just said, I am not seeing it for what it was, an insult because he was rejected. I am convinced I eat too much.

So I ram my fingers down my throat, scraping off the scabs on my hand but I am more determined after what he just said. I scratch my throat which is already sore but I don't care.

I vomit and choke and dry heave into the toilet but it's not so easy without a bottle of water or some salt. I need my own bathroom for this. I reach into my bag for a bottle of water and glug half of it and then ram my hands down my throat. That's better, it's easier now. But home is best for this or at least the theatre toilets where someone else is either crying or throwing up in the cubicle next to me, from nerves usually.

I leave the toilet cubicle and wash my face and hands before getting my coat from behind the door. I am so obsessive about hygiene. One of the reasons we are in this restaurant is the toilets are so clean; always somewhere to hang your coat and bag in the spacious cubicle while you throw up. And the floors are always clean enough to kneel over the toilet bowl.

I didn't choose this place because of the food. It is good Italian cuisine and expensive, but I am more interested in how to throw it all up again in comfortable surroundings. Nothing worse than bulimia in a dirty toilet cubicle.

I am gone 15 minutes and when I emerge into the restaurant again, Carlos is gone and I feel absolutely nothing. I feel broken and the waiters are concerned. *Am I okay? I don't look well. Very pale. Maybe a taxi?*

I nod and sit down while I wait. They bring me a shot of limoncello. I don't want it. It burns going down, burns through the scratches on my throat but it is kind of the staff.

I cradle my hand which is bleeding. I don't want anyone to see. I wrap a tissue around my knuckles and put on my gloves.

I hear one man say to his wife. *Isn't that the opera singer we saw in Il Trovatore?*

I don't know, she says. *She doesn't look so happy. Maybe she just looks like her. That girl looks ill.*

I don't look at them.

AIDA

Amneris in *Aida* is me. Like Carmen I feel this is a role created for me. Daughter of the King of Egypt. A goddess in black and gold, only I am not feeling the strength and power I did back when I first performed in the summer. I don't even remember it is my birthday I am so absorbed. I tell Kriszta a few days later and she surprises me the following day with an unusual silver bracelet in the shape of a snake wrapping around my wrist. It really goes with my Egyptian goddess look and I even wear it for the rest of the performances. The costume designer says, *It is beautiful, where did I get it? A boyfriend? It is perfect for my role. I have to leave it on, it is so right for the role of Amneris.*

Just a friend, I say. *A birthday gift.*

It is expensive and I say this to Kriszta as I touch the snake on my wrist, even his eyes are jewelled with tiny rubies. "Oh, it's nothing, nothing, I know you like your poison spider ring so a snake seemed very you," she says dismissively. But on my wrist it is beautiful. Not nothing; this is lovely. No one has ever given me jewellery for my birthday apart from my family. I am very touched. I put it on my left wrist so it doesn't interfere with me sticking my hand down my throat.

"Can't give you chocolates, Natalija. You would throw them all up again," she says with a playful laugh. "And flowers are for opening nights. But seriously you do know that Carlos was being nasty. He knew your weakness and he went for it. You do know you do not eat enough, don't you?"

"I don't know. I don't know what is enough and what is too much. I have no balance. I am afraid of eating too much. Unless I know I will throw it up," I say. I fiddle with my bracelet.

Kriszta touches my hand. "I am telling you and I know you better. You do not eat enough, Natalija. And when you do eat more than you should for emotional reasons you stuff and stuff full of trashy food and then you throw up and throw up until there is nothing left. No wonder it is making you ill. And God, Carlos who the hell does he think he is? As if he would be good enough for you. No man is good enough for you," she says with just a trace of angry ownership. I am her toy. She accepts I have lovers, she is married after all but I know something in her doesn't like it although everything in her denies her jealousy.

I shrug about the food thing. Because I do not know. I honestly do not know what is the right amount of food. I have no perspective. And it's hard to take advice from Kriszta who also throws up although sometimes only once a week, sometimes twice, sometimes she goes longer without doing it.

The première is dazzling and if anything I perform even better than I did in the summer, or maybe I am more confident. But my throat is not so good. It holds through the dress rehearsal but I am having to take antibiotics again by the time it is première night. The company doctor has looked at my tonsils after the performance and written me a prescription immediately. Kriszta is there for me as soon as I am off the stage, knocking on my dressing room door and I am drenched with sweat and emotion. The company doctor is saying to Kriszta, *Make sure this girl looks after that throat. She must get those antibiotics tonight.*

Kriszta promises him she will make sure we do. When he leaves the room, my costume lady asks can she help? I tell her I will be fine. Kriszta will help me.

Kriszta embraces me and tells me I was amazing. The

audience loved me. More than Zita. More than Philip the British man who plays Radamès. I own the stage. She sits happily on the sofa in my dressing room as I change out of my costume into a gold evening dress and gold high heels. I am wearing her snake bracelet she gave me for my birthday. I am tired and feel as though the life has been sucked out of me. I want to just lie down and have someone stroke my hair like a child. But I don't like to ask her what I really want tonight.

Tonight I am not up for fun or passion. I look at the prescription for antibiotics the doctor has given me. We will have to go to a late night pharmacy on the way home.

"Come on, you look wonderful," she says. "Let's get some drinks, hey?"

I nod and she protectively wraps her arm around my shoulders. "Takes it out of you, doesn't it?"

"Yes," I say. I feel very different to the girl who lit up the stage tonight and in the open air theatre in the summer. I am absolutely drained more than I ever felt in my life.

And to make it worse, Ádám, the stalker manager is hanging around outside my dressing room. He has already sent me flowers with a card saying something like 'fit for the Queen of Egypt, you are wonderful'.

I am Amneris, daughter of the King of Egypt. I am not the Queen. The flowers are huge, an enormous bouquet you would send to a lover. I am uncomfortable. I want to give them to my costume lady who is still in the dressing room corridor but I don't want Ádám to see.

Kriszta senses I am uncomfortable as Ádám gushes something congratulatory or other. She holds me to her and just roughly pushes past him as I murmur some kind of thanks for the flowers.

I wander around the stage in a daze, aware Ádám is

watching me, everyone congratulating me, even Zita maybe because I am quiet tonight, not acting like the diva I often do. Kriszta hangs on to me protectively, sensing I am not strong tonight, seeing that I am having trouble walking as I am weak. I stumble in my heels leaving the stage and get the stiletto caught in the gap in the wooden flooring where the stage set rises into a pyramid in the opera and Kriszta has to pull me out. The amount of shoes I have wrecked on this damn stage already with these slits and holes in the floor. She laughs as I sprawl flat on the floor breaking the champagne glass. I am not in a laughing mood, I want to cry. Tonight has taken everything out of me.

She knows my tears are close and quickly hauls me into the dressing room and closes the door where I just break down and cry and cry and cry.

"Hey, hey, what's this? Why are you crying, lovely girl? You were amazing tonight? What's with the tears?" She says handing me a box of tissues.

I don't know, I really don't. I am just not feeling so well, I tell her. *My throat hurts.*

"Don't let those bitches see you are weak, don't let anyone see it," says Kriszta as she reapplies my make-up before we leave. "Don't ever let anyone see that or they will eat you alive."

I know.

"And you?" I ask.

"I am not your rival, Natalija. I don't want you out. Besides you're my little girl, you need someone to take care of you. You're just not well tonight, that's all. It is a big role to play, you gave so much of yourself, too much. You must always hold something back. This giving yourself, it is wonderful for the audience but you will break in the end if you don't hold some of you back." She says this last bit seriously with some thought.

I don't really understand her logic but I get in the taxi. We head past one of the late night pharmacies to get my medicine and then to my apartment. I tell Kriszta who is holding Ádám's monstrous flowers to take them home with her. I don't want to have them in my apartment but I ask to please wait until I sleep before she has to leave, I don't want to be alone but I just need to sleep, and sleep and sleep. I swallow a pill from the bottle of antibiotics with some hot lemon and honey and I fall into the bed still in my dress and shoes. I can't even make the shower. Kriszta does what I want without me asking and strokes my hair, whispers something sweet in my ear and it is the last thing I remember as when I wake up it is morning and she is long gone.

I feel like hell. My shoes are on the floor but I am still in my dress and make-up. My face feels horrible, stuck to the pillow with my thick stage make-up still on it. I feel as though I have been drinking when I didn't even finish my first glass of champagne.

I see a text on my phone and reach for it, ***Why?????? Why her and not me? What does she do to you that I don't? You will be sorry for this, you and that whore Krisztyna. Opera House sluts, both of you.***

Damn Ádám. I didn't wake up but he sent it at 2am and this has moved the stalking to an unpleasant level. I reach for my medicine and take another pill with some painkillers. My throat is like the goddamn Egyptian desert they have designed outside the theatre. I might as well be in Egypt as I feel as though I have swallowed a load of sand, gritty and painful. I store the text on my phone. I want to delete it but I need evidence as this is threatening behaviour and if he says it to me alone, I have no evidence. Here I have the written evidence and it is direct from his cell phone. Not an anonymous number.

I am run down and tired, still ill with tonsillitis three days later. I don't even notice Christmas Day as we play in the morning at 11am and I never know if it is day or night over this Christmas and New Year period where they are packing in two different operas a day. I seem to arrive or leave the stage door in the dark and my body clock is totally confused. There is a different opera that night and I go home after the show and sleep and sleep and sleep and wake up disorientated to messages on the answerphone, wishing me a Merry Christmas. I had declined to go to my father's house to eat. They did manage to make it to my performance on the Christmas morning and we have coffee afterwards in the Opera Theatre café, which I guess is something. It was nice to see Levente, my brother who is over from Munich for the holidays. He embraces me after the show, and tells me I am a superstar. My father and stepmother are more restrained telling me I am taking on a bit too much maybe. I seem to be going from one opera straight into another. Even Lilla, hated stepmother, is looking concerned, although I doubt she really cares.

As for one opera following another, isn't that the idea? I am a raging success. I have to do this.

When I am not in the theatre I seem to be sleeping all the time. I have zero energy. I am even cutting back on nights of passion. I am just too tired. Kriszta asks me to attend her opening night of *Die Fledermaus* where she plays Rosalinde. It opens on New Year's Eve as this is when the opera's action is set. For one thing, I do not like *Die Fledermaus,* an idiotic light frosting of an operetta which I see fit for people who are too stupid to watch the real deal. I do not find comedy funny anyway. I have a cruel sense of humour. If someone falls off a piece of scenery or down a flight of stairs, I laugh without stopping to consider if they are hurt or not. I can't control this, another reason people hate me. One of the baritones was hit by a backdrop from the fly floor during our last few rehearsals of *Aida* when we had moved to the stage and everything was all new and fast and unexpected; having to adjust from cramped rehearsal studios to this echoing space, getting our entrances and exits perfect.

So when the King of Egypt is felled by the backdrop like a tree and falls flat on the stage and I burst out laughing, everyone looks with disgust. I am sorry I do it. Of course, if he was really hurt I would stop laughing but he is more stunned and dazed, uninjured as it is made of gauze.

I actually wonder at times if I am a borderline sociopath.

And in comedy, everyone is laughing at nothing it seems; only tired old jokes which I can't imagine were funny in the day.

I am sitting in one of the boxes and I actually fall asleep with my head on the edge of the box. I sleep right through the interval and I am woken up at midnight as celebrations take place on stage and the pyrotechnics violently exploding give me a fright and I wonder where the hell I am. After the opera finishes, I make my way backstage which is full of life and laughter and Kriszta is full of energy as I walk down the dressing room corridor at half midnight in a daze. Everyone is in good spirits and standing around drinking champagne in the corridors, running in and out of dressing rooms, sharing food and stories. Kriszta pulls me into her dressing room which is shared and I haven't the heart to tell her I missed half the performance, I can't even remember when she appeared on stage and what she did. Everyone in her dressing room is in an excited bubble of happiness passing around a bottle of champagne and even one girl who dislikes me hands me a glass. Kriszta whispers to me she will be able to stay at my apartment the whole night. As she leans in and I feel her sweet breath in my ear, I should be happy but I am just ill and tired and broken. I sip the champagne and immediately want to throw up.

She is smouldering with vitality and energy as she strips off her costume, ever the exhibitionist before changing into a red party dress although I see there are old and new bruises on her back. I want to ask but we are not alone and I know I will be met with dismissive lies about falling over in the shower or out of bed. Whatever the question, Kriszta has an excuse. We sit around some more as no one is in a rush to leave unlike the usual performance nights, but I am weak and exhausted. I don't have a performance tomorrow night as there is a New Year's Day concert instead, but the next night I do. The champagne rushes into my blood and I feel strange. Dizzy, but not happy. The antibiotics are not a good combination with alcohol.

Kriszta's taxi arrives on time and she doesn't even notice my quietness as she gabbles on like a glove puppet. I fall asleep at home, head aching and resting on the pillows, while Kriszta is pouring champagne in the kitchen, after showering the theatre out of her hair. She is only gone 10 minutes but I am deeply asleep. She wakes me up with a glass, shaking me roughly and tells me I am no fun tonight. The one night of the year she can spend more time with me and celebrate New Year and I am sleeping already.

"And all you have in your fridge was goddamn champagne, milk, juice and coffee, Natalija. It's bring your own food in this apartment. Oh, I suppose I did find a bit of wholewheat bread, honey and lemon in the cupboard. Just as well I brought us breakfast and chocolates. How you live like this, I don't know," she says with a touch of nastiness.

I feel tears in my eyes. I hate it when she is harsh. She doesn't notice, she is so intent on talking on and on and on about *Die Fledermaus,* the comedy, the laughs they had.

I try to drink the champagne and liven up for her. Kriszta is getting chocolates all over the bed, they are falling out of the box and melting in the sheets which she finds funny. Damn her, she is so selfish. The bed is a mess. I bet she wouldn't dare do that at home. Her husband would probably beat her. She is guzzling all the champagne, spilling it on the sheets, still on an adrenaline high from her performance. I eat one truffle and try to manage another before I run to the bathroom to throw up violently, chocolate and champagne and blood. I wipe my mouth and there is blood on the tissue. I am afraid.

Kriszta shouts angrily from the bedroom that this is out of order, throwing up after so little. *Why am I spoiling the night? This is her night too, remember. Where is the Natalija she met at the Turandot première, the lovely nymph from the woods who was beautiful and sensual. I am getting old before my time,* she continues, staggering into the bathroom drunk.

She sees me crying on the floor on my knees, blood and saliva on my hands and running from my mouth and it is obvious I am not a well girl at all. I am shivering despite the warm apartment.

"Natalija I am so sorry, I am a selfish bitch," she tells me. "You're still not right, are you? Your throat, is it hurting?"

I nod and she gathers me up all motherly and washes my face and hands which makes me cry more as I want to tell her I miss my long dead mother, and she is not quite old enough to be my mother but she is a mother to her own children and her tenderness is reminding me of what I missed but I can't tell her this. She dries my tears and tells me she will make me a milk and honey, I am still on antibiotics and she is so sorry for pushing me over the champagne, she didn't know I was still so ill. It means more for her and she gives up on the glass and just swigs from the bottle after she has wrapped me in the duvet and made me a hot milk. She talks on and on, still buzzing from *Die Fledermaus.* In the end we both just fall asleep, her constant chatter sending me far away until the empty bottle of champagne falls with a *chunk* to the floor. My throat feels as raw as sandpaper.

I wake up on New Year's Day at 8am and I am cold and the snow is falling thickly outside the window. I stare at the flakes for a few minutes. Kriszta is sleeping like the dead, still in a party dress from last night, her back to me as if I don't even exist and greedily swiss-rolled in all of the duvet. The sheets are sticky with melted chocolates and I feel totally empty. I haul back some of the duvet and she doesn't even stir. I examine the marks on her back I noticed last night, bruises faded purple and green with some fresh ones where the dress reveals them in the morning light. I touch them gently and wonder what she did or more like who did this; her husband or another man and does she really like it rough like she says or is she lying constantly? She always has the same answers about falling over drunk, slipping in the shower, liking it rough, falling out of bed. Then I drift away again until I am woken by Kriszta throwing up her champagne from last night in the bathroom.

I don't even get up to see to her. She is nearly 37 years old, for God's sake. And she brought it on herself.

I bury my face in the pillow. *Damn her for acting this way.*

I am guilty as I am thinking these angry thoughts and she brings in a tray with fresh juice, coffee and croissants and places it next to me saying I will feel better if I eat.

"What happened to your back?" I say biting a croissant.

"What?" she says sharply.

"I saw the bruises as your dress is cut away and I just wondered what happened."

She doesn't like my question but looks at her plate and waves her hand, "You know, I don't even remember. I think I fell in the shower when I was drunk."

"They must have hurt," I say reaching for her. "But they didn't all happen in one night, did they? Who hurts you, Kriszta? How can you put up with that?"

"Don't, Natalija, just shut up," she snaps. She sighs and says, "Sorry, I just fall over a lot. You know me, I drink more than I should."

I don't believe her. I know once she shouted at me not to come in to clean my teeth when she was in the shower. And she is not shy. More of an exhibitionist. But she likes candles, she claims she has cellulite and stretch marks from the children so she likes dim lighting. But I don't buy it. I have seen her body in the morning light when she is lost in sleep, twisted around the sheets and the skin on her thighs and stomach doesn't have a trace of cellulite. It is golden and smooth apart from bruises and cuts which could only be inflicted by a man's fists. At times she stands around in her underwear in her dressing room, other times she is fiercely defensive, hiding parts of her under her clothes, refusing to show me her arms or chest or back.

"If someone is hurting you….." I begin. "If your husband is hurting you I want you to leave. I can't stand it that someone would hit you, Kriszta. You….."

"Shut up!" she says cutting me off mid sentence and

grabbing my hair. She forces my head back and says, "Just drop it, will you? I told you I fall a lot."

Her eyes are angry and cold.

"Kriszta, I'm sorry. I just care, that's all. Can't you understand?"

"It's okay," she says. But the mood is gone. "I drink, Natalija. I fall over, you know what a party girl I am."

"Yes, I do," I say. But I feel sad and helpless as I sit there next to this lovely woman who lies and lies and lies to me.

We sit and eat in silence, staring at the white swirling snow through the window. I have killed the conversation. We always have so much to talk about but she seems down. I sense she doesn't want to go home, maybe she is afraid to go home and I tell her she can stay but I need to sleep. But she can stay, go and watch TV in the living room, read, cook in the kitchen, whatever.

She says she needs to get home besides what is she going to cook? I have no food in the apartment only scraps of things.

When she leaves I take a couple of sleeping pills and wipe out the rest of the day. I am not fit for anything. I hate New Year's Day. I wake up really early the following morning totally disorientated, not knowing what day or year it is. I have a vague feeling I am performing this evening. I have to check the dates and times everywhere, as I am paranoid I have missed a show with all this sleeping. I haven't, but I am performing later that evening.

I leave the apartment to go to the theatre early. I have a vocal warm up and I really need it.

Ádám is outside my apartment block. This throws me. How long, how long has he waited there? This is really out of line. He is not his usual doe-eyed pleasant self. After that text, I know it has moved up to a notch of unpleasantness.

I just say he shouldn't be stalking me and it isn't good for anyone. He follows me as I walk quickly to the tram. He is gabbling on about, *Why am I not good enough, why Kriszta?*

I tell him Kriszta is my best friend. And that is it.

Denial is the best. I am not giving away bullets.

I am hoping he is going to carry on the way he is as we get off the tram and towards stage door where I will have 3 witnesses from the men on the security desk. But Ádám is not dumb. He literally shuts his mouth at the stage door steps and walks away quickly.

CLOWNS

I am Lola in *Cavelleria Rusticana.* There are no mezzo roles in *Pagliacci,* which is paired with *Cavalleria.* This is a pity as the director has made efforts to interlink the stories of passion, betrayal and vengeance set in small town Sicily and Southern Italy. He is basing both of the operas in the same location to link up the operas better so we are all in Sicily, modern day, and the mafia is in full force throughout. I like this director and his approach. He has a bit of a crush on me and told me he would love me to be in *Pagliacci* too, but my voice range won't allow it. I watch *Pagliacci* in the dress rehearsal after my performance and I love how the lighting state grows darker and darker. I am reminded of Fiamma, the Sicilian girl, the fact my mother was quarter Sicilian meaning it is in my bloodline too and my hand drifts towards the phone and before I know it I have texted Fiamma. I feel guilty and want to make sure she is okay. Just that. Only she doesn't see it the way I do. A friendly ***How are you?*** turns into endless texts of adoration which I then wish I hadn't prompted.

And she comes over the following weekend unannounced, ever hopeful. Does nothing I do or say crush this girl's devotion? She says she has been performing *Tosca* in Sicily, taking the title role as she mentioned back in December and I am happy for her. She is getting the roles at least, even though they are not major venues. I sense a bit more maturity from her and she has actually booked a return flight to Napoli for the Tuesday morning. It is a problem as I am in a bit of a small time fling with Imre who is playing Pagliaccio. I have to switch my phone off as after the Saturday showing of *Cavalleria Rusticana* and *Pagliacci.* He is expecting to see me but Fiamma is waiting and Imre has already started to irritate me as he is one of the most arrogant singers in the company. He also has a wife, maybe kids, not that I care as I don't care about him but he really does love himself and I have no time for someone else who wants the limelight. I need that limelight and I need adoration, which is why I keep going back to Fiamma. I simply cannot stand men in particular who are wanting to be in control. He really thinks he knows it all because of our age difference.

I stand him up that night and switch off my phone. He is angry and he brags to the whole cast of both operas all about conquering me, about how I virtually lay down in front of him begging. He is pathetic. He also has seen me and Kriszta interacting with each other and quizzed me about it, which of course I deny. Rightly so he doesn't believe this so he goes one step further and tells everyone I was frigid as hell in bed as only a woman will get me off.

I am furious and try to avoid him, but on Monday, when I go down the dressing room corridor to get my coat and bag after *Pagliacci* finishes, there he is full of rage and he tells me exactly what he has told the rest of the company; I am frigid and inadequate unless Kriszta is around. I call him all the names I can think of. I tell him he is *pathetic for a 45 year old, just useless in bed. Maybe I should tell everyone that. You don't even know what to do with it.*

Everyone can hear us shouting anyway since we are in the dressing room corridor.

Slut, he calls me. *Vile little slut. Kriszta's little lover.*

I slap his still made up clown face and tell him, *Go back to your wife. You don't have a clue about me or any other woman, what would you know? You can't even find me in a bed, let alone do anything about it.*

That's because you starve and vomit all the time,

Natalija, don't think we don't know! You're too thin! he shouts.

The other singers have come out of their dressing rooms to see what all the shouting is about, they have heard it all anyway as we were shouting so much and it is entertainment for them. The stage manager slams the doors of the dressing rooms and tells us in a low angry voice to keep our domestics out of the workplace. *This isn't a theatre once we are off the stage,* she says.

I am so mad. Besides, he is wrong. I am not too thin, and not because I have an eating disorder. Okay, I am slim especially for an opera singer but that is the way it is now; slim and beautiful singers reign supreme, but my weight is just at the low end of normal. I know that. This is on account of the fact that when I do eat, I manage to hold down some healthy food. It is only on a binge, I vomit and purge everything from me.

I am shaking with rage about Imre and I go to meet Fiamma at the stage door. She had insisted on watching *Pagliacci* too which I knew was a big mistake but I guess I would have ended up in the same argument with him next performance night, on the Friday. Better to have it over and done with now. She sees me visibly upset and wants to know why but I hurry her out and just say one of the male singers has been hassling me, he wanted me and I refused.

More like I just had a meaningless fling out of boredom. But I do not want Fiamma to know this.

Protectively, she says she will go and confront him.

"No, Fiamma, the stage manager has told us to get out. Please, it will make it worse. You are a guest and you can't just walk in and start on the singers. You might be cut from the schedules forever. It is bad enough that I have to shout outside dressing rooms but please, Fiamma, think of your career."

I take her arm. It would make it worse. And worse for me too as the fling with Imre would be revealed. Kriszta's name would be thrown around and Fiamma would be hurt not to mention the stage manager and all the other cast overhearing more of my volcanic domestics.

I would then spend the rest of the night comforting Fiamma about my 'unfaithfulness' as if I should justify it. I do not belong to her. No one owns me but Fiamma would be whining in my apartment all night afterwards and this is just too much. I am tired. I need a good night's sleep.

She agrees. *Men are so stupid,* she tells me. *They really think they own women.*

And again, if I thought this visit from Fiamma was trouble free I should not have been so presumptuous. She cries again when she leaves that bitterly cold February morning. It is snowing and this southern Mediterranean girl is not used to the cold; from the weather or from people. She starts to text me 20 times a day saying how much she loves me, she can't carry on without me. Either I move to Italy and she will help me find work or she is willing to move to Budapest to live with me whether she is able to work or not. All she wants is me. She will look after me, she will cook for me, clean the apartment, support my career.

You stupid girl, I think. *You stupid sad girl.*

This last bit I find pathetic. We have worked ourselves into the ground to get as far as we are in Opera and will continue to give as much as it takes, and it does take. We are all exhausted, the lead soloists and I know that I have many more years ahead of me to continue to fight and push myself to the absolute limits. The idea of giving that up for a relationship which probably won't work out anyway disgusts me. Opera comes before anything.

I tell Fiamma to pull herself together and quit texting and calling. I need head space and she is screwing it up for herself more than anything. Her career should come first before everything and everyone, but she is not of my mindset. She will never be great. She has a beautiful voice, lovely stage presence but lacks the drive to make the big time. She will forever be playing in small Italian theatres, and occasionally guesting abroad. It is a waste. She also has problems with French and German, particularly German so her repertoire is limited. My French is good outside of the roles. Fiamma only learned French for roles such as Frasquita, she cannot speak the language.

Ádám follows me into my dressing room one evening soon after Fiamma's visit and I tell him firmly to please leave, I need to get changed.

The next moment I am pinned against the mirror. His hand is on my throat, his other on my breasts groping at them so hard he tears the top of my lace dress and he is full of rage.

"Why don't you want me, Natalija? You've been with everyone else in this goddamn company, you are just a whore. And I think the theatre director should know that his young star is into women. I know about you and Kriszta and that hot bit of Italian ass who was just here who looks so adoringly at you. I know everything. You think I can't do anything about you? I can poison everyone's minds against you. You need to start playing nice with me, sweetheart," he says. His blue eyes are ice and his face is pressed against mine but I am being choked by him as I am trying to shout for help which is not far away.

I am dizzy as though I will pass out and the thought of being strangled to death by such a bastard gives me the power I need and I summon one last bit of strength and manage to grab between his legs and twist. Like a martial arts expert told me. Grab as hard as you can and twist and it will floor any man. Especially as he is wearing a suit so there are no jeans to protect his anatomy.

He drops and I wrench open the door and scream for help. I flop to the floor dizzy, my windpipe feels crushed.

I am sitting outside my dressing room and a whole load of people from the costume lady to crew and the stage manager come running.

"He choked me and threatened me," I say. "Ádám attacked me and I thought he would kill me."

The musical director and some violinists are also on the scene.

It helps my dress is torn, showing my underwear and there are bruises coming up on my arms and my neck. Ádám is getting up from his fallen position.

"Bitch," he is saying. "You bitch."

This doesn't help him and his defence.

I am shaken as I never thought he was dangerous or threatening.

"She is a lying slut," he says. He has lost it. "She asked me into her dressing room. She asked for it!"

I bring on the tears which don't need to fall, but I need to make it absolutely to my advantage. Ádám is vicious and I am afraid of what he will do now, afraid he could get me out of my job.

I am crying and the musical director leads me away. They know no one ever comes to my dressing room other than Fiamma or Kriszta. Unlike some of the others, who have sex in their dressing rooms I have not even kissed anyone in mine.

The stage manager who is a tough female and not a fan

of Ádám's is saying this is going down as a serious incident. Everyone has seen my bruises. He will be fired for sure.

I have also kept every single text he has sent. Okay, I can't prove what else he said or how he stalked me outside my apartment but the texts and also the time of them are crucial. Always late, always threatening.

"I will kill him," Kriszta says her eyes flashing with rage. I have called her after the show and asked her to meet me. I don't want to be alone tonight. She is beautiful when angry and I know she would fly at him as well, like a tigress. She is strong. Way stronger than me.

"Don't say anything to him. He has threatened me, everyone knows, they saw my bruises but he has said he will tell the theatre director about us," I tell her in the dressing room.

"So?" she shouts. "So what! They know nothing. We say we are friends. Anyone who says otherwise is just jealous and gossiping."

"Please, Kriszta," I say. "I just need you to be with me tonight."

She calms down and sees the purple fingermarks on my neck and arms. "Oh, Natalija," she says gently drawing her fingers along the marks. "My Natalija. I could kill him."

She hugs me and I cry for real this time. Exhausted, ill, traumatised and so messed up.

In the taxi I lean against her and say, "I don't want to be alone. I don't want to be alone any more."

"You are never going to be alone," she says firmly. "I promise you, you are never going to be alone. I swear on my life that will never ever happen."

The incident is logged. The theatre director speaks to me about it. He is fortunately one of my biggest fans. He is not about to listen to the whinings of Ádám whatever he says, he now simply looks like the stalker he is, and dangerous with it. I hear from someone else that Ádám has been fired and if he stalks me again, the opera company are going to act seriously. Ádám just looks like a pathetic schoolboy telling tales, whatever he tries to say about me and my many lovers. And no one can prove who is a lover and who is just a friend. Some people have sex in the dressing rooms, or backstage, some people get caught in the act. It is something I have never done and never would. Another one of my rules. Don't give them any bullets. They don't see anything, they can't prove anything.

BLUEBEARD'S CASTLE

It is István's birthday at the end of February and Lilla has asked what happened to my hand, and I always say, *Oh stage accident* and dismiss it as nothing. She sees it as I reach for the bread.

Liar, her cold eyes tell me. She says it in front of my father to see if he will notice. But she doesn't care enough about me to tell him. She wouldn't care if I died.

István is not really noticing. He never notices anything these days. He is becoming a hollow shell of a man. He says very little and toys with his food and glass of wine. I feel almost angry at the person he has become. I want to shake him back into his old personality when he believed he was István, the first King of Hungary. I know he was ill, that it was delusional which was a result of bipolar disorder but I preferred that to this zombie of a man, bossed around by Lilla and medicated heavily. This is his birthday for God's sake and he can't even make enough conversation to be civilised.

I am lucky not to have suffered bipolar myself since both my parents had it. But, I think gloomily, there is still time. What if I do get it? Who would really take care of me and would it ruin my career? I know my father has the serious type, bipolar one whereas my mother had the less severe form, bipolar two. However, it still didn't stop her ending her own life, or more like the fall from the bridge shocked her heart and she died when she was recovering. I try not to think about it. We never talk about it. My father told me once and choked with sorrow and we never discussed it again.

I am putting my coat on to leave and Lilla puts her hand on my arm. I look at her as if she has burnt me. Her eyes are still cold, her manner still careless. But she says, "Natalija, you should get help you know. There is a doctor at our surgery who specialises in eating disorders. Please will you call him and just try to give it a go?"

"What would you know?" I say jauntily as though it is nothing. I look at myself in the mirror as I button up my midnight blue Langiotti coat with the dyed fur of chinchillas that shimmers and changes colour from inky black to deep blue according to the light and free my long black ringlets of hair that are trapped in the collar. I smile at myself. *Looking good,* I think.

"Natalija, I......" Lilla begins again then holds her hands up and walks back into the kitchen.

I let myself out.

I am almost relieved to have a smaller role again, one I played before, as Rosette in *Manon* by Massenet. It was one of my first big operas in London but I like it so much. Manon as a character is not really me but I would be wanting the role badly if it was mezzo-soprano, so every performance of the run, I watch the lead soprano receiving the loudest applause in the house and I do feel envy. I should be there, always centre stage. I know it is not healthy but I crave it like a junkie.

I am exhausted and to play demanding roles is stressful until I sort out my health. I am seeing a shrink. Kriszta has recommended this doctor and actually admitted she is worried about me and my bulimia and I need to cut back. This doctor is also an eating disorder specialist and with his help, for once, I am able to curb the bingeing and I take the appetite suppressant anti-depressants he prescribes. This is supposed to stop me feeling the need to stuff my face.

But I am like a demon unleashed. For one thing the anti-depressants are a little speedy and make me hyper and without throwing up I am feeling healthier and I have this craving for people. The amount of lovers in and out of my smart top floor apartment in the XIII district that spring leads me to think the neighbours must think I am a hooker. Some know I am an opera singer but they must have their doubts at times. I am literally taking back a different lover every other night. The lack of stress on *Manon* is having an adverse effect on me. But I sleep well anyway, I sleep so deeply once my hunger is satisfied sometimes taking sleeping meds to knock me out as the anti-depressants keep me awake otherwise. But I know it is not helping me. I feel disgusted and if the opera company knew, they would not be happy. Keeping it in the opera family as it were has its advantages. No one will give me negative media coverage but I am already becoming a star in the Hungarian Opera World and I do have to guard my reputation.

So I stop. But I can't really stop, like a dry alcoholic. I demand more of Kriszta. She is a safe bet and my favourite but she can't do it. We argue and she says she can't give me any more. I tell her I don't want any more of her except as a lover. *You are nothing more to me, Kriszta, you never were and you never will be. So much for all that rubbish you told me about me never being alone. It is okay for you; you and your wonderful family life. Get the hell away from me, why don't you?*

For once she actually looks really hurt, as though I said something insulting.

My family life is not so good, it is nothing like you think, Natalija. You are so wrong, she says.

I just can't give you any more than I am doing. My husband, he gets angry when.....

She is upset and turns away. What the hell for? Isn't that what it's about, meaningless flings?

Kriszta, isn't that what it is after all? And what was that, 'you are never going to be alone' bullshit the night I was attacked by Ádám in the theatre and you promised me in the taxi I would never be alone.

I meant that Natalija, I still mean it. Give me time, please. I am very busy right now and you are not for once. Try to rest at home, give me some time but remember you mean so much to me.......you....

Oh, go to hell, Kriszta, I say interrupting her angrily. *Go home to your perfect life and perfect family.*

She walks away, unable to say any more and we fall out for the first time and I feel like Fiamma. I do not like this feeling of needing someone however shallow the feeling is. Kriszta's birthday is on 20th March and I choose to ignore it to show how in control I am and go back to the anorexic baritone Mikki who is having to take roles in northern and southern and eastern Hungary to get work; the opera company have scheduled him in for so little. Mikki, who was once one of my early conquests. We lie in bed one night and both stare at the ceiling. The anorexic and the bulimic, so much in common and yet so unwilling to admit anything to the other. A text comes through as I am lying in bed. I look. *You forgot my birthday. I would never do that to you. Why don't you trust anyone, Natalija? Why are you so full of venom like a cobra? Why don't you listen to me when I say that my life is not perfect, when you need to give me time?*

Mikki is so depressed he doesn't even notice me looking at my phone. I look at my snake silver bracelet Kriszta gave me for my birthday next to the bed and feel horrible. She is right. She would never do that to me. The bracelet is still so precious to me. The bracelet is fitting, being a snake. I am a cobra, she is right.

"So did you eat anything today?" I ask Mikki hoping we

can find some common ground in our eating disorders.

"A banana," he says. "And an apple. You?"

"Oh, you know, just some salad, a bit of chicken," I say. "I'm trying to be healthy, trying not to throw up."

"Right, that's good. It's so bad for you, you know. And for your voice."

And starving yourself is robbing you of your voice, Mikki, I think.

But he knows full well. He knows what he is doing. And like me, he can't stop.

Neither of us stops staring at the ceiling.

We last a week or two and it fades out. We are both worried in our own ways about our careers and it isn't working. I am reluctant to go to anyone else's apartment for entirely selfish reasons; I need my own bed to sleep and be fresh for rehearsing.

I resolve to try to get help like I did before. I resolve to try to limit my binges and vomiting to every third day.

But I have been here before. It has been on and off since I was 14 and I was so hungry but had to stay thin to be an ice skater and once the 30 hours of skating a week cut to nothing, I gained weight.

The illness came back when I was training in Italy at a prestigious academy for Opera in my early twenties. I was homesick and surrounded by everyone who wanted to be the best; everyone as cut-throat as me. Now and then it would go into remission; when I got the lead, when I got praise from directors but it never lasted. The buzz would wear off like crack-cocaine and the pressure to be slim and beautiful took over any health concerns. And I could not stop eating after shows late at night. I was so full of hunger and adrenaline, forever sitting in the kitchen or standing by the fridge and stuffing the biscuits and cakes and all the junk I could find and feeling so disgusted it was not hard to throw it all up. I drink salt water to make sure I get rid of it all even after ramming my fingers down my throat.

Now I am worse than ever. I cannot be a fat opera singer. I will stop getting the roles I love so much, I might spiral out of control and eat as much as an African elephant. I will get bitchy comments from the other singers. I will feel self-conscious on stage. And I will lose the lead of Carmen.

I overhear people talking about the older singers in the company at premières. "Yeah she sings well, but how can someone so fat play Madama Butterfly? She is supposed to be thin and 15 years old not an overweight middle aged lump."

And these women are not fat. Just the wrong side of curvaceous, maybe nothing losing a few kilos wouldn't solve. The girls who bitch are slim and mean and nothing special. They have faces like rodents and they all hate me. Their voices in chorus are long and lingering collectively but they lack the perfection, that elusive magic of soloists. They will never be beautiful. They will always be chorus, or at the most in minor supporting roles.

That cannot happen to me. I will not be fat. I would sooner kill myself with this bulimia than be a lard ass. My heart is already going into palpitations sometimes, as the lack of potassium is causing it to beat irregularly. I am playing with my life and not just my career.

My dentist has replaced my tooth enamel on some of my teeth several times, grabbed my right hand where my knuckles are permanently grazed from hitting the back of my teeth and told me to stop throwing up, I am ruining my teeth, my voice and my health. He is not stupid and not fooled, this dentist. Ironic that my father was a dentist and never picked up on the enamel problem. He saw to my teeth until he retired early due to poor health. He was puzzled but put it down to grinding my teeth in the night and made me a mouth guard to solve the problem. He didn't think to check my knuckles, covered in old and new sores, always bleeding as I am run down all the time and my immune system is preventing my body from healing.

My new role is one of the most demanding yet in *A kékszakállú herceg vára* or *Bluebeard's Castle* by Bartók and the first time I will perform in Hungarian. Despite it being my mother tongue, I am not so comfortable using the language for singing. It demands surgical precision on each syllable unlike the lingering sounds of Italian and French I am so used to. I have not trained in Hungarian opera unlike Italian, French and German. It is alien to me and it is showing. I am regretting taking this role. I should give it up but I can't. Something in me always refuses to give in. I already started rehearsals during the *Manon* run so it is a relief to be overstretched as usual and stop from feeling emotions.

It is also intense. Only me and Bluebeard on the stage for a dark, edgy opera. I am against a much older bass-baritone, Lajos, who looks down on me and tells me I am too young for this.

Two people in an opera and I am stuck with this hateful Lajos. Why can't it be Mikki or someone neutral? Mikki sang the role before. I really need support in this one as it is so new. It makes sense Bluebeard's wives are all stuffed in a room and I end up there too. *What the hell did they ever see in him?* is all I think as we are rehearsing. Him and his depressing castle and his wives.

Traditionally Lajos has performed with a mezzo 20 years older than me. But she is away in New York guesting long-term so I was given this chance. He constantly undermines me telling me Judit has depth and I do not. I do not have the power and feeling for the role of Judit.

"Stick to Carmen, love," he tells me patronisingly. "A shallow little tart, dark gypsy that you are."

I tell him to go to hell and I am glad to be dark. Unlike him and his milk-white complexion and straw coloured hair. Who would find that attractive? He is paler than a theatre ghost.

"Been moon-bathing again?" I say to him one morning as he is looking particularly pale.

Lajos is about to answer with another insult but the director stops us.

The director says this is brilliant. We already have onstage chemistry. Good, we don't like each other. Very good. It will make for intense viewing. There is a strange kind of love between Bluebeard and Judit, not a passionate one and maybe we will hit it right in this opera. I am studying so hard for this, but try as I do, I know this role is not one I am fitting into and Bartók's opera is giving me nightmares. Every night of rehearsals I dream and dream that I am in a house, a forbidden castle and behind the doors lies something so sinister I can't even explain it and although I mustn't go there, I have to. I am compelled by obsession to force Bluebeard to open all the doors just like Judit does in the opera. It is a miserable March and I am just so tired knowing that after the performances in April, we are straight into *Carmen* again.

It will be the only time I do not perform as well as I could, *Blubeard's Castle.* And the only opera I will ever sing in Hungarian. Although the audience response is warm, the directors know I am not right for the role, I am too young and I am never a Judit. Lajos says he never ever wants to work with me again.

I let him down, he says. *I am just not right.*

"Fine by me, you arrogant dick," I say and walk off.

"I am never ever performing on stage with her again. She is a self-obsessed little diva," he tells the director so I can hear him. "Who the hell is she screwing to get all these leading roles?"

"No one!" I yell at him from the stage steps. "I don't need to, I have all the talent I need right here! You're just jealous because I will be better than you at your age! I will be a star and you are still here in Hungary, paleface!"

I stalk off still mad, as I know I wasn't good in the opera. I am surprised the director didn't chase me after I insulted Lajos. But he has heard how nasty Lajos has been during our intense rehearsals and he has had to tell him to lay off a few times.

But I know someone older would have done it better. For once, I know I wasn't up to the mark. I am as angry with myself as I am with Lajos. I should not have agreed to taking the role. It has cast doubt in my mind about ever performing in my native language again.

And there she is, Kriszta. Somehow I have avoided her for two weeks but here she is in the dressing room corridor.

"Hello," I say awkwardly. I feel like shit. I am burnt out after the awful show and my throat is sore from vomiting. I have wanted to call her every single night and resisted the urge. I missed her.

"I watched you, Natalija. You were so good. Judit is not you, but you were so passionate in the role," says Kriszta.

"I was lousy, Kriszta and I am sorry for.....And I missed you, I really missed you the last two weeks."

"It's okay," she says gently, taking my hand. "You don't need to say sorry for anything, I missed you too and I thought maybe you had bin-bagged me. I actually cried quite a lot," she says seriously.

"Kriszta, you cry over some lover? That doesn't sound like you," I tell her.

She looks at me, and I look into those dark eyes which are serious and wonder what other secrets I could find if I looked hard enough. But she is ashamed of admitting to this so she quickly looks away and removes her hand from mine.

"And I meant what I said about you not being alone. There is just nothing I can do about it right now."

What the hell does that mean? I want to ask. *What are you going to do?*

"Come on," she says smiling with her voice full of mischief. "I know just the thing in the meantime." She leads me by the hand up the corridors and into the men's toilets backstage and hands me a black magic marker to scrawl some childish sexual drawings on the wall and some graffiti about Lajos and his impotence. It is Kriszta's idea. Lajos is double my age and has been viciously insulting throughout the rehearsals and after every show, so Kriszta and I huddle together in a cubicle coating the wall with obscenities. It is the first time I laugh all month and she holds her hand over my mouth as someone comes into the bathrooms and relieves himself loudly, sighing as he does. Kriszta draws obscene pictures on the wall and writes ***Lajos*** in huge letters.

I have no idea about Lajos and the bedroom department and have no intention of finding out but Kriszta is right; doing something so immature is light relief from Bartók's dark opera and Lajos barking out, "She's no good, she's too damn young."

And those endless nightmares about Blubeard's awful castle with his rooms of tears and blood, all that for feeling shit like I do. As soon as the curtains close between us and the audience after our curtain call, Lajos is dropping my hand like I am dirt and telling me I fucked it up for him *again*.

We argue so much the musical director has to send us off separately after every single show.

I think Lajos is the worst man I have ever worked with.

And now, after our childish graffiti in the men's room, me and Kriszta run out and down the stairs laughing like children but I am dizzy. The stress has been awful, making my bulimia worse as I actually did feel I wasn't up to the cut. Every night after rehearsals I have been bingeing and vomiting at home. After every performance I have stopped off at the Turkish 24 hour takeaway and bought masses of food and eaten in 15 minutes in my apartment, throwing up and purging with salt water until I am exhausted. After all the help Kriszta's doctor gave me I am too ashamed to tell him. And her.

"Are you okay?" Kriszta asks as I stagger along the dressing room corridor holding on to the wall for support.

I tell her I am fine, just tired and overworked.

"You should slow down, Natalija. Maybe get married. You'd be a good mother," she says.

I turn to her in a rage and say, "Go back to your husband. I never want kids, Kriszta. I hate them. And I hate you too, for being such a liar and a cheat. Get married and then go and have affairs with women everywhere. You are full of shit! Look at yourself. Hiding behind a man, more like."

She grabs my hand. "You can't have everything, Natalija. This is Hungary. You have to have a man behind you."

"I don't because I am not staying here unlike you! I can go anywhere, anywhere! I don't need you, and if having a man behind you means you get bruises all over your body that you have to lie about then you can keep it, Kriszta. I do not want to be beaten by anyone, even if you do," I say walking away.

Kriszta opens her mouth to deny it all again but doesn't. I carry on walking.

She stops me again this time hugging me, "I'm sorry, I'm sorry," she says into my hair. "Don't go."

"I'm sorry too," I say. But I don't know if I am. I am angry as I am guessing about her constant excuses for marks on her arms, neck and back. She showed up one day with her shinbone bruised virtually all the way down to the ankle and said she fell down some stairs in high heels.

Two male musicians pass us on the stairs. "Lovers!" says one laughingly to the other.

We take no notice. "My mother died in April," I tell Kriszta for the first time. "I never knew her. I was only just over a year old."

I realise I want my mother so badly it hurts. I hate April so much.

Kriszta wipes a tear from her face. "No wonder you are so angry, so driven, so full of pain. My poor lovely Natalija. You never told me."

"I'm sorry about your birthday, I didn't really forget. I was just mean."

"I know," she says. "I understand."

"But, Kriszta. Please don't let your husband hurt you any longer. You can stay with me. I am not trying to possess you, I don't want to see you with bruises you are lying about all the time."

She says nothing. She just takes my arm and we leave.

I take her straight into one of the designer shops where there is a simple black dress in the window. I know it is something she would like. I pretend to be looking at it myself and then I ask for her size.

"No, Natalija. You don't need to repay me like that. I got you that silver bracelet for your birthday but really, just some flowers would have been fine."

She gets the dress. I tell her I will buy it in my size unless she agrees to try it on and she will need to lose weight to fit it. Better try it on and get the right fit or it means more vomiting in the theatre toilets.

"Bitch," she says laughing. But she puts it on in the shop. In the daylight I see light bruises on her shoulders, and I touch them lightly and ask for the hundredth time what happened. I have already told her I have guessed what is going on so I wish she would just admit it. She says so honestly she fell out of bed after a nightmare and hit herself on the bedside table. I want to say more but I don't. I just admire her in her dress. Glamour and glitter suit her but this simple black shift dress really accentuates her dark beauty with its V-shaped neck. And it is in the sale.

I always remember that day, the childish schoolgirl feel of graffiti on the toilet wall, drawing obscene pictures of Lajos in black magic marker and writing obscene words to go with it. Laughing like children and then my emotions changing into sorrow and sadness as if someone snapped off a light in my head, snapping back again to happy as I took Kriszta to the dress shop. My illness and overwork are really starting to affect my moods badly. I am finishing *Bluebeard's Castle* in a week and I can't wait to be shot of it. I hate it so much.

I have been offered the role of Charlotte in Massenet's *Werther* in early September in Roma and this is an extremely demanding role, mainly because of the amount of acting I have to do. Charlotte is the absolute polar opposite of me. She is saintly and pure and good. I am not a Charlotte. But the opera is not that frequently performed and I do not want to pass up this chance with a big theatre who have been hearing about my reputation. The pay is good and I should be more flexible with the roles or I will be forever Carmen until that is all I am doing. The competition for mezzo-soprano roles is fierce, it would be easier for me as a soprano. And as I have effectively refused britches roles I am unable to pass up the big mezzo roles I am offered even if I really do need a rest.

CARMEN AND WERTHER

I am ready and hungry for *Carmen* again when it returns towards the end of the opera season in May. I have stopped seeing the shrink, thinking I am cured apart from the Bartók episode since I stop the bulimia again and start to feel better. I am also closer to Kriszta after our argument and me admitting for the first time to anyone about my mother and how her death affects me, how I feel I caused my mother to kill herself when I was just a baby. *She must have hated me,* I had said.

No, no, Kriszta had told me. *She was ill, Natalija. She was ill. It wasn't your fault. It wasn't her fault and she would be so proud of you now, she would be so happy to see how beautiful and successful you are.*

The story makes her cry every time she thinks of it. It is the first time I have actually let anyone in and seen a small part of weakness, if you could call it that.

And the memory of me and her huddled in a toilet cubicle writing obscenities about Lajos on the wall was something which still makes me smile. Treating her mean and forgetting her birthday was the best way to feel in control, but it wasn't right. I don't need to treat her mean, like I do with the others. I need to lose this control.

Fiamma is taking the role of Frasquita again and I have decided I do not care what she says or does, I will be meaner and harder than before. I still cannot lose my cold-hearted behaviour. It works with the men and it should work with her. But she is still hurting from last time. She doesn't fall at my feet although by her looks at me during rehearsals she wants to. We haven't been in direct contact since I put her in the taxi in February in the snow, with her crying and pleading. She has just sent texts and letters which I ignored.

But it doesn't take her long. By the end of rehearsal week one I find her crying in a toilet cubicle backstage at the end of the day. Or more like I hear her. I knock the door and gently ask her to let me in. She refuses. So I go in the cubicle next door and just climb over, scraping my legs on the divider.

"Fiamma, come here. I'm sorry, I'm sorry I made you feel bad," I say holding her in my arms. I am not really so sorry but I want her back. I can't deal with her moodiness but I need her adoration. I need Fiamma, just not in the way she wants.

She weeps into my neck and says she missed me so much, and this is making her crazy seeing me again she wishes she hadn't come back.

For God's sake, girl. Make your mind up.

I say some sweet things instead and promise to make it up to her. She notices my hands as she wipes her eyes. "Your hand is better. You are better? You don't do that any more?" she says hopefully taking my right hand with its now healed up skin, free of scratches and scabs.

I hand her a tissue and say, "No, I am cured."

Like hell. I know it will come back. I don't believe for one minute I am cured for good from my bulimia. Like a demon, I know it is just waiting for its moment to return when I am weak.

I am kinder. I have learned something from this shrink. I have been kinder to Fiamma and when she begs me to come to live with her again, instead of being cruel, I just say, "We'll see."

I even manage a smile. I am lying, of course, I know I have no intention. But she doesn't deserve me to treat her the way I have done. She is not a rival. She is not a bitch.

She is not after my limelight. She would be happy to sit there and let me shine and applaud my every performance from a theatre box if it meant she could be with me.

I can't be so heartless.

I even take her to the airport in a taxi. It is delaying the inevitable. The constant refrain of, "We could be together forever, Natalija. I love you" is grating. But as Fiamma disappears up the escalators back to Italy and turns to wave at me sadly, I feel something akin to emptiness.

She is gone. She is sweet, she has a good heart. Why am I not acting on it? Why when I badly need someone to take care of me am I resisting? I don't understand. Someone so pure, so beautiful and so giving. And I could easily find work in Italy. But I cannot let myself feel so I don't.

The urge to stuff my face in the nearest café is crying out to me and it takes everything to get back into a taxi and away from the cakes in the airport departures. They are waiting for me, these evil cream confections, their faces shining with grease and silky soft chocolate and everything that will slip down so easily. I go home and I am about to eat a giant jar of Nutella without even tasting it and bring it all up again, when I smash it to the floor and drop on my knees in relief looking at the shards of glass mixed with temptation. There is nothing else in the apartment. I am so relieved. I was so close to losing it again.

Nutella was always one of my first ever binge foods. That glossy hazelnut chocolate which slid down without even swallowing. I could empty the jar in two minutes. I make a note to never ever have this in the apartment again. It is the easiest and best binge food I ever found. Peanut butter sticks in the throat but Nutella glides down like gloopy satin.

I am also sad because I realise part of the reason Fiamma

is the way she is. Why she wears such a haunted expression. It isn't all about me. Being the diva I am I assume it is but this time we have had more of a chance to talk and over dinner one evening Fiamma tells me she was once violently sexually assaulted some years ago in her first ever opera role. It was a small place in Spain and one of the stage managers had spiked her drink and tricked her into going to his house saying the rest of the cast would be there for a party. They had just finished the run and there was no reason not to believe him. She had been working with the company and he had never given her much attention, never been anything other than professional. Once back in his house, as the spiked drink kicked in and she looked in horror at the empty place as he locked the door she knew exactly what he wanted. He had planned this. He tied her up although she was too drugged to struggle, sexually assaulted her for what she thinks was about 7 hours and beat her. It was only when he fell asleep and the drug was wearing off, she managed to escape, climbing out of the window of the ground floor house and running away dazed until a taxi found her wandering on the road.

"Didn't you go to the cops, Fiamma?"

"No, I just wanted it over. I wanted to forget, never go back to Spain and forget it ever happened. I could not deal with seeing his face again," she is looking down as she says this. For once her green eyes depthless, free of tears, but I think how damaged it made her.

I think if she ever did like men, no wonder she doesn't or can't now.

All I want to do those last few days is protect this girl. Which is why I am sad to see her go.

She has clung on to the one person she adores, but a cruel person who has also hurt her but in a different way.

I don't feel good about myself. I feel very guilty knowing what I do now. Poor Fiamma. I wish I had been there to have helped her, made her go to the cops, sorted out that piece of trash stage manager for doing what he did. She will not even disclose the theatre, or the name of the man, she knows I am vengeful and she is afraid of ever seeing him again. And I would too. I would go and see that stage manager and kick him to the ground and spit on him just to show him, I would threaten him with the Hungarian Mafia, I would make him afraid for his life. I do meet Hungarian Mafia. Of course I do but I never use them. One car followed me home from the Opera Theatre one night. The man wound down his window and called to me. The tinted black windows prevented me from seeing who was in the back but I knew there were a couple of men there as well as one in the passenger seat. The driver asked me did I ever need any help. I knew what he meant.

I said, *No but one day I might.*

I still have the business card. They had seen me perform. They said they could help me progress.

I thanked them as the whole interaction seemed so threatening and I had to be polite. I had no intention of calling the number on the card. I knew about the Mafia, I had seen and heard things over the years in Hungary but it was best to stay away. But looking the way I did, being the person I was, I seemed like a magnet for trouble.

But I really believe I am cured of bulimia for now when in August I head to Roma to start rehearsing *Werther.* I have really cut back on my binges and I am feeling healthier. The theatre itself is like all theatres in August, in a long dark while they maintain the building and we should be maintaining ourselves, having a much needed rest. But not me. We are pushed into some cramped rehearsal rooms down the road with a deadly pasticceria on the corner which I have to walk past twice a day. I will not look at the cakes, the cornets of cream and chocolates. I know I will not stop after 1, 10, or 20. Kriszta is taking a break; she is in Lake Hévíz with her family. She calls me several times over the 2 weeks she is there and I am in Roma. She calls late at night down the road from the guest house she is staying in, pretending to her husband she has gone to get some chocolate or milk or some other excuse. Her calls are tender and concerned.

"Natalija, don't you think you are pushing yourself a little too much? You are so young, so young to have this demanding role in a big opera house. It is great you have this role but the August rest break was designed for a reason."

I tell her I am fine. I will rest in bed.

"All alone?" she says playfully. "You are all alone in that big bed in Roma?"

Yes, all alone. And it is not good, but I leave that part out.

She laughs when she tells me her husband found my photo in her handbag in its frame the other day and asked who was this mystery woman, so beautiful and exotic and fresh, was she a film star from Italy?

And she said, "Oh, just a friend, a friend from the Opera."

He innocently put it back. Of course, what else. I am a woman and it has not occurred to him she would take me as a lover. That she is cheating on him right now if only in her head. That she cheats on him in her sleep. She laughs again at the thought, like a wind-chime. I love her laugh. I just picture her as she speaks twirling her dark hair round her fingers and sitting on some bench near the supermarket in this thermal spa town in the summer warmth of night where she is pretending to buy something she doesn't need. She sounds happy and relaxed despite her protestations of boredom and wishing I was there. She can't be missing me that much.

I hope he is not hurting her. She still denies and denies and denies. I have offered her my spare room, I have done everything to try to get through to her but like me and my illness, we are both unable to accept help when we so badly need it.

I am kind of flattered she tells me about the photo though. I don't carry her photo around. I have some photos of her in my apartment in a drawer along with some of Fiamma. I have photos of many beautiful people.

But the fact she has taken my photo to Lake Hévíz is touching. I imagine her looking at it as her husband sleeps and she is bored with him, maybe beaten by him which I can't bear to think about and the teenage children are in their own dream worlds in the room next door after swimming all day. I try to imagine Kriszta's life but I can't because I just cannot get inside her head. All I know is I am very much inside her head despite being lost in the frenzied heart of Roma and one of the most heartbreaking operas ever. It is taking up all my headspace.

And I am lying in this dark apartment in Roma in the merciless August heat. Alone. I fall asleep holding the sheets of music, dreaming myself into the sad heart of Massenet and *Werther*.

I cry in my dreams a lot that August. The pillow is damp with my tears. I wake up with the music sheets all over the floor each morning. Sometimes I have nightmares and fall out of bed, one night hitting my head hard on the bedside table and wake up sprawled on this dark marble floor. I cry not so much from the pain but from frustration and loneliness. I never knew Opera could be so lonely. And why are theatre digs always so dark? Why do they never have anywhere light and bright with a beautiful view? How are we supposed to perform when we are stuffed like animals in dark cages?

The opera company are okay. The cast of *Werther* are not as ruthless as Budapest but not particularly friendly either although I can't speak for the rest of the opera company as our opera is mainly a cast of 4 leading players with Werther and Charlotte the leading soloists. The Italian girl playing Sophie really hates me but I couldn't care less. She is nothing to me, my dear sister in the opera, bitch from hell outside it, a tall Venetian 30 year old with a sheet of glossy dark hair, a chest just as flat and a face which could be attractive if she wasn't so sexless and haughty. Someone who I figure just needs to get well and truly laid she is so rigid and frigid no doubt. If she wasn't so dull I would offer to help her out but she is just not attractive to me. She is unsure how much everyday Italian I know outside of the Opera World since *Werther* is in French and our artistic director is French. So here she is bitching to one of the others outside stage door about me when I have to go in on the first day to fill in the paperwork. I tell her in perfect Italian she should get a life and it is not my fault I am playing the lead, I am just more beautiful and more talented than she could ever hope to be. "Take a good long look in the mirror, honey. No one could find such a sour face and flat chest attractive and you make the Virgin Mary look like a hooker."

She is speechless with rage. The girl with her says, "Who is that bitch? Who does she think she is? Hungarian gypsy girl. She really has a nerve coming here and talking to us like that."

I do have a nerve.

I could have made it easier for myself by being less bitchy, but she started it all. Now all I get are resentful looks when the director praises me in rehearsals. Too bad for her. Would she really want my life, our lives? Werther and Charlotte are amongst the most demanding roles I know; me and the Milanese Werther, GianCarlo, are so physically and mentally drained even before we open for the dress rehearsal. There is not even a thought of romantic life here, despite GianCarlo being handsome. We are all battered at the end of the day. Battered by the intensity of *Werther* and it leaves no room for anything. I remember a quote from an older mezzo who told me that she liked the mix of tragedy and comedy, 'Because to die on stage every night is so exhausting.'

She never understood why I only wanted tragic roles, even *Carmen* is tragic as you have to die at the end of each performance. I am understanding her thinking only too well these days.

The small cast makes it difficult and intense for all of us and the opera is extremely demanding. And depressing. Massenet has a sadness which rips into your heart even more than the saddest of Puccini arias and by the end of the first week I am with my head over the toilet in my dark rented apartment throwing my guts up. I still have time for this in my life obviously.

Each time I pass the pasticceria and have managed to avoid these 'trigger' foods for a long time, well since April, it is so difficult. Aside from the *Bluebeard's Castle* run, where I lapsed, I have managed to get a grip on this bulimia. But that day I have gone in and bought 15 small cakes and taken them back to the apartment and stuffed myself until I am physically sick. I don't even need to force it. I feel so disgusted and fat I throw up immediately.

I put it down to stress and working abroad, being in an unfamiliar place. I resolve to stop there and reason it was a one off, due to extreme loneliness. But I throw up every single day of the second week. The same pattern, always a pasticceria and if I walk a different way I find another. Always after rehearsals. Always desperately stuffing the sugar and frosted coatings in so fast I hardly taste them, a shark feeding frenzy and then throwing it all up again, drinking salt water to rid my insides of everything. And then a few hours later, I eat my controlled meal of one avocado pear, a yoghurt drink, 3 plain crackers and a hot milk and honey. Very carefully. It is important I do not feel full.

I make lunch of protein packed food my main meal, eaten in a safe environment in the theatre or a café nearby because my body has to have some nutrients or I will not have the energy to sing.

I am surprised when I am heading into the theatre one sizzling hot morning and Marina, the soprano I met in London is coming out. She remembers me immediately, greets me enthusiastically and laughs. "Tosca's crucifix," she says. I am wearing it for luck. She will be performing Mimi and is in rehearsals next week.

"Natalija, you look so good but tired. Are you eating enough? I just saw your name on the sign in book and I remembered you, the beautiful young Hungarian mezzo I met in London. So pretty and so talented. I am happy to see you again, especially in Italy as your Italian is perfect. You really are doing well for yourself to have got this major role in our wonderful opera house. But please, remember to eat!"

She kisses me goodbye, saying she has to go. *I do eat,* I tell her.

And that is the problem. I eat and eat and then throw it all up again. No wonder I look like shit.

But Marina, for such a world-renowned diva is actually a very lovely person. She gets problems because idiot journalists are forever probing into her personal life, particularly the London ones so she gets argumentative and defensive often refusing interviews altogether or walking out, rightly so. It is no one else's business, your personal life. And it always seems to work that way. When a man is demanding and talented, well he is a star. A woman with opinions and star status obviously is just a spoilt diva.

By the time we open I am not in the best of health. My throat is inflamed and hurts every night after singing. The Opera House demands so much of us, the crowd is restless and noisy although appreciative and after every show over the 3 weeks of performances I binge late at night in the gloomy kitchen and vomit in my dark bathroom, sleep in my lonely bed wondering how and why I can have it all and not have it at all. It is too late to think of all the sacrifices we make. They are made and we carry on. I am losing track of the seasons, of day and of night.

I didn't tell Fiamma I was coming as I knew she would give up everything in Napoli and spend all her time here. I couldn't deal with that as I had to give this role absolutely everything. I needed to live it, I needed to be absorbed in it more than my familiar roles. Charlotte has taken me over. I am her.

But as I rest my aching head against the cold marble bathroom floor that September night, I wish Fiamma could just appear and rescue me now. I am not coping too well.

I have overridden the effects of the anti-depressant

medication which is supposed to suppress the urge to overeat.

In the end Fiamma does know I have been to Roma. She sees glamorous photos of me in an Italian fashion magazine and an interview with the leading young mezzo-soprano from Hungary who has just played in *Werther* to high critical acclaim. I am paid for the shoot and the interview. I am looking healthy and lovely in the arty black and white shots in various famous locations around Roma. I glow with health and happiness in the interview. I am a true diva. No one reading it or seeing the photos would see anything else but *a beautiful, successful opera star just 26 years old and already commanding the European stage, who speaks fluent Italian, loves Italy and is going to be one to watch in the future. We want Natalija as our own, she owns the mezzo-soprano world, this stunning Hungarian with Sicilian blood.*

I even lie to myself that this is the real me. They wrote this, so it must be true.

My mother was a quarter Sicilian. The Italian magazine have seized upon this snippet and turned it into possession, wanting to claim some ownership of me like everyone else does.

I am fine. I must be fine.

Fiamma's text to me arrives when the magazine is printed. I am back in Budapest, reading through the edition they sent me.

How could you? How could you come to Roma and not tell me? Why? Why, Natalija?

She wouldn't understand. It is all or nothing. She wouldn't have just attended one night and left me alone. She would have driven me mad when I needed my concentration.

I have finally made her crack. And this time not through

cruelty.

Why? She screams at me down the phone. *You were in Roma all this time and you never once called me to see you. How could you? I hate you, I hate you!*

"Fiamma, listen," I tell her. "That role took everything I had. I knew you would want to see me more than I could manage. You demand too much. You wouldn't be happy with one night seeing me as Charlotte. I am stressed." I don't know why I am explaining and not telling her to leave me alone forever. Maybe because I do care about this lovely vulnerable girl, but she is just too demanding, too pushy over wanting to see me. If she could only ease off, I wouldn't need to push her away.

As it is she is the one who says it. Through tears on the phone she tells me she will leave me alone for good now. I have broken her heart too many times. *I am leaving you alone forever, Natalija. Your heart is dead and cold.*

Fiamma, I say. *Listen...*

But she is gone.

AUTUMN AND WINTER OF THE DAMNED

Kriszta leafs through one of the Italian magazines I brought for her and breathes out. "Natalija, you really are making the big time." She says it without a touch of envy. She brushes her hand over my photos. "Wow, you are so beautiful."

The tonsillitis is so painful this time I can hardly swallow. It has been threatening all through September and my throat is scratched so raw I literally cannot get out of bed. The rehearsals for *Cavalleria Rusticana* and *Pagliacci* have started and I am unable to attend. I promise I can still sing Lola, I can hardly speak but I promise the director I will be able to do it; it opens next week in October and I can sing, I promise.

After missing half the rehearsals I am back too early. The company doctor says, *To give this one up. It is one role in a short opera. Give it up, Natalija or you will lose out on the big time.*

No, I say.

So I sing, he sighs and writes me a prescription for more antibiotics. Pagliaccio gives me evil looks as I exit the stage and the cast of *Pagliacci* are in the dressing room corridor ready for their glory but he says nothing.

Clowns, I mutter.

I miss you. Three simple words. On a postcard from Taormina. It is a month since she said she was out of my life forever but she can't let go. She is weak.

I put the postcard from Fiamma on the kitchen mirror. Taormina looks nice.

And we are straight out of *Cavalleria Rusticana* and into *Il*

Trovatore. There is no rest. Somehow summer in Roma has turned into autumn and winter is looming and the seasons are beginning to melt into one and I need more antibiotics. As the weather starts to slide into autumn gloom and the sky is beaten lead, the Duna River is shrouded in a funereal grey fog. My opera schedule is just as punishing as last year, even more so. I hardly have a break until the end of June. I should be happy.

La Damnation de Faust as Marguerite. The rehearsals start on New Year's Day, the most insensitive thoughtless thing they could do other than Christmas Day. They are making the schedules as dense and varied as possible to bring in the crowds, especially the winter tourists. I hardly see Kriszta who is Musetta in *La bohème's* long Christmas run, because in between rehearsals I am travelling to Bratislava to rehearse and play *Carmen* and I actually feel as though I have lost myself somewhere. I see me on the train as I travel the journey, a ghostly reflection in the glass and I don't know which direction the train is going in half the time. I put it down to playing two polar opposites. There are only 5 performances of *Carmen* over December and January. We are rehearsing for *La Damnation de Faust* as I am still on *Carmen* but it is enough and punishing enough to make me ill again. I have to travel to Bratislava and stay overnight and return on the earliest train the next morning to make it to rehearsals in time since three of the five *Carmen* shows are in January.

To break as Marguerite on stage, to weep full of betrayal is no longer acting. I feel all her pain. I am finding it easier to act the roles I never thought I could. I thought I was forever the careless Carmen. But I am digging deeper all the time, digging into my soul to give every fibre of my existence to this theatrical performance. I forget it is a performance. I am unable to switch off at the end of these shows, in the same way as I was with *Werther.* Of course, I am buzzing after performances but these sad roles take hold of my spirit and hold it like an electric current. I am always having to resort to the sleeping pills in the end.

On the opening night the bouquets shower down when I take my curtain call. The audience have been taken to the place Faust takes Marguerite; they have felt my pain. At times the theatre seemed so quiet as though everyone was collectively holding their breath when I was on stage. I hold the moment to my chest looking out into the blackness of noise and applause from a house of 1700 people and shouts of *Brava!*

But it is taking everything from me. The hellish visions Faust sees towards the close of the opera are projected on a cinematic backdrop and there are burning fires everywhere. The director has made the production particularly dark and I am having nightmares. I am having nightmares they are going to execute me as they do to Marguerite. I wake up every morning at 3am full of horror.

I am too involved in the roles. It is dangerous. It takes me over so much.

The theatre director tells me I am absolutely magnificent and that I have the power to captivate the entire auditorium. I am one of the most talented singers he has ever seen and heard in his life. I am flattered, I know I am good. I know I am exceptional but I wish it didn't come with so much sacrifice. It isn't hard work that is the problem. I am laying my life on the line. Literally.

I can't say no to performances. I can't say no to big parts which follow immediately on in an unbroken line from the previous opera. I cannot stop and take a rest. *I am 27,* I tell myself. *I am okay and I have to live as if this is my last day on earth.* It is mid February and I am taking on a German language role as The Queen of Sheba, the title role in Goldmark's opera.

Even Zita, the senior soprano I sang opposite during *Aida,* who will perform as my love rival in *Die Königin von Saba* and should care nothing about me really, has tried to give me her experienced advice to cut back, to take a break, to save some of my talent. *I am too young to be taking on role after demanding role. And now Natalija, you are* in *Die Königin von Saba. How can you keep going like this?*

It is burning up fast like a fire, she says. I am not going to make it to Kriszta's age. I am not going to make it to 35, or even younger.

Take my advice, Natalija. Listen to me even if you don't want to. I have been where you have and I was not bulimic and I still nearly lost it all. Your body and above all your voice will not take all this pressure. Each time you throw up you bathe your vocal chords in acid, not to mention the scratches from your fingernails on your throat.

She is looking at my hand. I hide it self-consciously. I can cover up everything else, but this scratched up hand will not heal and I tried once with a spoon and lost the spoon. I thought I was going to die when I swallowed it. I was 18 and the hospital had to remove the spoon. I told them afterwards I was eating a chocolate mousse and slipped but they just looked at me sympathetically. They knew no one loses cutlery eating chocolate mousse.

They didn't believe me. I didn't believe me either. I am afraid of choking to death if I poke around with something like a toothbrush or spoon. And I do not want to die like that on my bathroom floor. I live alone and therefore no one is around when I throw up. No one would be there if I choked to death. I imagine all the bitches in the Opera Theatre saying, *You know how she died? With a spoon down her windpipe!*

And they would shriek with laughter. Who wants to die like that? I think maybe there are worse ways to go. I can never go to the bathroom on a flight as I am afraid there will be turbulence when I am in there and I will crack my head on the ceiling and die, my jeans round my ankles and that is how I will be remembered.

How did she die? Everyone would ask.

With her bare ass in the air, her pants round her ankles in a plane toilet. Everyone saw when the air hostesses unlocked the door after some bad turbulence and she just fell out in front of the whole planeload of people and everyone gasped until they covered her dignity with a blanket.

No, that is not how I want to end up.

Roma Opera have asked me to return to play Charlotte for a week long performance of *Werther* in March after its success last summer but there are six performances over a week, way more than we are used to. It is two days after *Die Königin von Saba* finishes its run and I can just about do it. I should say no, but I can't. The Royal Hungarian Opera tends to run shows over a two to three week period and I would perform no more than 6 times, including the dress rehearsal unless I am in a Christmas show. It is getting to the stage where I am not having a day off. I am straight out of one and into the other.

I know I am way over my healthy limit of performance nights in a year recommended by the company doctor, I have actually lost count.

I like *Die Königin von Saba* but I don't love it and I think I am having trouble connecting with the language. German is just not in my heart. Which is another reason for keeping strong links with Italy. Hungary puts on a lot of German language productions, usually not involving me but they see me as The Queen of Sheba herself, regal and elegant. I float along in the beautiful costume they have made but the language is just not suiting me and it is showing. I am so exhausted I even wonder whether to step down from the role but it is the dress rehearsal and I can't.

The dress rehearsal is not good. I am not good. I get the applause but it isn't tremendous, not like the reaction I normally get. I am hoping it is because the house is only two-thirds full but in my heart I know the reason is me. Zita is my love rival, Sulamith and she performs magnificently. Her applause is how I wanted mine to be.

I am not envious, I am just broken and angry with myself. I just make it into my dressing room and as the costume lady is helping me, I am a wreck. I am crying and crying and she is asking, *Natalija, what happened? Nothing went wrong did it? What's wrong, darling, are you ill?*

Where the hell is Kriszta, she promised to be here. Did she even come tonight?

Someone knocks the door and I tell my costume lady, *Send them away, I can't let anyone see me!*

I hear Zita's voice on the other side and she is asking, *Can she please come in, she is worried about me.*

Okay, I say.

The costume lady leaves us to it. I am so broken, I do not care.

Zita comes over and wraps her arms around me. I cry into her and say, *It wasn't good was it?*

No, Natalija. It wasn't your standard. It wasn't anything the audience would notice but you usually perform with such heart-breaking intensity. And that wasn't you tonight.

I cry more.

Look at me, she says taking my face in her hands so I see the intense blue of her eyes. *Listen to me. Listen to your body. You are ill, Natalija. You are breaking yourself. When I was ill, I dropped my shows. When I had tonsillitis, I dropped out of performances. You sometimes have to do this. I am not your rival, Natalija. I see a lot of my younger self in you but you are at breaking point. The doctor will tell you the same. The directors will tell you the same. No one will hold it against you if you have to drop out.*

Someone else knocks on the door. *Who is it?* Zita calls.

It is Kriszta with the doctor. I feel like sending them away. Zita has turned into my mother tonight and I don't want to be disturbed. I want her to hug me like she just did, full of maternal love and concern. *Mama, don't leave me,* I think.

Zita goes to open the door and the room swirls and I fall to the floor.

She's burning up, Zita says. *Please take her off the show. She is ill.*

I just thought it was a bit hot on stage tonight, I thought the heating was high, or my costume was too warm. I don't realise I have a fever.

"Natalija, can you sit up?" the doctor is asking me. "Can you sit on the sofa?"

Kriszta is helping him get me up. "She's ill," Zita says. "She is working herself too hard. She's killing herself."

The doctor looks into my throat. "Natalija, you need to step down. You can't sing with that inflamed throat."

"No, it is only four performances," I am telling the three of them.

"Exactly. And how many lots of antibiotics have I given you since you joined the company. Let it go, Natalija. Zita has in her time, listen to her. Listen to the advice. She cares about you."

"Please, Natalija," says Kriszta. "That wasn't you tonight. And it wasn't because it was German."

Zita goes to leave. "Zita," I call after her. She pauses at the door still in her glittering costume.

"Thank you. You didn't have to be kind to me."

"I've been there, Natalija. I was you once." She leaves.

And I let it go. I actually spend a week in bed I am so broken and exhausted. I am too ill to move. Kriszta comes to visit bringing me soup, to sit with me. I am too ill to even think about bingeing and vomiting. For once I listened to three people who knew better than I did and I gave it up.

I have to get well for *Werther* in Roma.

I call Fiamma to invite her to see *Werther*. I am trying to make it up to her.

She is cool on the phone and I tell her if she wants, she can have tickets for any night of the week.

"I don't know, Natalija. I really don't know," she says.

"Please, Fiamma. I want you to." I actually mean it. I really do want her there.

The tickets remain uncollected. I actually feel hurt. I am not supposed to feel. I am still fragile after my illness.

Damn you, Fiamma. I would never do that to anyone. Either say you're going or not. I hate that. Guests not collecting the tickets. It is as rude as those retreating backs of the ignorant people who sit through a whole performance and then just have to be first out before the curtain call, their lives so important they can't waste 10 minutes to applaud the performers who have let them escape their dull little lives for the evening. I always want to scream at those people who do that. I got into a big argument in one of the boxes when a couple left as soon as the show came down and

Kriszta was performing. Or more like I was shouting and they were trying to leave without confrontation.

"Oh, you're so important you can't wait for the curtain call, can't waste 5 minutes more of your precious time. Look at you, can't even waste 30 seconds for an argument." I had stood in the doorway of my box and yelled down the dress circle corridor after these idiots.

"Don't bother coming next time. We don't need people like you here! Stay at home and watch TV, it's more on your level!"

They must have known I was one of the company. They must have seen me in productions but they tried to get out without saying too much. I had shouted curses after them as well which the front of house staff on the dress circle level heard. Not good. But I hate people like that. What if everyone did that?

Fiamma arrives on the final night on her own ticket. I know she is there because a bouquet of roses is delivered to my dressing room, signed by her with love.

I cry on the stage at the end with Werther dying in my arms. It is not hard to cry. I am so emotional, so broken, so fragile. I cry into his dead body and the applause is deafening. People throw rose after rose at me during the curtain call. I am the star but I am still crying. I have achieved everything I wanted and something is still hurting, an aching emptiness inside because this moment will burn up like crack cocaine.

"Fiamma, I can't," I say. I am removing my make-up and she is sitting on the sofa in the dressing room and once again pleading with me to come to Italy to live full-time.

"Natalija, they love you here. You speak perfect Italian. We can live here in Roma, I can find work here maybe. I can leave Napoli. La Scala will want you now, you could get some work in Milano too. I heard people talking in the audience. They loved you. You would be perfect here. You belong in Italy."

For one split second I almost consider it. The flash before my eyes of me in Italy, away from Budapest, my devoted Fiamma there....

But I know I would break her heart. I would cheat with 1, 2, 20 something people. I know me too well. And I think of the dark-eyed smoky Kriszta and I know the real reason I can't do it; Kriszta. Imagine never seeing Kriszta again or only very rarely.

I also imagine the screaming, the tears, the arguments, all the cups and plates smashed in our apartment when Fiamma finds out I am a cheat.

We will be drinking coffee out of champagne flutes over breakfast, me tired and resentful, her sulking and hurting.

And I know I just haven't got the space in my heart or soul for another person, especially one who demands so much. Opera has taken it all. With an unforgiving, unrelenting greediness, the Opera has taken my whole life and it will not give it back.

"I love you," she says. "I always will. I can take care of you. I can help you, you are not well."

She knows she is losing and gets up to go because I never answer, never say the words she wants to hear; *I love you too.* I don't and I can't.

I stop her. Isn't she coming back to my hotel? I am flirty, still wanting attention. My greedy soul craves more, shrieking on and on for attention when I have hardly left the stage with all the adulation I received less than half an hour ago.

"No!" she screams. "No! You just use me and go back to

Hungary. Your heart is dead. You are ill, Natalija and all you want is passion. You will never get well if you cannot love or accept love and help. Look at yourself, look at your hand. You are making yourself throw up again. You only just dropped out of *Die Königin von Saba* because you were ill and you are making yourself worse.".

"Fiamma, I need you tonight," I say. I do. I am not lying. "I am not well, Fiamma." She is right about me not being able to accept love, but adoration and love are so different. I crave adoration but shun love.

And she stays, this lovely beautiful girl who is offering me everything. She follows me to Hell and back but each time she does, it breaks a bit more of her. I am so bad for her. I am not a good person. I should come with a health warning to myself and everyone else who comes near me.

I dream that night in the hotel room amongst the purple sheets that I have left Budapest, and I am living in Roma. I am running through the Trevi fountain as Lilla, my stepmother made us do once when I was so young I could hardly remember it. We got arrested and my father was mad. But now in my dream, the sun is burning hot, unlike the winter's day I jumped in aged 4 or 5. I am in the centre of the Colosseum looking up through the sand and beautiful stones and I hold my arms up to the sun feeling its power and everything is going so well, then the sky is getting darker, the sun turns to deep venous red and it drips blood on the sand and I feel a sense of dread and fear. The lions are going to be released, I will be mauled to death. I am alone in this arena of death. And then the shouts of people in the distance, the cries of *Toreador! a*s the music turns into *A deux cuartos!* from *Carmen.* One of the toreadors runs at me with a sword and I am speared to death as the crowd cheers. *Carmen* is mixing in with ancient Rome. I am screaming and lying on the ground dying in this arena of pain.

Fiamma wakes me and I am sitting up in bed terrified, like the moment I see my death card in the fortune deck in *Carmen.* It takes her five minutes to calm me down, I am still in the nightmare.

"It's a dream, a bad dream, it's okay. You are safe, Natalija," she says smoothing my hair.

But it was so real, so real. Is it a bad premonition of what my future would be in Roma? I can't move to Roma now. Not after that.

I have to sleep with the light on. I have to tell Fiamma to watch me sleep before she does so I can feel safe.

"Are you going to come back?" she asks me the next morning. Her face is clear and lovely and without make-up she looks about 15. I feel way too old for her, despite her actual age being two years more than mine. I am packing my bag. She is pouring out coffee into the cups by the bed, placing biscuits on the saucers, handing me an orange. It is a blood orange and it freaks me out after the dream I feel I am still in but I eat it anyway.

"No," I say quietly. "I can't." I look at the orange in my hands and its bloodied flesh. "Why did you buy these red oranges? They remind me of blood."

I drink the coffee while she looks at me with such hurt and despair, I can't even say anything.

If I meet her dark tearful eyes through the silence of the hotel room I will weaken and promise her things I just will never do, which in the end will hurt her more.

So we say nothing as I get ready, not even goodbye. She just sits in bed and watches me, the ghost of the girl who once stepped shimmering onto the Opera Theatre stage in Budapest, who had everyone enchanted. I have broken her time and time again.

I close the door and I do not feel good about myself but I do not know how to change.

I leave the hotel room and hear her crying.

It hurts me when I think about her brutal assault in the theatre in Spain, how it must have damaged her so much. I want to tell her I am sorry, I will try to make it work for us. Even if I am lying, I want to stop her from hurting right now.

I hesitate at the door and as I am about to go back in, to tell her I will try and give her what she wants, the morning cleaner pushes her trolley along the corridor. And it is enough to break my tenderness. I just walk away to reception and check out, take a taxi to the airport and sit on the flight to Budapest still reliving the dream, which is more real than anything that happened on stage last night or last week.

I had it all; the adoration, the flowers, the cheering crowd, the devoted girl waiting for me afterwards.

And I left it all there. Because I am still hungrier for the big time despite all the exhaustion. Because I am afraid to give myself to anyone in case I lose any of my soul. Because I had a bad dream that I am afraid is a premonition of my death.

And without meaning to I hurt Fiamma again.

And the nightmares continue. Always the same, always the Colosseum; sometimes I am speared by a toreador riding a horse, sometimes one runs at me with a sword, but always dying to the shouts from the crowd under a huge blood red sun, grotesque and frightening. The sand is red with blood; mine and others before me. Sometimes, I am setting out the fortune cards as I do in *Carmen,* drawing the death card and I know it is predicting the inevitable. And then I am killed.

I wake up in panic and full of horror many nights.

BREAKING - APRIL

"Get out!" I scream. "Get the hell out!"

I am lying on the bathroom floor after throwing up and throwing up and the room is spinning like a carousel and I feel delirious. The glass of salt water is lying spilt next to me and the salt shaker is on the edge of the bathroom sink. I am in István and Lilla's house. I had gone over to see him as he is not feeling well, Lilla was in work for a few hours and he ended up just sleeping on the sofa soon after I arrived which made me mad, so I cannot stop. He wanted to see me, he wanted me here and now he is out cold. He doesn't care about me so I have raided the fridge and eaten and eaten until I am bursting and then thrown it all up again. There is a hundred times more food here than I would dare to have in my apartment. I have rammed and rammed my fingers down my throat and drunk salt water to get out all of the food and the signs of my binge are all over the kitchen, empty or half empty packets and dishes.

Only I am feeling worse and worse after these episodes, I sometimes pass out on the bathroom floor and I am lying there now. From my flat position I can see Lilla is standing in the doorway in shock. I must look awful, my heart is pounding, I feel like I am going to black out and there is blood on my hands, on the carpet, down my clothes, over the toilet seat. I don't want anyone to see me like this but it is too late. Without a word, Lilla drops her bag and kneels on the floor and holds me. She holds me like a mother and I let her and I cry and cry into her chest as if the world is ending. I am clinging onto her, getting blood and saliva and vomit on her designer dress but she holds me tight and strokes my hair back. I inhale her perfume and I surrender and say, "I'm sorry, I'm sorry, please don't tell István. Please. Let me clean the carpet, I'm so sorry, I got blood on your nice carpet."

"Natalija, forget the carpet. I will clean it. You need help. You are killing yourself. You think I don't care about you? You think because we hate each other I don't love you? I know you are making yourself throw up, I knew for a long time but I didn't know what to do. You hated me, I wanted to help and I wish I had because you are dying like this, you are dying."

I cry like the 3 year old I was when I first met her. I cry after years of holding everything in, I cling to her like she is my mother and I can't let go. I am like a cat, claws clinging into her long hair tangled up and not letting go.

Mama don't leave me. Don't give up on me, I cry.

She is cleaning me up, gently untangling my hands from her hair and taking my top off like I'm a child and I won't let go of her as though this gentle Lilla I haven't seen for all those years, might change and become the cruel Lilla and laugh in my face. She wraps me in a bathrobe and half carries me to the bedroom that used to be mine and brings me honey and warm milk and a sleeping tablet and I drift away as she sits there on the bed.

I feel her sitting there as I am drifting away. She pulls the covers higher and strokes my face.

"It's okay, Natalija. I'm sorry too. I am so sorry. I should have been there for you. This is my fault too. I haven't taken care of you, this is my fault. I was messed up myself when I was young, I took an overdose which damaged my liver. I should have tried to help you, this is my fault, Natalija. I've been lousy towards you. I've been a terrible mother." She actually wipes a tear away from her eye.

No, Lilla. It isn't. You didn't do this to me. I would have done it anyway. No one would be able to stop me. I slide under and don't dream of anything.

"Your daughter is ill. Can't you see that? Don't you see, István? All this stress is killing her, do you know what she does to herself to stay thin? Do you know what she is doing to her body?"

I hear this as I wake up. It is late, it is dark, I have been asleep for hours, I feel terrible, everything hurts, my throat, my stomach and my head is fuzzy. I am disorientated and wonder why I am not in my bed in my apartment.

"Listen to me, you stupid man. Your opera star daughter is dying in front of you. She is 27 years old and you ignore it because you think it will just go away. She's been at this since she was 14 years old, throwing up and you are a fucking dentist and didn't even spot the signs. Why? For God's sake, say something, do something. She needs urgent help! This isn't some teenage phase that will pass. She is at it all the time. She cannot stop. It is going to kill her or ruin her voice or both. Is that what you want? Listen to me!"

I can't hear István but he is mumbling something and for the first time I am mad at him and not Lilla. Why didn't he notice something was wrong? Why didn't he know years ago, when he wasn't so sick himself, when he had the frame of mind to see? Why? I came over to see him today and all he did was pass out on the sofa and didn't hear me raiding the kitchen like a demon and then throwing up all my life fluids as if the world would end. He probably had just woken up now.

He stumbles into the bedroom a few minutes later and he looks pretty spaced out. I can't imagine he can help me or himself. He sits on the bed and sighs. Stretches out his hand and strokes my hair.

He says nothing and if I wasn't so wiped out I would

shout at him myself. *Say something, do something, anything, shout at me, scream at me, just notice me.*

I collapse on stage during the rehearsals for the second time that week. The company doctor tells me I should not be playing Carmen at the moment. I have to go to hospital, my pulse is very weak but I force myself into a taxi instead of the ambulance he wants to call. I have let my rivals see enough. If they think I am fragile, they will eat me alive. My heart is racing and then beating a strange fluttery rhythm. *So I have a heart after all, it is beating,* is all I can think of.

I tell the doctor that we are 2 days away from opening night, we are already on the Opera stage, this is not the first week of rehearsals. I can't and won't stop.

I lean against the taxi window, sweating and shaking. I know exactly what it is, I know when the doctor in hospital examines me and checks my heart and my blood and tells me my heart is beating irregularly due to dangerously low potassium levels. I could go into cardiac arrest.

He takes my right hand and holds it up and says, "This will kill you if you don't stop. We can help you now, but you must stop. A girl 22 years old was in here last week. She died. Her hand was not as bad as yours. She looked healthy but her heart was not. This is killing you. And if it doesn't kill you, it will rob you of everything you worked for; all that stardom will be gone and you will be left with nothing in less than a year. How much clearer can I make it for you? Are you listening, Natalija? You will either die or be left with nothing, only memories of a brilliant career that ended before you were 30 years old. Do you really want to listen to someone singing Carmen when your voice has gone for good. And I mean for good, we are not talking about recovering from this once the damage is final. The bulimia will kill everything and you will never ever sing again. You will feel like you are dead even if your illness doesn't finish you off. Are you listening? Why don't you get help? Take months off, take time out, go to a clinic before it really is too late."

They keep me in overnight for observation. I want to leave but they don't let me, I am trying to get out of the bed and they virtually push me back in it. I am distressed so they ask if they can call someone. I give them Lilla's number. I pass out. I am exhausted and my heart beats in an unsteady rhythm.

I am running out of time.

Lilla arrives in her cloud of Coco Chanel. I can just about hear her talking to the doctor but I smell her perfume before I see her. She comes in and we don't speak, we don't know what we can say.

She just holds my hand.

In the end I say, "Where the hell is István? Where is my goddamn father? Doesn't he know? Doesn't he care?"

He does, he does know and he can't talk about it. My mother died from heart failure. He thinks if he starts talking he will break down and cry. Okay, but I need him to tell me he cares. Not through Lilla. He needs to be there for me.

"Why did we ever fight, Lilla, how did we waste all those years?" I say.

"I don't know. I was messed up and I never thought of anyone but me. I know what it's like to be messed up, Natalija," Lilla says. And she looks out of the window. She looks far away, beautiful and sad and the hard bitter face is nowhere to be seen.

She takes out a sandwich she has made with chicken and avocado and a vitamin shake, freshly squeezed. I do eat, I am getting good food but when I binge I do it so much it is cancelling out all the potassium and minerals in my body.

Lilla doesn't understand this but I eat a little of the sandwich.

"You should call Fiamma," she tells me as she is leaving. "Or Kriszta. She really seems to care about you. You know we don't judge you for being the way you are. Love is love. Do you want me to call either of them? Kriszta maybe since she is in Hungary? Don't you think she would want to see you?"

I shake my head and I am too weak to ask how she knew, why I should call her and how much does Lilla know about my love life or more like not able to love life and I pass out.

And she is wrong about me. From what she says she assumes I fall in love with women. I don't fall in love, and men, women are all the same. She's telling me she understands or she and my father understand if I date women.

I am not anything. I don't buy these labels. I am greedy. I just love beauty. I could be with a man one night and a woman the next. It makes no difference as long as they are besotted with me, but I can't stand public displays of affection. From either gender. If they try to act possessive or romantic I hate it.

I wake up and realise how Lilla knows about Kriszta. There is a bunch of red roses which have been delivered to my room. The small card inside says simply; *'your Kriszta'*.

I never knew she even cared. And gossip travels so fast. She wasn't even in our rehearsals but word has reached everyone the great Natalija has collapsed twice in a week and been taken to hospital. The vultures in the company are already circling my dead body, just waiting for me to be too ill to sing. I can't let them win. I would sooner die first.

I am touched in a way by Kriszta's gesture which is so

out of character for her. She must have had them delivered to me immediately. I never thought she would give a damn.

And of course, there are the rumours I have had heart failure. When I return the following day against all the medical advice I need to rest for at least a week, I return to the stage.

"Still here, then, Carmencita?" one of the chorus girls says and laughs. "Thought you might have died on us!"

"Kriszta has been asking about you," says someone else in a bitchy knowing way.

"I didn't eat breakfast and I fainted, fat ass, that's all. You can all shut the hell up. There is nothing wrong with me apart from I don't like food. Get a life and maybe a day job because I doubt if your salary is enough to keep you in cheap bread and rubbery cheese. Losers!" I push past them and down the dressing room corridor.

"What a bitch," someone else says low and angry. I don't make it any easier for myself when I insult them and call them all pathetic and fat and talentless losers. I could make it better by not being such a bitch, but I don't know how.

Good, let them think I am a bitch. Better than weak. Let them hate me, I really don't care.

Their hatred is my fire. Whenever people hate me I know they want to be me.

I strut onto the stage and say to the director, *I am absolutely fine, I just hadn't eaten enough and I am fine.* He is worried I am going to collapse during a performance but he knows there is no one else who could take my place and I assure him I will eat on the show days. It is not so punishing due to the operas alternating; 5 performances over two and a half weeks.

But as I say to everyone I don't like food, I think of food and I know I love food, and I want to stuff my face there and then full of fat and sugar and then throw it all up again. It has been 3 days since my last binge. I love food. I dream about it. I dream I am stuffing myself with chocolates even when my fridge is empty.

I look at myself in the mirror during a break and I am pale and sickly without the make up. My golden skin is starting to look bleached and dry and there are sores around my mouth. In contrast to my black hair I look like a gothic girl on a bad day. I go straight to my bag and plaster on some sunkiss foundation to hide the evidence that I am not healthy, that I am ill.

I am Natalija, the opera diva, I can't be ill, I can't be any less than beautiful.

And Fiamma is not here. Someone else is playing Frasquita.

She has given up on me. I don't blame her. All I did was take and take and break and break her and smash her heart to pieces and walk all over the fragments.

I don't deserve kindness. I don't deserve her adoration.

I am not a good person.

Kriszta is waiting for me afterwards. She is rehearsing *La bohème* in the rehearsal building down the street but she wants to take me for coffee and cake. Danger food.

For once her flirty, seductive manner is serious. Her dark eyes don't smoulder with mischief and she looks worried. I want her to be the Musetta she is playing in the opera and dance on the tables but this is never going to happen today.

"Natalija you look so ill, I'm sorry I couldn't get to the hospital, I sent you flowers as they told me you were only in overnight for observation and you were leaving the next day. I just couldn't get there, I'm sorry. My husband, he was being very difficult last night. It's this role; it's a big role and he hates me playing it. I swear if you had been there one more day, I would have come," she says. I believe her. I don't see the big deal. No one knows how ill I really was, what exactly the specialists said, and the fact I left the theatre in a taxi just looked to many people like the company doctor was being cautious, just sending me for a check-up.

No one knows the truth apart from him, the hospital and me. And maybe Lilla.

"Kriszta, I'm fine," I tell her. I look at the cakes on the table. "Thanks for the flowers. Red roses, Kriszta," I say leaning closer. "Are you in love with me?" I whisper seductively and then I laugh like crazy and slide my hand towards a cake. My emotions are all over the place.

She reaches for my hand and holds it before it reaches the cake. "Don't even think about throwing that up. You are not going to throw up after eating it. I won't let you. Eat one and sit here with me and don't dare throw it up. One cake will not hurt, take the plain sponge. I ordered plain sponge, no cream, no chocolate. No chocolate because I know chocolate is your worst trigger and cream. If you really have to get rid of it, have you tried laxatives?" She is avoiding my question about the flowers, about my question over her feelings.

"You throw up too," I say. And she knows laxatives and being on stage do not mix. It is a crazy desperate idea thrown out to me. Doesn't she think I tried that? Even without being on stage, I need the food out of me and not having to wait for it to go through my digestive system. When I binge, I have to throw up immediately.

"Yes," she says. "I throw up, now and then. But not when I have had heart failure twice in one week. Not if I was as talented as you, with lead after lead going from one opera to the next. I wish I had your talent. You are really something else on that stage but you're killing it. And you think your voice is going to last with the bulimia? You're running out of time, Natalija."

"I didn't have heart failure, I fainted on stage. I was just tired and hungry and everyone wants my role. They are all lying. The whole company is full of liars and cheats. Who said heart failure?"

I try to pull my hand away and she grips it and says, "Your stepmother called me today. I asked her to tell me the truth. She called me in the rehearsal break and I was worried sick all afternoon. Promise me to get help. What good are you to anyone dead or unable to sing? Mikki asked me about you. There are people who care about you, Natalija, you just refuse to see it. Even Zita, the soprano asked me recently if I could stop you doing what you're doing to yourself. And Zita is not one to give a damn about anyone in this Opera World. Fiamma cared so much for you and I do. Fiamma loved you. Or still does."

I laugh but Kriszta doesn't. *Care, my ass.*

"You don't even care about yourself, Kriszta being beaten every night," I say staring at the bruises on her chest. She pulls her cardigan over them and looks upset. She won't admit to anything as usual.

"What would I do without you?" she says. "What would I do without my Natalija?"

"You'd find someone else, Kriszta if I died, you always do, why don't you call up Fiamma in Italy? You would be good together and you like them young," I say breezily and force another laugh, but I can feel the tears coming as I am shattered. We open in 2 days and I am afraid I will collapse on stage during a performance.

I don't want Kriszta to see I am weak. But I am still dizzy. I try to get up to hide the tear glistening down my face but I stagger into the table and Kriszta places her arm around my shoulders to steady me. She insists on taking me home, she has her car and she wants to make sure I am not going to throw up. She also wants to bin bag everything I would binge on in the kitchen. I am lying on the bed too weak to move as I hear her dumping all the cakes and biscuits and chocolate in the trash and to be sure, she is taking it with her. I can always buy more. There is a 24 hour shop and a 24 hour Turkish takeaway within minutes of my block. Failing that, I can dial for anything. Pizza, fatty greasy pizza stuffed with pepperoni and evil cheese.

I look at the red roses she sent me in the hospital and feel empty. They are on the dressing table. Kriszta comes in and says she needs to get home. She rearranges the flowers and looks at herself in the mirror and tells me to call if I need to. She leans over the bed to kiss my face and her long dark hair brushes my cheek, but I roll away from her so she just places her finger on her lips and then on mine. She stands for a minute looking at me with those lovely eyes no longer sparkling with fun and mischief but showing sadness and worry. Is she thinking I am no good to her now, that I am broken and weak and ill, or is it more. Does she actually care, even if a little?

"You never answered my question when I asked you if you were in love with me," I say. But I don't expect an answer as I say it so carelessly and cover my head with a pillow. Damn her and what she feels. What do I care really? Do I need anyone? Do I really want to be hurt, because all relationships hurt in the end? And I can't deal with hurt.

I want to say, *Stay, please stay with me. Just for an hour or so. Don't leave. Never leave.*

But I don't. I close my eyes and her image remains in my brain. Beautiful, sensual Kriszta holding a black bag full of forbidden food. Hurt, damaged and beaten at home. I want to hold her there and stop her going home to this monster.

But I don't as I know she won't stay.

She leaves dragging the bin bag full of my trashy chocolate and cakes behind her and closes the apartment door. I put my face into the pillow and cry. I wanted her to stay. I wanted her to stay and tell me it was okay, everything will be okay.

I wanted her to tell me what she really felt. Even if I do not or cannot feel anything for anyone.

SUMMER

The *Carmen* run finishes at the end of May and I turn up at the rehearsals for *Farnace* where I am due to play Selinda. The directors and the company doctor are waiting for me. I smile and say hello. They look serious when they tell me I am not to perform in *Farnace.*

"It's not a major role, it's only on 4 times and then the season ends, I can't step down, I can't," I am telling them.

"Let it go, Natalija," says the doctor. "This is not a popular opera. This is not your big moment. It won't matter if you let Anna play the role. No one will judge you. You need a rest before the big season begins in September. You haven't taken a break in the 2 years you have been here. You need to rest. We know how ill you were and your performance in *Carmen* was still wonderful but you are risking your health if you carry on like this."

I am protesting and begging and pleading but the artistic director shakes his head. I am overworked. He actually thought I might collapse and die during *Carmen* as I gave it everything.

I won't let anyone see me cry. I don't even like *Farnace,* I just can't seem to stop working.

Twice I've had to step down. On *Die Königin von Saba* and now this.

I sit in on the final performance of *La bohème* that night and watch Kriszta, the enchantress, spin out Musetta's waltz. The tears drip down my face as I am alone in the box.

I go to find her afterwards.

She already knows. She is partly responsible. She told them how ill I really was, that they must cut me from *Farnace* for my health. She looks down and she says, "I am sorry, Natalija. I did it for you. Because I care. Because I was afraid for you."

"Double crossing bitch!" I shout and shake her by the shoulders. "I hate you, Kriszta, I really hate you for messing up my last opera of the season." I shake and shake her and she doesn't get angry, just tells me, "Please understand. Please understand how much I care about you."

I slap her face and walk out.

"Natalija! Please!"

I slam the door and run through the dressing room corridor so she can't chase me, and down the stairs. How could she? How could she do that?

And how could I hit her? I am as bad as her husband. I feel awful.

Kriszta has also called my father and told him how sick I really am. That I have been pushing my body to breaking point and the company doctor is telling me I need to go to a clinic and I am refusing help. So I am in this clinic in Vienna for eating disorders. Kriszta has actually driven me there to make sure I don't run away. My father has paid to make sure I don't just say I will go and then not turn up. It costs a fortune this private clinic. It better be worth it. It is the 15th of June and I tell them 6 weeks is all I can give it. They are asking me to stay at least 2 months but I say no, it is out of the question as rehearsals will start in August for the September season. I have been asked to perform in some concerts but I pretend I am in Italy having a month off for holiday on doctor's orders and it is easy enough over the summer as the opera houses all go dark in July and August. My vocal chords are already showing signs of damage. The company doctor has written to the specialist in this hospital unit, detailing my problems.

When Kriszta drops me off, she hugs me and I try to get back in the car so she has to drag me in. It is too real now, too much and I don't want to be locked up. The staff come out to help and I am shouting, "Please don't go, Kriszta! Please!"

She is emotional, about to cry so she gets in the car and drives away fast before it gets worse.

The staff gently lead me inside, one of the nurses taking my suitcase as if I am too weak to carry it.

The specialist in the unit wastes no time. He shows me photos of my damaged throat and tells me this damage is going to be permanent pretty soon. We are talking months not years. It is a big wake up call. I can actually hear it. Even my voice is huskier in speaking.

I am institutionalised. Of course, it is easy inside not to be bad. This is the whole problem. I am a model patient. I am not having to be watched in case I vomit secretly. I am compliant. I do what they ask. It isn't difficult. Unlike many of the other younger girls, I am not desperately trying to starve or binge. I am here as though nothing is wrong. I eat the food they give me. They weigh me, they check me for signs of vomiting. I don't even have the urge. But they do not understand. This is easy. I talk in group, I talk in private, I do all the activities and yoga and everything they ask like an obedient little schoolgirl.

The danger point is when I am stressed and stretching myself to the limits and there is no clinic and no one to stop me when I have a late night craving for food. No one to stop me stuffing myself. It is easy to feel cured in this place. I attend therapy and group therapy every day and I inspire the younger girls who see me as a star, an opera star with problems who is facing up to them and if I can do it, so can they and when I leave a month later, they all crowd to hug me goodbye. The staff in Vienna think I am cured, I truly believe I have cracked it. It was easy. Too easy to be true.

I do believe it. I actually think as I leave the clinic feeling healthy and happy that I am cured for good. And Kriszta surprises me by coming to collect me. She didn't tell me, I was about to get a taxi to Westbahnhof but the staff said a friend was coming, she would be here for me.

"Don't you have better things to do?" I say to Kriszta.

"Like what?" she says. "Like spend longer in that overstuffed, radioactive crater of water, Lake Hévíz? I left my husband and kids there. I told them I am sick of every year being in that place. Besides I am singing in the summer festival in Pécs, tomorrow night. I'm taking you with me. I don't want you to get into trouble when you are just released. I hope you have forgiven me for taking you out of *Farnace*. I did it because I cared."

"Okay, I did forgive you but I was mad at the time," I say. "Besides, I don't even like the opera."

"I know, you just can't stop yourself, that is the problem. You will work yourself into an early grave, Natalija."

She gives nothing away though. Glammed up, beautiful as ever but matter of fact as though I am an afterthought and I might as well go with her to the concert since she is going anyway.

"Why do you do all this for me, Kriszta?" I say as we head over the border into Hungary.

She turns to glance at me with a smouldering look and then looks back at the road and says nothing.

I am standing in the beautiful square in Pécs, in the burning evening heat which is still 42c. I have such mixed emotions here. I was okay as last night we arrived and just had dinner in the hotel. I ate well, not too much, just some chicken and vegetables and nothing sweet. Kriszta thinks I am cured when she sees me eat. I think I am. I have been wandering around as Kriszta went to her rehearsals and I pass all the ice cream parlours without a thought. But I never really liked ice cream. I still think I am cured. But tonight, I think of my university days and of my mother. I am only half listening to the concert as Kriszta sings fairly early on so I get bored and restless after a while. Afterwards, Kriszta has drunk a few glasses, enough to make her loud and obnoxious. I am not drinking, I am afraid of my emotions although I want to have a glass or two.

"That's my husband there," she says to the musical director loudly.

She points at me and blows me kisses. He is about 75, dressed in an evening suit in the heat and he looks like he has been slapped by her comments. He is speechless, this conservative man with a red face too hot in his black suit and even more hot after his soprano has just made some outrageous comments. What can he say to this loud-mouthed diva who wants the world to know tonight I am hers? Other people stare too. Some are amused, others embarrassed. I reach for Kriszta and say to her, "What are you saying that for? What the hell are you doing?"

"Oh, come on now, sweetheart. Don't be like that," she says putting her arm round me.

"Kriszta I am not your fucking husband!" I say.

"You're better than him in bed!" she says brazenly looking at me direct, dark eyes flashing dangerously as though daring me to tell her not to say any more. This is also really loud. Everyone around us turns to look. I want to slap her I am so mad at her for being so badly behaved. This is an opera festival. People know who we are. We aren't in Vienna, nameless and faceless.

"Will you shut the hell up! Do you want everyone to know

about us?" I am angry with her for doing this. It is attracting attention but not in a good way, although the men seem to find it entertaining. This is my career too, she seems to forget. I am more famous than her and she does have a husband and family to hide behind. I don't. I don't want my private life shouted out to this audience of people in this horrible heat of southern Hungary. It is making me irritable and I am still ripped raw with emotions. The facade of the good girl of the Vienna clinic is crumbling and falling apart.

I walk away, pushing through the crowds and then break into a run, despite Kriszta calling after me to come back. I run and run through the hot dark streets, oppressively narrow in the heat, hating her so much and end up in the cemetery at my mother's grave. No one is in sight so I sit by it and tell her everything. "Why did you leave me, mama? Why? Did I make you do it? Did you kill yourself because you didn't want me? I don't blame you. I wouldn't want me either. I am so sorry."

I cry on my knees and keep saying the same thing over and over again. "I must have ruined your life for you to kill yourself. I must have ruined it."

Maybe I will sleep here tonight and not in the hotel with Kriszta. I cover my face with my hands and howl.

Then through my tears a hand is on my shoulder and I feel my mother's presence at my side. "Mama, please tell me you didn't do it because of me?" I say my eyes closed, face heavenwards.

"Please forgive me, mama."

She has come back to earth to talk to me at last, all my prayers have been answered. I feel her fingers run gently through my hair and I wait for a sign, my eyes still shut.

"What are you doing?" says Kriszta. It breaks the

fantasy, I really thought my mother had come back to be with me.

"Leave me alone," I say. "Just get out of my way!" I try to get up but I am crying so much I can hardly see.

"Shhh, it's okay, it's okay. I am so sorry, Natalija, I am so sorry for acting like that." She is holding a butterfly balloon. "I got you a helium balloon, look."

I let Kriszta hold me as the purple butterfly balloon sways gently in the air. Pillangó is slang for prostitute. I ask Kriszta if she got this butterfly-shaped balloon after behaving like a tart.

She laughs and says all the children shouted, 'Pillangó, pillangó' as she ran through the square with her shoes in her hand and the balloon floating after her. "Maybe they thought I was selling myself."

"How did you know where to find me anyway?" I say through all my tears.

"Where else would you go in Pécs? You told me about your mother. I had to take my shoes off to chase you up here with your balloon. God you run fast, Natalija. Lucky I knew where the cemetery is." She smoothes my hair away from my face and ties the balloon string to my wrist.

As she stands at the gravestone, she traces my mother's name. "She was too young, too young to die," she says. She looks sad and beautiful, like something ethereal in her dress in the warm dark of the cemetery. I have visions of my mother looking down on us. I almost want to introduce Kriszta to her.

"Why did you act like that tonight, Kriszta? Why did you say all that in front of everyone? Why am I even here?" I ask her instead, drying my face with a tissue.

Her eyes grow darker, sadder and she seems to have sobered up. The glitter shines in the darkness on her evening gown and all the diamonds in her hair. “I missed you,” she says. “I really missed you.”

I arrive at the theatre in Napoli unannounced. I have done what I should have done before as I still have a bit of time before returning to work after the clinic and decide to spend a week in Italy. There are cheap flights to Napoli and after Kriszta, I need to see Fiamma because I don’t know how I feel. I am having emotions I really don’t know what to do with. And I need a break which for once is not jetting off to work in Italy. Kriszta drops me at the airport in Budapest. She is not happy. I just say I need to sort some work out in Napoli, and yes I might see Fiamma, but no, I haven’t told her I am coming. But I need a bit of a break away, just a week. I also have a meeting in Milano which I have not told anyone about. I am afraid it will ruin it if I breathe a word to even Kriszta so I say nothing. Just I need some time to relax.

If I knew what explosions I would cause by my presence alone, I would not have gone to Napoli. Only direct to Milano and never contacted Fiamma again. I should have left her, it had been a while and I shouldn’t have gone after her again. I should have let her heal as she was doing without me.

Kriszta is jealous. But she is just greedy. I don’t think for one minute she is truly jealous of Fiamma. She used to find it amusing this lovely Italian girl was so obsessed with me. It seemed to increase my worth in her eyes. But she is acting weird at the moment. She is very protective of me, such as making sure I got treatment and kindly taking me and collecting me from Vienna but after what she said that concert night in Pécs, well that was just crazy. And how can I take it seriously when she shouted it in front of other people? Maybe she was just bored after the summer, had a few drinks and was playing around. She likes to be centre of attention and it certainly got her that. She is so unpredictable.

"I'll bring you some limoncello," I tell her. "I will only be away a week."

She doesn't answer as I get out.

"Well, see you soon," I say. She doesn't look at me. I slam the door and she drives away.

I know Fiamma is rehearsing for a one night concert as the Opera Theatre have told me, so I know she will be there. I want to surprise her for once. I am feeling guilty and superstitious that if I behave as I should, my throat will heal up. I even have some blue roses for her. I don't bring red, but blue is unique and different. I wait at stage door, chatting to the man on duty and there she is, coming out of the building escorted by this stud in a suit who is holding her hand like a goddamn toreador.

So to see her, Fiamma with a man and a diamond engagement ring is a shock. She is leaving the theatre with him and her face flashes a hurt then cold angry recognition of me. She tells me she is getting married in a month. She tells me in front of this Giuseppe. She takes pleasure in telling me.

I shrug, but it hurts even though just a little. I tell her where I am staying and she says she will come by later, we should catch up. Her concert is not for a few days. She seems cool, together and not happy to see me. She takes the blue roses without thanking me.

But when we meet in my hotel bar she suggests we go to my room, as she has to talk in private.

In the elevator she moves away from me when I try to

take her hand. She won't even look at me. But in the safety of my hotel room once I close the door, Vesuvius erupts and she loses it, screaming at me, throwing my towels around the room and everything else she can lay her hands on and actually shaking me by the shoulders shouting, "Why did you come here? I was trying to get over you! I am getting married to get over you and you arrive here and my head is messed up again!"

"Do you love him?" I ask her. "Do you love this man? Or is it all for show, Fiamma? After what you always told me I never thought you could even kiss a man unless it was on the stage. How do you do it?"

She doesn't answer. She looks away and sits at the desk by the window. She gazes at the view. It is beautiful, of the Bay of Napoli, in contrast to this ugly moment.

"Do you love him, Fiamma?"

"No!" she screams getting up. "I love you and I told you that and I always will! How can I marry him now? How can I? I can hardly bear to hold hands with him!"

She puts her face in her hands and sobs. "I would give up my life for you, Natalija. But all you do is hurt and hurt."

I am a terrible person. All I can do is comfort her, she pushes me away but eventually gives in and lets me hold her and I tell her she means everything to me. I am lying. My work means everything to me, Fiamma is way down the list and now way below Kriszta but I have to sort out this mess. I created it all and coming here has made it a thousand times worse.

I am unable to sleep that night. I am lying in this hotel room in the July heat in southern Italy, the noise in the street of bottles crunching all night from bars and restaurants. The heat is oppressive and men are drunk and shouting. And Fiamma sleeps next to me.

She has 40 missed calls from her fiancé.

And a hundred promises from me I know I won't keep.

I know I will try to be good but I will hurt her again. She has already torn off her engagement ring. It lies sparkling next to her on the night stand as she sleeps, her face so unhappy, tears still on her cheeks. She saw my cell phone ringing with Kriszta's name displayed as I was in the shower.

And then the tears, the hurt and me telling her, "Fiamma for God's sake, she is my friend, one of the only ones I have in the Opera there. She was calling me to see I am okay."

Yes, and maybe more. But Fiamma knows about Kriszta and she weeps half the evening saying it is always going to be like this, me cheating and lying and having lovers call me and never knowing if I am faithful when I perform away from home and I have the first glimpse of what it must be like to be someone's husband and I do not like it one bit. One call that I didn't even answer is the catalyst of this night of melodrama.

But I have caused all this pain for Fiamma in the first place. I just tell her, *She has to stop her jealousy. She has to stop, because it will destroy her. And it is so unhealthy.*

Just like I am destroying everything in my life.

"Kriszta knows about you, Fiamma and she knows where I am. She wouldn't hurt you. She wants to see I am okay, that's all," I say. "I promise. She has a good heart."

Another lie. Kriszta wouldn't give a damn if Fiamma wept all week. She is careless, like me.

That is why she likes me so much. I crash through life, not caring about hurting anyone else.

Why don't you answer me? What are you doing tonight?

I roll over in bed and text Kriszta back, that I am just

resting. It is hot in Napoli.

Resting in peace or resting with her?

Goddamn Kriszta, what is with you?

I am sleeping, Kriszta. I will call you tomorrow, I promise.

"You are so cruel, Natalija. So cruel. Texting her when you are with me," says Fiamma.

I don't love this poor passionate girl. But I am selfish, I don't want her with someone else, not him, not married to this lawyer. I want my devoted little toy back.

And I have ruined her chances of any happiness just by visiting. I owe her.

I sigh, "I am doing it in front of you just to show that I have nothing to hide. Or I would be going to the bathroom. For God's sake, Fiamma. I have friends. Not many but I do. And I just got out of hospital. Cut me a break."

"Hospital! Natalija, what happened?" And she is back to her devoted little girl persona. So worried when I tell her that I collapsed during rehearsals, that I have been in a clinic for my bulimia.

She is then crying and saying I should have called her, she would have taken the first plane out. She is so sorry I was ill, she had no idea.

Then hysterical that the reason I didn't call is because she doesn't matter to me, she is nothing.

I sigh and tell her I didn't want to worry her. A lie. I didn't want her involved. Kriszta was too involved.

And I do what she asks, I go into the theatre in Napoli the next morning and I speak to the directors. They have heard from Roma about my reputation. They would have work for me. They know about the audition with La Scala. I would have to travel between the three cities, I would have to return to Hungary to guest every few months in order to make up my schedules but it is possible. Roma Opera has the most for me, so I will base myself there, finding a small apartment. I have Marina's phone number after I met her again when I was last performing in *Werther* in Roma, I will call her and ask if there is somewhere which is light and bright. I cannot stand to be in any digs the theatre give me with no light. I will go crazy. Marina will help.

Fiamma is waiting in the opera café, her eyes raw and red from crying. Her parents have told her she is making a mistake. She has called off the engagement. I didn't ask her to and now I am responsible.

And her fiancé knows about me. He swears at me when we leave the theatre, where he knows I am and where he will find me and Fiamma. He is in my face spitting and shouting I am a bitch, a slut and I am a thief. I have stolen Fiamma from him.

I am a Hungarian vampire who does nothing but suck the life out of everyone I meet. I am arrogant and vile and if I wasn't a woman he would punch my lights out.

And I am sick and twisted, he carries on. "I don't know who corrupted her but I blame you and your country. She is a good girl. She is not into women. And I bet you are not either, you just want everything you think you deserve. Fiamma was right about one thing; you are a real opera diva. You can never love anyone like you love yourself."

For once, I don't shout back. I take his anger, this handsome lawyer who thought she was his. No one is his. She is not his possession. No one owns anyone else.

So Fiamma has told him something about me, that I am a greedy, arrogant diva. Well why shouldn't she? She is right after all, and that is how the world sees me too.

And he is so stupid, Fiamma is not into men. I don't think she even had a man in her life, apart from that horrible Spanish stage manager who raped her and beat her but I keep my mouth shut. I let Giuseppe get it all out. I am in the wrong here and I will not make it worse for anyone.

His last words are, "She will break your heart, baby." He grabs Fiamma by the chin and forces her to look at him. "She will use you and throw you aside. You are ruining your life, Fiamma."

I tell him to let her go, stop threatening her and leave. I want to hit him for touching her like that, forcing her head up. What else would this man force her to do once they were married? This poor damaged girl. He looks at me with more hatred than anyone in The Royal Hungarian Opera ever did. He lets her go and walks away.

In her apartment she makes the dreaded call to her family to say it is definitely finished with Giuseppe. Her parents are mad at her for calling off the wedding and want to know why. She has been crying that night as she called them from her apartment. I am sitting there at the table mashing the pasta she has made into a glutinous mess, wanting to throw it all up again. I hear the shouting from across the table. These small town Sicilian people who have no idea their beautiful daughter is unable to love men and unable to tell them why; the shock would kill them. She is blaming work, saying that Opera is incompatible with a relationship and everything always fails due to the demands of the job.

I would agree with that. The Opera World destroys everything in its path like a raging fire, splitting up marriages and relationships and friendships and normality.

PAIN

That night Fiamma locks herself in the bathroom and no amount of pleading is getting her out. I think she is just acting up but I am worried when she isn't responding to me.

In the end I am desperate to use the bathroom myself so I kick the door as hard as I can and the lock creaks. One more crash and I kick it open. And she is sitting on the floor like a rag doll, half-conscious, her wrists both cut and bleeding into the cream coloured rug.

I forget everything stupid she ever did and scream, "Fiamma, what did you do? Oh, darling what have you done?" She is bleeding dark venous blood almost purple in colour and the razor blade lies dropped to the floor. I grab towels and press them into her wrists. I know from the dark blood, the slow bleeding that she has reached her veins and not the arteries. Thank God. She probably literally has just done it as the blood is oozing out slowly from her wrists as she murmurs, "Leave me, just leave me to die. I want out. Life hurts too much, you hurt too much."

"Stay with me, stay awake, Fiamma," I tell her. I run out to get my cell phone and call the ambulance. I tell them please hurry, my friend has cut her wrists, no she hasn't hit the arteries but please come fast as she is barely conscious.

"Your friend...... that's all I am...." Fiamma says and flops to the floor.

I hold her wrists high above her head padded in the towels as the blood soaks through them.

"Fiamma, I love you, Fiamma can you hear me? Darling, stay with me please," I am hysterical. I never thought she would do anything like this.

She doesn't answer. She is unconscious.

I don't love her but I am willing to say anything to keep

her from dying. I keep telling her I love her, that I will stay forever if she just only stays awake.

I ride to the hospital and despite the paramedics telling me I did well breaking the door down, padding her wrists, she has not lost too much blood, hopefully her wrist tendons are not damaged I am crying in the ambulance. Why did I come here, why did I make her do this? Why, Fiamma?

She didn't cut deep enough, thank God. But I am distraught. Because I feel I caused all this and as I sit next to her bed I know I can't hurt this girl again. She wasn't being attention seeking. I think she just couldn't deal with the mess in her life. She didn't know where to turn. She can't turn to her family and she seems to have few friends in her life.

I wish I hadn't had this holiday. I should have just gone direct to Milano and back to Budapest and told Kriszta about La Scala, because now I am smashing up other people's lives more than my own. And people who don't deserve it. Already I have destroyed the dreams of two families, caused Fiamma to attempt suicide and I do not feel like a good person. And I have to take care of her now. She will need me.

She wants to leave the next day. Her wrists have been stitched, her bandages fresh but the hospital insists she stays for psychiatric help. I return to her apartment to collect some of her things and Fiamma's wedding dress is hanging in the closet. It is beautiful. I want to see her in it but now is not a good time. After two days the hospital release her on the condition she returns to see the psychiatrist every week. That she will call immediately or I will call them if she is in danger again and she is given some anti-depressant medication. I tell them I am worried as she lives alone and I have to return to Budapest where I live. They then look doubtful and want to keep her in but she insists she is released.

I hug her and tell her I will make everything work. *I will, I promise, beautiful Fiamma. It will be okay, I will never hurt you again I swear. I love you, Fiamma. Truly.*

Another pack of lies. Of course I will. And of course I don't.

That night I do try on her dress myself. I slip out of bed and take the fitted slim dress off the hanger and into the hallway. I pin up my hair and wonder what it would be like to be married in this lovely cream white which although a little too big as Fiamma is curvier than me, is strapless and figure hugging and towards the base, it ruffles and falls to the floor so prettily.

And I just cannot imagine it at all. Maybe because I can't imagine who I would be with or want to be with or maybe I just don't face up to who I really want to be with and hide all my emotions under my work and bulimia.

But for now I rustle along the corridor for a while and laugh at the mirror and me in this dress. It is just some light relief, I desperately need it after the darkness of the past few days. I am not really in a laughing mood, my emotions are all over the place.

"What the fuck are you doing?" Fiamma asks me. I have woken her up and her face is an expression of rage like I have never seen. I have never seen her angry like this and I kind of like it. It stirs something more in me than her whining and crying and moping around.

I want to say something stupid like, "You're beautiful when you're angry in your lovely black silk nightdress," but I bite this urge as it would sound even more mocking and say, *I am sorry, I had to.*

She rushes from the bedroom door frame and slaps me

across the face. It hurts her wrist to do it and I see the pain on her face for two reasons.

Bitch, she says. *Bitch!*

She runs back into the bedroom and I follow her tripping over the white froth. "I'm sorry, I was stupid, I just wanted to see what it felt like to be married."

And she grabs her abandoned engagement ring from the box on her shelf and jams it on my wedding finger as her eyes blaze fire and hatred at me. So she does have fire after all. Too bad I never see it because it makes life more interesting.

"Fuck, Fiamma, that hurts," I say trying to pull my hand away but she grips my wrist so hard her scarlet nails leave bruises. She stares at me and I actually think she wants to kill me now she is so mad. She is still holding my wrist, twisting it, but she lets go; her wrists are hurting her.

Her eyes are not the girl I know. Beautiful, green and clear but so full of hate and rage.

She leans over me as I am lying in this frothed up dress.

I look at her and wonder if she will spit at me, slap me again, bite me. I don't touch her as her wrists are still delicate.

Instead she says in a low voice, "Well now you are married. To me. Are you happy?? I have never even been with a man apart from what I told you happened in Spain. I never wanted to before him either. I never even slept with Giuseppe, I said I would wait until the wedding night. I could hardly even kiss him, I had to think of you, I had to think of acting on stage, anything."

She lets go of me and turns away.

"You really think that would have worked? You are not even attracted to men, Fiamma. God, why did you think you could cover it all up? Besides you got the wrong hand," I tell her sitting on the bed showing her the diamond rock she has rammed onto my left hand.

"In Hungary you put it on my right hand." I smile at this. But this has her incandescent with rage. She is so angry she can hardly speak. She grabs a fistful of my hair and forces my head back so she can look at me as she says, "I know that, I am not stupid," she is barely audible she is so mad.

"But you would probably swallow it and choke to death when you stick your fingers down your throat. Maybe then we'd both be better off." She has never been so nasty. It is not her at all. She wants me dead. First herself and then me. She rolls away from me as far as she can and falls asleep.

But I did ruin her life. She tried to kill herself.

For once it is me crying myself to sleep, still in this stupid wedding dress.

Marriage is awful. One night of it and I hate it. One stupid fake night and it is horrible.

I wake up and it is morning and I am so stifled by this wedding dress I can hardly breathe. I have moved closer and put my arm protectively over Fiamma, touching her bandaged wrists. The creamy white lace is rustling and hot. I need to get out of this dress.

The ring doesn't come off either. It is stuck so she insists I keep it. I can't get it off my left hand even with soap so I give up.

"Giuseppe won't want it back, even if he does I will not give it back. You gave yourself to me, you promised me you would be mine, Natalija," she says still with a touch of angry ownership.

"You told me you loved me, I heard you as I was half dead

in the bathroom. And you said it when you brought me back to the apartment. You can't say you didn't."

I did and now I have to live with it.

And this engagement ring will cause more idle gossip and questions in the theatre. This stupid goddamn expensive ring I don't want. And I regret promising anything. I just did it to stop her dying, I really thought she might die that night. And then I had to make her feel better, I would have promised her the world just to make sure she was safe as I can't be here.

And I don't want her to do anything when I am gone. I can't have her death on my conscience.

And I do really care about her, just not as intensely as she thinks or wants.

I want to leave earlier and spend a few days in Milano but I know I can't. I stay to support Fiamma. I have had to lie and tell the theatre she had a road accident; that she was knocked down and got concussion. She is going to be okay but she can't sing in her concert. What else could I say? Besides the directors are interested in talking to me more about the roles I can play in Napoli, after they express concern over Fiamma and are reassured she needs just some rest. She will be fine. I am a good liar. I even believe my own lies.

Fiamma won't leave my side in the apartment. She is quiet, sad and seems so unhappy, a ghost of the girl I first met. I thought she had got what she wanted. But she knows it comes at a price.

I ask her did she really mean to die that night, did she really want life to end?

She shrugs and says, "Maybe."

"I told the Opera House you had been in a traffic accident, that you had concussion. You need to get that story straight. They must not find out. How will you hide your bandages?"

She looks sadly at her wrists. "I guess I will have to wear sleeves."

"And what about when you are in costume, Fiamma?"

"I don't have any roles until September, the bandages will be off in a week or two."

"You're going to have to pray you don't have bad scars or wear a lot of bracelets. No one must know, Fiamma. I mean this, you cannot let anyone but your psychiatrist know what you did."

She nods, sadly. She knows.

Whenever I answer my phone and speak Hungarian to anyone, she sits downcast and silent, waiting for me to finish knowing it is probably one of my conquests and she can't understand a word.

She has even booked us tickets to the ballet. I do not like the ballet. Every time Fiamma was in Budapest, she would ask me would I go with her to The Royal Hungarian Ballet Theatre and each time I refused. I admire their skill, their beauty and especially their thin bodies. Thin is beautiful in my eyes but sitting through a ballet with no singing was dull. I was taken as a child to *The Nutcracker*, to *The Sleeping Beauty* and everything Lilla and István thought a girl would like. But I never really did; that is why I liked ice-skating so much. The ballet classes I did were just to help my skating. Ballet was so rigid, skating felt like flying; dangerous, reckless and thrilling.

And now on my rare evenings off, I do not want to waste it watching a ballet. Okay, if Kriszta is in an opera I would attend if I could but even then that is tiring.

So I have to go to the ballet in Napoli. At least it is a plot-driven ballet instead of those showcase ballets. It is *Romeo and Juliet* and it is pretty but I am not moved. Fiamma is in love with ballet. She cannot understand why I am not. In the interval I disappear on to the outside balcony to take a call from Kriszta. Fiamma comes out with the champagne and sees me laughing and talking on my phone and she places the glasses sadly on the table, looks at the starry sky and says nothing.

She pulls at her bandages and looks so broken.

I tell Kriszta I have to go and Fiamma hands me my champagne knowing who I was talking to but she can't even ask any more as she could push me away back to Hungary forever and be left with no one. She has resigned herself to the fact I am a liar and a cheat and a heart-breaker. And she knows I will not change. She has resigned herself to accepting my careless and reckless attitude towards anyone who ever tries to love me. She folds up the wedding dress and when I am packing to leave Italy I am surprised that it is in my suitcase.

"You might as well wear it, Natalija. Wear it to a première, do what you want with it, I can't bear to look at it in my closet. Just take it with you, please."

This means I have to leave out most of my clothes since this cream confection takes up half the suitcase. This is what she wants. She knows I will not live with her all the time, that I am taking an apartment in Roma and she is too broken to argue. She is satisfied that I will at least be close, that I will be staying when I perform in Napoli, that I am not in a different country. She hangs the clothes I leave behind in the wardrobe, places a pair of my shoes inside. Then shuts the door and sits on the bed looking at me with such despondent sadness. I have a flight to Milano and La Scala have been wanting to see me for some time. I will fly back to Budapest from Milano. I am superstitious and I do not tell anyone about La Scala, only Fiamma knows because she is here but not Kriszta. If I tell just one person other than Fiamma, I believe I will fail. Fiamma believes I will have the work in La Scala, that I belong there, that Italy is at my feet. This is not the time of year they would be hiring though. It is probably just a little talk with the directors.

"Fiamma," I tell her. "Promise me you will not hurt yourself. Promise me that you won't do that. Because I can't do anything from Budapest. If you threaten on the phone, I cannot do anything. It is not fair on me. Please go straight to the hospital if things are that bad. Just go. Promise me?"

She looks at me and agrees, "I promise. I'm sorry, I am sorry you had to find me like that."

I tell her she means the world to me, I tell her I love her, I tell her everything I do not feel because I want to keep her safe. Of course I don't love. But I care about her.

I still do not love and I definitely do not love her. I don't think she even loves me. It is pure obsession. She is like a schoolgirl with a crush. I don't think she developed properly. Repressed little Fiamma. Beautiful girl in small town Sicily and with crushes on girls she could tell no one about as it would be devastating for her and her family. So she just let everything turn into obsessions. She told me about a teacher she had an affair with, some beautiful married lady whose husband worked away a lot in Torino and then one day he came back and caught them when Fiamma was 15, and her teacher was 26 or so. He beat Giulia and shook Fiamma, choking her until she thought he would kill them both. He said if she came to their house again he would kill her and Giulia. And then Giulia never ever spoke to Fiamma again, not in school and when Fiamma tried to talk to her, she said she needed to get a life. She was cold and cruel.

I told Fiamma, Giulia was protecting them both. She

probably knew her husband would kill them.

But when Fiamma told me the story, she still got sad. She never really got over Giulia, even after she moved to the other side of Sicily a year later to work in a different school. No one knew. Fiamma just carried her secrets around in her sad heart.

As I fly to Milano for my secret meeting before Budapest, I regret taking on this girl with her puppyish adoration. Yes, it is nice to be adored especially by someone so lovely looking but I want to shake her myself sometimes. I want more of the Fiamma I saw when she was so angry with me for trying on her wedding dress. I want more spark, more life from this girl. Her name means flame so where is it? I want her to show it more often. Even her singing has a sadness and she always has an affinity for sad characters like Madama Butterfly or Mimi. I really regret it now as I feel responsible for her suicide attempt, feel I can't hurt her, can't tell her that I do not love her. There is someone else who means the world to me I can't tell either; I am a mess. I also realise like Mikki, me and Fiamma really have nothing in common other than our Opera World. With Kriszta, I feel alive and energised and the conversation never stops. We have so much to talk about. Yes, there are moments but these moments are not through lack of common ground, more through emotions; jealousy, irritation, frustration and hurt.

I know that the Opera season opens soon with rehearsals for *Nabucco* where I will play Fenena which is the first opera in September and I am looking at the schedules and this year will be more gruelling than last time. I also have to study for *Nabucco* as it is not often performed and I am unfamiliar with it. But I always love

Verdi so it makes a change to play a different role. And I don't die at the end. It is August and I am fresh and ready for rehearsals after my break, ready to give everything. I am cured of bulimia. I am healthy. I will be okay. Kriszta says, *I am looking so much better but what happened in Napoli? I was away longer than I said. I must have been having a good time.*

"Nothing much, just I will have some work with them this season, after New Year and Roma Opera," I tell her. I nearly tell her about La Scala but decide to wait.

"And Fiamma, what about her?" she says tensing up.

"Oh, you know," I say.

"No, I don't, Natalija. What does she want from you?" Kriszta asks sharply. "And why are you wearing that ring? Did she give that to you?"

Kriszta has even tried soaking my hand in cold water and soap when I told her the story. She laughs about it after hearing the fact I wrecked Fiamma's forthcoming marriage to Giuseppe and even more that I put on Fiamma's wedding dress and made her mad. But I leave out the horror of finding her slumped in a pool of blood in the bathroom. I can't even bear to think about it. What if I hadn't broken the door down? What if I had just shouted through the locked door, *Okay Fiamma I am just leaving* and picked up my case and gone? I could have easily walked out, just a stupid mistake which I would regret for the rest of my life.

She would have died and I would never, ever forgive myself for that. I would have gone to Milano and she would be dying, lying in her apartment for days, a week before friends or her neighbour would notice.

Kriszta is cruel. She likes the fact this poor girl suffered and I was careless. She likes the fact I smashed up a wedding before it even got to the altar. In Kriszta's eyes it makes me more desirable like reckless, cruel, impulsive Carmen who is possessed by nobody and breaks everyone's hearts by her free spirit and inability to love everlasting. Carmen does love, but more than the love itself is the entrapment. Once she has someone's heart, she soon restlessly seeks her next victim, like an addict searching for the next fix.

I also leave out the part about bringing the wedding dress back, about what Fiamma said to me. About what really happened in Napoli, how I am now stuck because I feel I caused it. I don't tell anyone because I am still so traumatised about finding shy, gentle Fiamma bleeding to death in her bathroom. All because of me.

"Don't worry, Natalija. You got a free rock. And you could always flog it if you ever manage to remove it, buy another Langiotti coat. Maybe red this time," Kriszta smiles breaking my thoughts.

I just agree. *A free rock.* I hate Kriszta at that moment, however fleetingly, I hate her.

"Who's the lucky man?" ask a few people as I am in the Opera Theatre with this stupid diamond on my hand that I can't take off.

"Kriszta probably, her little girlfriend," says one girl and laughs. "And this is the mezzo who thinks she is too much of a lady to play bitches' roles." Her laugh is a witchy cackle.

"Kriszta is already married, you idiot," I say. "And I am too beautiful to play those roles, you are right. Pity about you, though. First time I saw you I didn't know if you were a man or a woman."

The bitches are not taking this from me like they used to; they are forming their defences, moving into a circle around me as though they want to burn me at the stake.

"What would you know, Natalija? You don't even know

what you are, you have that many lovers, you must wonder if you are husband or wife."

"Opera slut," someone says. "Kriszta too. She's a whore. You think you're the first girl she's had, Natalija? You think you are special to her? She doesn't care. She takes anything with a pulse."

I turn round and shove this one to the ground. "Jealous, jealous because I had an audition for La Scala and they want me! I am going to be the star; I am her, you are all nothing! You will never be anything other than useless!"

"Come on," Kriszta says pulling my arm. "Don't even talk to them, they are not worth it. Think of your own life. Don't listen to their lies about me either."

She tells the circle of witches to work on their singing techniques, to lose weight, get some teeth whitening, anything other than blame us for their lack of ability and ugliness.

No wonder we are both hated.

"Kriszta's such a nasty bitch. And that diva Natalija, she's lying, she can't be going to La Scala. No one gets there. Not at her age. She thinks she is better than she is," one says as I leave them debating this.

Kriszta says quietly as she pulls me away from the coven, "Don't let them get to you. You never did before."

I shouldn't have told them, I wasn't going to tell anyone. Maybe it is best they don't believe me. It is a secret I have guarded that I travelled to Milano and La Scala have offered me work from next April. I already have Napoli and Roma and initially I will base myself in Roma, returning to Budapest for guesting. I could still fail.

"La Scala?" says Kriszta. "Really? So that's why you were so secretive."

"I don't know, I really don't know," I tell her.

"Wow, I could visit you in Milano. I have never been to La Scala. That is one trip I do want to make," she tousles my hair.

"I know what they said is true, Kriszta. About you. About me."

I face her.

"Yes, it's true. You are not my first. But you weren't there before, remember that. You are here now. And you are special. You think I have some other bitch's calendar on my kitchen wall, photo in my handbag?" She laughs at this, the sparkling flirty Kriszta. "You are so damn special, Natalija. Don't listen to their lies. You are one in a million. And you're the best I ever had." This last sentence is whispered like a ghostly bubble surrounding me and when I open my eyes again, Kriszta is gone. Maybe I imagined she said that, maybe I just need to be adored.

I have visions of Fiamma arriving at my opening night in La Scala with Kriszta in a box opposite. Fiamma calling and calling me as I am in Kriszta's hotel room and then the arguments, the tears, the broken promises.

And nothing to drink the coffee out of in the morning as Fiamma has smashed all the cups.

It could work, I could buy us plastic, she won't be able to smash those, I think. But I guess she could melt them on the fire.

I have a magnet in my heart for trouble.

The thought of all the possible arguments, all that broken china makes me feel exhausted. I am relieved that I will at least have my apartment in Roma despite the fear of being alone.

Meanwhile the Budapest arguments carry on into rehearsals. The vultures are circling again. It is affecting the whole mood of the cast. It is unprofessional and not what any of us should be doing.

The director tells us he has never known such fighting and backstabbing between singers and he is telling us all but looking at me. We should be ashamed. We are professional opera singers and we are behaving like a straggly cast of a school pantomime production.

"If you want to mess this up, fine," he says. "But all of you will be cut from the schedules after this for the remaining year unless you shut up and just work together on this opera which the audience love. They come to see something to forget their arguments and fighting at home. They come to see beauty. This is a poisonous wasps' nest! This is not opera. We haven't played *Nabucco* for years and if this is how it is turning out, I doubt we will ever play it again!"

He knows this is not an idle threat. The company is big enough to do this. Even to me, their star performer.

It is fitting I am arrested when I play Carmen the wild gypsy girl for slashing another girl's face.

We are all that close to fighting in reality. *Carmen* returns in March. The directors decided to cut the September show and go with *Nabucco* for a change. The musical director tells me he hopes I am getting treatment for my bulimia. He knows what is going on. He tells me if I start any more arguments, illness or not, I will be axed. I am the catalyst and whatever they are saying, I need to rise above it. There are inevitably going to be jealousies at this level of performance but I don't need to get involved in it all. Let them argue with each other. The artistic director of *Nabucco* does not particularly like me although he rates me highly, but this musical director is one of my biggest supporters.

I am leaving his office and he says more softly. "Natalija,

please get the help you need. Your voice is lovely, the best in the mezzo-soprano range you could be, but it is showing at times. The damage is starting to show in rehearsals. You must think of that voice. That is your living, your dreams, your everything. Lose that, and it is not like tonsillitis. It is gone for good if you ruin it with throwing up. Please go and see a specialist and take time off after this show if you need to, you have to get well. You need to take a month's leave if you have to. You can still carry on, but you can't keep pushing yourself like this."

I nod and thank him and close the door. I think I am not performing as well in rehearsals because it is a new opera to me. That's all. My voice is just not so familiar with singing *Nabucco*. I even lie to myself.

He doesn't know I have just been in treatment for my bulimia in the summer but they told me I needed longer for my voice to recover fully, that to take a big role in September was too soon for my vocal chords to heal. I can't tell him this, I might lose my role. I can't lose this role because then the directors might start questioning if I am actually up to performing at all, Italy will find out and it will be a downward spiral and I might lose everything. I am too afraid to step down once in case I fall all the way.

So when Fiamma visits me a couple of times that season, I am kind. I don't hurt her. I am trying to be good. She shows me the scars, small and thin across her wrists. She is wearing bracelets to hide them and tells me she is so sorry for that night. She swears she never did it to hurt me, or to make me stay, just everything got too much. She had argued with her family, her life seemed a mess and she couldn't deal with it. Well I can relate to that. I deal with it the only way I know which is hiding all my bad feelings under my bulimia and throwing my life fluids up to avoid all the feelings I should feel but won't let myself. Fiamma seems less needy now she is certain of me moving to Italy. She has already made space in her wardrobe, she says. I am still way busier than her, so all my focus is on my performances. But she is telling me I should be with her in Napoli full-time.

That is impossible. "Please, Fiamma. It makes no sense to base myself in Napoli when many of my schedules are in Roma and Milano. Roma is halfway. You can come and see me when you are not performing."

The real reason I need my own apartment is because Fiamma will drive me crazy and also for Kriszta. I need somewhere she can visit in Italy. I am pretty sure I will be in some dark rental apartment when I perform in Milano. One dark apartment is enough.

TURANDOT

During *Aida,* Zita tentatively asks how I am. This is a big deal for her, to actually honestly ask about my health. Zita is renowned for being an absolute diva who cares for no one in this company. But Kriszta had told me when I was ill, both Zita and Mikki showed concern. I am touched that this senior soprano who should hate me like the others do, actually does have some motherly concern.

I tell her I am doing better. I actually come clean and confide in her I had treatment in a clinic in Vienna and she says she is thrilled to hear that. I am doing well.

I know I can trust her. We never will be friends, but I know from Kriszta that Zita will never tell anyone about the clinic. She is not one of them. She has risen above the backstabbers long ago.

But I am so exhausted; when I am not on stage or rehearsing I am asleep. My body just seems to shut down because it is so starved of nutrients. I still don't eat properly as I am afraid to trigger an eating binge so I have actually cut back on the food and it won't carry me through my day to day existence. I am absorbed by the Opera World. I am having trouble differentiating between day and night and theatre and reality. When I am not in the theatre I am passed out asleep. I have nothing in my life but Opera.

I spend December in *Don Carlo* rehearsals as Princess Eboli, which is a gruelling five act opera. Every rehearsal gives me a migraine. It is just too long, and I wish that our director had chosen to cut the running time as many directors have. It is not a massive role so I shouldn't be so tired but I am and I find the whole opera so gloomy and the music of Verdi I usually love so much is heavy in this dark opera. I have worked and worked to get where I am going which is to the bright lights of La Scala in April. For once it is Kriszta who is playing the lead; okay she is the lead on alternate performances but she is actually playing Turandot and not a supporting role.

"It's only 4 nights, Natalija. Andrea is singing 5 nights over the run. It isn't so big," she tells me.

"But Turandot, Kriszta. The first time I saw you I knew you could play her. I just didn't think you wanted to. You always seemed happy with supporting leads," I say. "I can't wait to see you in it!"

"I regret many things. I regret not working as hard as you because I did have the ability. I wasted it. I regret my husband," she turns from the mirror to look at me.

"And I regret losing you to ....."

With this she hides her tears and leaves the bathroom.

"Kriszta, wait!" I grab her arm.

She shakes me free and runs out down the dressing room corridor.

"Kriszta!" I call but she disappears down the stage door exit and is gone.

She doesn't answer my calls.

I end up with Mikki for a night or two, trying to make sense of it all, but he is not in a good place.

I actually want us to talk but decide not to. He is troubled himself and it isn't fair to start on my private life. How I messed up some naive Italian girl's heart and now I seem to have messed up with Kriszta. This troubles me more as I haven't done anything other than the usual.

He has no roles at the moment only some oratorio performances and a New Year concert. He is depressed and I see his meds in the bathroom. For once I am in his apartment as he is living on the same road as Opera and like me, he has no energy to do anything. He has a cabinet full of antidepressants when I go to clean my teeth and a fridge full of nothing in the kitchen. The only edible thing in his apartment is a packet of coffee in the freezer so I settle for that. *Don Carlo* is so long I have to eat sushi every night for energy. I drink vegetable shakes and pop vitamins for energy but I am not cured.

Even that day when I get back to my apartment I find some hidden chocolate and bread and cakes. I throw them in the trash. But the trash bag is clean, I changed it earlier so I am on my hands and knees stuffing it down until I can't feel any more. Until everything stops hurting and then I throw it all up and I am ashamed. I was cured and I am doing it all over again.

It was a one off, I swear I will not do it again. Kriszta brought this on, it is her fault, messing with my head. Intense and acting as though she was in love with me. She did this. I won't ever mess up again. I do my best, I really try to eat healthily but something keeps going wrong. It always does.

And the next time I see her she is breezy and mischievous, the old Kriszta a few days later. I want to ask her more but I know the conversation is closed. We can't talk about it. Maybe we won't.

She is stunning on stage. My opera has already opened so on her first night I have the night free. I should rest but I would never miss this chance to see her and for once I don't fall asleep. I love *Turandot* but I especially love Kriszta in it. Okay, I notice her voice still hasn't quite got the heights of the vocal range demanded of it by this opera, but she makes up for that by her stage presence alone and her impeccable acting. When she gazes out at the auditorium blackness, her eyes reach everyone in the 1700 sold out house. She is chilly, intense and every bit the cruel Chinese princess who has all her would-be suitors beheaded. She plays cruel very well, because I know she is cruel and vengeful. I think of her scrawling obscenities about Lajos on the men's bathroom walls after he was nasty to me during *Bluebeard's Castle* and I smile. I am in the company box but as it is popular I have to share it with 3 others. One I hate and the other two I don't really know so well but I just lose myself in Kriszta's performance and the wonderful flowering oriental score of Puccini.

She is cheered the loudest during the curtain call. Roses are thrown from the staff from the proscenium box and she gathers them up, holding them tight to her chest and waving at the crowd.

I am so proud of her. She applauds the orchestra and blows kisses for the audience and she looks every bit the star she deserves as she stands and blows an extra kiss through the darkness towards the box she knows I am in, although she can't see me. There is not a shred of jealousy in my heart. She deserves this and more. She deserved it a long time ago.

I head to Kriszta's dressing room as soon as the curtains close. The biggest and best dressing room, no more being shoved into a shared room furthest from the stage. She is still in costume and the blue roses are in a vase, the ones I sent her for luck. Blue is always good. She opens the door looking regal and beautiful as the cruel princess, more even than on stage.

I hug her and tell her no one could have done better, not ever. "And the blue roses match your outfit," I say. "You were the best Turandot you could ever see. Everyone loved you."

She holds me back and her expression changes,"Natalija

you look lovely too, but what is that you are wearing? A wedding dress?" she says looking at the full beaded ivory glory.

I am wearing Fiamma's wedding dress. I thought why not, it's Christmas.

"Yeah, I thought I might as well," I say.

"You are planning on getting married?" she says with a touch of hurt in her voice. "Who to?"

I laugh and tell her it was Fiamma's and she can't bear to see it again so I had to bring it back to Hungary.

"I see," she says and looks down. It has rattled her and I think maybe I shouldn't have worn it. I thought she might like it, since it is evidence I am a heartbreaking homewrecker. The dress has put her in a reflective mood. It has punctured her happy bubble. I am anxious to get her back.

"Can you leave that on, Princess Turandot?" I ask her.

"No, the costume has to be cleaned." Besides, she is drenched from her performance; she needs a shower.

"How about we have a drink, Natalija, it is Christmas and we are not on stage for a few days," she says brightening up as she slips off her elaborate blue and silver costume. She is trying to get back to happy again, on a high despite the demanding role she has played. "And I know you are dying to take me home and put me in the shower," she says seductively, back to being the old flirtatious Kriszta.

"Sure," I say. "You must be tired. Come home, I have some champagne chilled ready. You can shower at my place."

"Perfect," she says, and just takes off her headdress, forgetting the dramatic eye make up as she slips into a black fitted dress and we leave the theatre quickly.

I get plenty of stares as I exit in my wedding dress and

the theatre bitches are hanging around stage door like a load of vultures, all nasty and jealous.

“Told you she was with Kriszta,” says one. “Fancy wearing her wedding dress to the theatre, how obvious. She doesn’t give a damn what anyone thinks. What the hell does Kriszta’s husband think?”

No I really don’t give a damn, not about them, not about this husband or what he is thinking. So what if he is hurt she told him he wasn’t to come tonight, he probably wouldn’t anyway. So what.

I wonder if she did tell him not to attend. Or whether it is just work to him, and he doesn’t have any interest in it. If that’s so, it is very sad. He is a wife-beater. I hate him. I hate him for what he does to her, and also maybe I am jealous that he has her as his possession but I do not admit this to myself. It is something I cannot deal with.

We are in my apartment, and she showers as I open the champagne although the make-up is still there when she comes into the living room. After gabbling and laughing initially, she seems to have slumped and looks tired.

“What did you mean the other day about things you regretted?” I say as the conversation has gone quiet.

She looks down into her glass and grabs at the champagne bottle to pour some more. “Nothing, I shouldn’t have said anything. Haven’t you got anything more than toast and bits of fruit and cheese in this apartment, Natalija? I am really hungry. You still eat like a mouse.”

She is trying to change the subject as she reaches for her phone saying she will dial us some home-delivery sushi. That is low fat and healthy, I will not stuff my face.

“I mean your career is possible, you could still make it big Kriszta. But what you said about me....”

"Stop it," she says her voice low and dangerous. "Stop it now, Natalija. I told you I don't want to go there." She is punching the sushi delivery numbers into her phone.

"You started it, and I want to know. You started it back in Pécs in the summer."

"Natalija, it's too late! It's too late for me to regret it, stop talking about it." She puts down the phone and gulps a whole glass in one go and chokes on some of the fizz.

"Tell me!" I shout. "I am sick of your games! I am so sick of it, Kriszta!" I fly at her and pin her to the sofa, holding her hands above her head. "Tell me what you were going to say and stop with the games, the flirting and tell me what you really want!"

"Get off me!" she shouts, pushing me aside. She is stronger and I flop to the floor, hitting my head on the coffee table and the wedding dress spills over me like a waterfall.

"That hurt!" I say. I hold my head.

"I love you! I love you, you stupid girl and you need it spelled out to you because you hate yourself so much!" this ice Princess Turandot says as she stands above me, magnificent and regal before dropping to her knees. The first time I see the Kriszta underneath her facade, the first glimpse ever in the whole time I have known her.

"Don't touch me!" she screams as I try to hold her. "It's too fucking late, Natalija. It always was. And you are wearing her wedding dress, her engagement ring, you are already fucking well married to her!"

She cries into her hands, tired and emotional. She touches my face, "I'm sorry I pushed you. Your head, it's bleeding a bit, let me get some ice." She tries to get up.

I hold her still and say, "Forget my head for now. I'm sorry, I'm sorry. I shouldn't have worn this dress, but I swear it means nothing, like the ring and I can't even get this goddamn ring off, we tried, you know that."

I don't know why I am sorry. I don't know what I should say. I don't even know what I feel.

I don't know if she really does love me or thinks she is losing me to Italy and to Fiamma.

If I wasn't leaving would she say all this, if she wasn't tired and drunk and emotional would she really care?

Is she like Eugene Onegin in the opera who only wants Tatyana when she is married to someone else? When he is broken because it is too late. It is human nature, to want what we can't have and who we can't have. So many operas are so relevant hundreds of years after because of this.

The fire of jealousy will burn for centuries.

"It's not too late, Kriszta. Please believe me." What else can I say?

But she cries harder at this and whispers, "It is, it is. It is now. Because you don't love, Natalija. And your heart is closed and you don't love me. Maybe you really do love Fiamma."

And for once it is her crying in my arms, Princess Turandot.

"No, I don't love Fiamma," I tell her. "I honestly do not love Fiamma. But listen to me, Kriszta and swear this is just between us; Fiamma tried to kill herself in the summer in Napoli. She cut her wrists and I had to take her to hospital. I could have walked out of the apartment as she had locked herself in the bathroom but I sensed something was wrong. She wanted to die. She wasn't doing it for attention. If I had left that night thinking she was just being difficult she would be dead right now and I could never ever forgive myself for that."

Kriszta stops crying for a minute. "Oh, God. Natalija, I am so sorry. Is she, is she okay?"

"It wasn't deep, she didn't damage any arteries or tendons but it feels like my fault, do you see why I can't be cruel to this girl? She didn't do it for attention, she really didn't. But I do not love her, Kriszta. I don't and I can't and I don't know how I can make anything right."

Kriszta is back to crying again. Heartbreaking and I am lost for words as I am with Fiamma.

I could make it okay if I just told Kriszta what she needed to hear but I can't. I can't make this okay because she is right, my heart is closed and I don't know if it can ever truly feel.

"You don't see things, Natalija, you never did. You never see because you are so reckless. You are killing yourself too with what you do, you are damaging your voice and you could ruin your career. And you don't care about anything or anyone only success."

"That isn't true, I thought you didn't care! I thought I was just always your bit of fun to spice up your marriage, just a bit of excitement in your life. You never once told me how you felt, not once Kriszta; I thought I was just fun for you. I thought that's what is was, fun and friendship and a bit of passion thrown in. You never told me and you should have done!"

"Well now I have!" She screams and cries harder, the champagne tears of Princess Turandot. "Now you know everything! Me and Fiamma both in love with you and you do nothing, just lead us on. You are cruel. Your heart is not even beating!"

She should be angry, she should tell me to go to hell and stride out of my apartment and I won't stop her but she doesn't. She lets me hold her because her tears are hysterical and she is lying on the living room floor, the champagne bottle spilt and she is crying so much, she can hardly catch her breath. I have never said *I love you* to anyone apart from poor Fiamma lying there with slashed wrists but I didn't mean it. I didn't know what to say other than lie. I just can't love. But now I want to say it just to stop this lovely Kriszta crying. This is not the Kriszta I know. I want to stop her hurting, but I don't know how. Just like I wanted to stop Fiamma's pain that night.

"You were wrong Natalija, you were so wrong, ever since that first night when we met. We went to the woods, left the stage and everyone else just disappeared. It was so magical, so beautiful, so celestial like an amazing dream. I never had an experience like that. I loved you there and then. All this time and you never knew," she says crying harder. It is so loud I think the neighbours must hear. I wonder if she is just tired from her role and I say this, maybe it has taken it out of her making her emotional.

"No!" she screams. "I don't know how I can get it through to you, Natalija! You don't even love yourself! How can you love me if you don't love yourself?"

But I don't say what I feel either and I never do.

She disappears to the kitchen and comes back with the ice wrapped in a cloth and puts it on my forehead, soothing the hurt.

"Stay, Kriszta, don't leave now," I say.

She shakes her head and doesn't speak.

She leaves when she has stopped crying, she won't meet my eyes, won't say anything else.

I tell her that she doesn't have to go, she can stay as long as she wants.

"Stay, please stay. I don't want you to leave tonight," I tell her. I try to take her hand but she is putting on her coat and shakes me loose.

But she wants out now.

I am on the verge of standing in front of her and telling her why she shouldn't go, that she is wrong about me; that I don't want to be alone. Not now, not never. I want her to stay but I can't say it.

I just can't find the words.

I let her out and tell her to please call me tomorrow, I am worried about her but she descends the stairs without speaking or looking at me, her blue and silver and black eye make up has run into a clown's mask with all the tears.

"Krisztyna!" I call down the stairwell. "Krisztyna, please don't go!"

But she has disappeared into the darkness.

I cry and cry as I lock the door; 2 double locks and a bolt and I feel like I am pulling the bolt across my prison.

I can't bear to feel this.

And I find my hidden stash of chocolates in the wardrobe. I do have more than bread and fruit and cheese, I have just hidden it to stop me eating it but I can never stop, can never stop myself buying it and then hiding it or thinking I will save it for visitors. It just never works that way. It always goes horribly pear-shaped.

In desperation I am heaving my guts over the toilet bowl again. I cannot deal with my emotions. Everything I learned in the clinic, coping strategies, everything they told me seems to be overridden by this urge to block my feelings by stuffing myself to bursting point. And once again the trigger is Kriszta. I don't want to feel, I don't want to feel anything. I drink glass after glass of water and throw up and throw up until there is blood in the toilet bowl.

And the feelings are gone because I am too tired and weak to feel anything. I purged it all from my body. Right down to my blood. I deserve to bleed after hurting so many hearts.

She avoids me for the rest of our performances over New Year. She doesn't even come to watch me perform. She avoids my calls and texts. Nothing.

I am angry with her now.

There was so much we still needed to say. She knows I am unfaithful to Fiamma. She knows I will be cheating, she hasn't lost me to anyone. She knows I will return to Budapest to guest. She knows she can visit me whenever I am in La Scala or Roma Opera. Yet something in Kriszta dies that evening. The smoky flirtatious fun loving Kriszta is nowhere to be seen. I try to call her again to meet for a coffee in early January but she doesn't reply. She refuses to see me backstage after a performance of *Turandot.* The costume lady tells me and stands in front of Kriszta's dressing room protectively to block me from entering. "Natalija, I asked her. She won't see you. She asked me to tell you to please just leave. She won't talk to you. I told her you are here. Please, she is tired. Go home. She is hurting so please respect her wishes. Please," she says gently touching my arm.

"Give her time."

And Kriszta sits behind the dressing room door hearing all this. Knowing I want to see her and knowing she could open the door and talk to me, but I do as the costume lady asks, and I leave the building. I don't want to cause a scene. Not with other people around.

I want to shout out to her but I don't and I just leave quietly.

So I do the only thing I know how. I can't sleep that night she refused to see me in the theatre. She is not going to get rid of me like this. I won't let her, it is hurting and I can't deal with it. Even the sleeping tablets are not knocking me out, even throwing up is not calming me down. I have to see her. If she won't answer me, I will find her and try to talk this out. I don't want to lose one of few people I do trust and care about.

I turn up at her apartment in the XI district the following night as she is not performing. Her few shows of *Turandot* have finished now. I turn up to see for myself what is this married life and dull husband and family she has. It may be stupid and risky but I can't carry on with her silence. One of the children answers the door, the boy; he is a good looking well-mannered 15 year old and there is also the 17 year old girl who smiles from the back of the hallway, a pretty younger Kriszta. They go to fetch her, asking me please come in. She appears from the bedroom, fresh and beautiful, shaking her long hair loose and asking who is here. She puts her hands to her face when she sees me taking my shoes off as I sit on the floor. "Natalija," is all she says. "Natalija what are you doing here?"

The children have disappeared back to their own rooms.

"Are you alone?" I ask standing up.

"Yes, but you shouldn't be here," she says pulling me into the living room. "You shouldn't have come here," she whispers.

"Well what else do I do and you told me where you lived. You gave me the address ages ago. What else do I do when I am even outside your dressing room and you tell your costume lady to ask me to leave? Honestly, Kriszta you tell me all that stuff and then you avoid me for the next week, not even answering my calls or texts. And your life looks pretty damn good here. Why would you question it?" I look at the plush apartment, the view out of the windows and I am not being bitter or sarcastic.

"Natalija, you are leaving to go to Italy. Fiamma loves you. She needs you."

"And so do you," I say to her.

She opens her mouth to speak then holds her hand up.

"No, not here, Natalija," she says.

"Kriszta," I say taking her hand. "You haven't lost me. Fiamma doesn't own me. I will be over for guest performances, you can visit me in Milano or Roma. I will have an apartment in Roma. I will only stay in Napoli with Fiamma when I perform."

We sit for a long time not speaking and the life seems to drain out of me. I have thrown up twice today, I hardly slept and I am exhausted, I need to lie down. I start to fold myself into the plush sofa as sleep is calling. Emotions are exhausting and this sofa is so soft.

"Come on, you need to lie down, Natalija, you look really pale," she says more gently. "We'll go to the bedroom. I'll make you a hot drink. You don't need to tell me what you've been doing today and I'm sorry if I caused it. I should not have run away from you that night. I should not have refused to see you last night."

"But, your husband," I murmur.

"We are just going to sleep a bit. He told me he was not back until tomorrow late morning. He is visiting his parents in Miskolc. Don't worry. He will call from the car as he always does on his way home, and I will set my alarm early just to be sure, besides the children have to be up early for school."

The warm milk and Kriszta next to me is so nice. So soothing, I could just lie here forever.

"I don't deal well with my emotions or rejection," says Kriszta.

"Neither do I," I say. "So don't reject me."

"I was afraid you would reject me once you knew, that's why I behaved like an idiot. Acting stupid and loud and obnoxious like I didn't care all the time and I realised I did care, so much. I always did."

"It will be okay," I say as I drift away. Actually it probably won't but I am too tired and broken to think otherwise. I pass out for an eternity and I feel so safe.

At first I wonder if I am in the Opera House. My head is fuzzy and someone is shouting. I am in someone else's bed and I think I took a sleeping pill. I am sleeping so much these days; I just see a bed and climb into it. The shouting is coming from a man, and then I realise; it is Kriszta's husband and I am in their bed with Kriszta. All we are doing is sleeping but this is enough for him to see us together in his bed. He has come home early, it is early morning, some grey hour around 3am and for a dull man he has a hell of a temper.

"I knew it, I knew it! Do you think I am stupid?!" he is screaming at Kriszta. "I knew you were having an affair. All this time but I never knew it was her, this siren who is on that goddamn calendar, on photos you had in your handbag, this opera diva! I thought it was a man and I thought I could just deal with it, but this I cannot deal with, this is disgusting. You are disgusting!" he shouts at me.

I am still fuzzy headed so I don't say anything. I feel disgusting but not because of that, because of my insides and throat from throwing up yesterday.

He rips off the covers and Kriszta shouts at him to stop. He stares at me in my underwear like I am a cheap slut. I try to pull the covers over me again but he tears them off and hurls the duvet over towards the window. Hauls me by my arm out of the bed like a rag doll and drops me to the floor and tells us both to get out. He can't look at Kriszta tonight.

She shouts at him to get his hands off me, I am fragile.

"Don't you touch her! I will hurt you if you put your animal hands on her!" Kriszta leaps out of bed and flies at him like a tigress and grabs him round the neck.

He pushes her out of the way in disgust and she falls back on the bed. Then he swings his fists and hits her across her back so hard, I can hear the breath knocked out of her as he beats her, shouting obscenities as I lie helpless on the floor. She cries out with every smack and curls into a ball.

We are just weak women. We could both be flattened by this man if he carries on.

"Take her with you then Kriszta, you little whore, take her to Hell, just get her out of my sight! And take your goddamn trash with you!" He pulls the calendar and the photo of me in a frame out from Kriszta's bedside table. She takes them and holds them possessively to her chest as though he would tear them to pieces given the chance.

"You make me sick, Kriszta," he says turning away and going into the bathroom. "I just thought you were frigid as hell all these years. No doubt you were laughing about me as you always lay there with as much passion as a corpse whenever I touched you. And all you did was go out into that theatre singing your way into everyone else's beds when you should have been at home caring for the children."

"She is a talented opera singer and you held her back. You beat her when she got the roles she always deserved. You hated her success," I say. I am burning with rage and for a minute I think he is going to hit me too. I fire myself up from the floor, ready to run, or kill, I don't know.

But he stares at me, fists clenched, eyes so full of hate. "And as for you, Miss opera diva, don't think you are special to her. She is a tart. Don't think you're her first. All these years I have put up with it, guessing that she was having affairs and not wanting to see but now I know. She is unfaithful and a heartbreaker. Are you surprised I need to beat some sense into her?"

I am holding Kriszta round her waist as I can see she is in pain where this hateful man hit her. If I was strong I would hit him back but I am not and I would end up halfway across the room. I figure it is safer for us to stand together and I pick up my clothes from the floor and holding Kriszta lead her out of the arena of pain she has lived in for her whole adult life.

The children are still asleep, thank God, as I quietly take Kriszta out of the apartment, wrapping her coat around her as the tears are already falling.

And as we sit in the taxi in stunned silence, I know I have screwed up someone else's life, allowed someone else to fall hopelessly in love with me.

I should never have gone over there. Kriszta sits still holding the calendar and photo and staring straight ahead as if I am not even there. Tears roll down her face and I want to tell her it will be okay. But I can't because I know it won't. I take her hands and say nothing. Her back must hurt badly but she doesn't say a word.

To her credit she doesn't blame me. We just go back to my apartment without saying anything. She could be mad at me but she isn't. She just wants to sleep and forget this awful night. She lets me put ice in a cloth on her back where the bruises are already coming up purple and blue. That bastard. I promise her no one will hurt her again.

Why did she have to fall in love with me? If she never had, or never said it, this wouldn't have happened. But I know what I knew before. That this man hits her, that he chokes her, that his fingers grip her arms so hard that he leaves bruises for days. I am burning with anger at the way he is. Okay, he found what he didn't want to find. But tonight wasn't the first time he has hurt her. She lies about her bruises pathologically, she lies about all of them and they have got worse since she got her big role as Turandot. He hates her success. I don't even need her to tell me. I know. But I have smashed my way through everything and set a blazing fire which has burnt through everyone who has ever tried to get close to me.

And Kriszta's husband comes over with all her clothes and boxes and boxes of her junk the next day. I answer the door and he says nothing. She is in the supermarket since I had no food in the apartment and I am performing later in dark, depressing *Don Carlo*. He throws the suitcases into my hallway and I just stand aside until he is finished. She has a lot of clothes. He hands me her coats without a word and gives me an evil look. I decide it's best not to say anything. It is done and I don't want him near Kriszta again after this. He might kill her, he is so violent. He pushes me against the wall as I am thinking this and tries to kiss me.

"Get the hell off me!" I say. "Stop it!"

I am weak and he shoves his hand inside my dress and feels me up. There is nothing sexual about it, it is just an act of aggression and violence. Just to show he can. I shut my eyes and feel his breath on my face, his hateful body against mine. He is handsome but I cannot bear him touching me.

"Not so tough, are you? Not so tough as you make out. You're afraid of men, you don't like being touched by them, do you? Well neither did she but she had to." He starts to put his hand up my dress, roughly grasping at my thighs and I scream for help.

I am afraid he is going to drag me into my apartment and do much worse.

The old lady in the next apartment opens her door.

As if he is burnt, he steps away.

I am shaking with rage. “I know what you did to her, you wife-beater,” I tell him. “And I know you did it all the time and I hope you burn in Hell forever. I curse you. I curse you to death!”

“You gypsy witch,” he says running down the stairs. “You’re crazy.”

“Are you okay, my dear?” the neighbour says. “Do you know him? Shall I call the police?”

He turns in the stairwell and points at me, “Tell her she is never coming back. Tell her that. She can stay with you, you home breaker. Tell her the children do not know and I don’t want them to know, I don’t want them to know about you. But she is never coming back to our apartment. Our marriage was over before she even met you but it is well and truly dead now. I hope you know what you did.” He doesn’t even shout. He is beyond it.

“She would never want to go back to you, not in a million years. Never!” I say to his retreating back.

I don’t even know his name. I tell the neighbour he is a friend’s husband, she left him as he is violent and has been beating her for years and she will stay with me. I persuaded her to leave so this man is angry with me.

A bit further from the truth than reality. But true enough. Violence is violence and Kriszta has suffered more than anyone should have to suffer. It hurts when I think about it. It hurts me.

“These men, these horrible men who think women are their possessions,” says the old lady. “Are you sure you are going to be fine? Do you need the police?”

I tell her it will be okay. My friend has her clothes now. He shouldn’t come back.

The neighbour says if he ever comes to this building again, she will call the police immediately.

I go back in, bolting the door, and look at all Kriszta's possessions. I am about to start putting them away but there is so much there I feel totally overwhelmed.

I go into the kitchen and I don't want to feel, I don't want to deal with this on top of everything and all the opera rehearsals and performances and Fiamma and La Scala and my head will explode any minute. I need to stop the feelings I don't want to feel. I sit in the kitchen and stuff a whole loaf of bread and Nutella down my throat in about 2 minutes and throw up and throw up until there is nothing left. Damn Kriszta for buying the worst trigger food for me. I have to stop her having this death by chocolate. And then I go and do it all again, with two packs of biscuits and a cake. I cannot stop. I flush myself with salt water until my insides ache. My heart beats a fluttery kind of beat and I feel dizzy, there are spots in front of my eyes. I am afraid Kriszta will return, that she will know what I've just done.

Then I call Lilla and tell her what happened. I don't know who else to call. My father owns the apartment and I tell Lilla I have screwed up even more and when I go to Italy, please let Kriszta stay here, I have messed up everyone's lives. Fiamma tried to kill herself in the summer and I found her bleeding in her bathroom. And now I have broken Kriszta's marriage up. I am a terrible person. She is in love with me and I don't know what I can do. But he beat her, he beat her. He was awful to her.

Lilla is concerned. I am husky on the phone from vomiting and she knows I am in a bad way. She says, *Of course Kriszta can stay, she can't go back to that horrible man, not to worry, to get well for April. I have to think of that. But don't let Fiamma down. Don't even think of cancelling Italy. For Fiamma and more importantly for you,* Lilla says.

You have the chance to get well. You have to go to Italy. Your voice is going to be ruined if you stay here doing what you are doing. Kriszta may love you, Natalija but this is your life. She is safe now but what about you? Remember what the throat surgeon said. If you don't get well, you will never be able to sing again. You don't have to tell me you relapsed, I already know just by hearing you. I'm not angry with you, but you were doing so well, I thought you were cured. And that poor girl, Fiamma, is she getting help out there? Are her family there?

I tell Lilla that Fiamma is better, she is on medication and she is seeing a psychiatrist. Her wrists are healed. But her religious Sicilian family will never know or understand. She is alone in Napoli.

She needs you, Natalija. Even if you love Kriszta, Fiamma needs you more, says Lilla.

I am about to say I don't love, I can't love but I realise that is a lie. I don't let myself feel.

But hearing that from Lilla, about my health and my voice which could be ruined next week, next month, punches through my chest more than the surgeon's own words ever did.

Of course I wouldn't dream of not going to Italy. I see it as the only way to save my health. Kriszta can't help me, she throws up herself. And as for Fiamma, I can't hurt her again. I might be unable to love but I am not so cruel as to do that. She would throw herself into the Bay of Napoli. She already tried to kill herself once. How can someone so beautiful want to die so badly? How could she do it to herself? And how could lovely Kriszta, so confident and carefree, hide that darkness from the world for so many years?

What a mess. I guess we all have our secrets. Underneath the stage persona, I have my own. No one who watches me perform would think I had anything less than a perfect life. They must envy us, the three of us who set the opera stages alight, who reach for the chandelier with our voices, who represent beauty and everything ethereal and otherworldly.

The audience have no idea.

TOSCA

Kriszta has lost her sparkle. From the delightful, fun-loving beautiful woman I knew until only a short time ago, she is sad and quiet. Instead of freeing her from her slave girl shackles and a life of lies and violence, she has turned inwards becoming withdrawn and depressed. She has phone conversations with her children, promising to see them, just she had to leave, her marriage is over. That it had been over for a long time, yes she is okay and she is staying with an opera friend, no not a man.

She might as well be, I think. I am that man who broke it all up. I smashed up their world. At least they are older. 17 and 15 so they will be able to deal with it better. Unlike my broken up childhood with my stepmother and father and their messed up relationship.

But he has been beating her for her whole life, he has hurt her. He is an evil man. Each time I try to talk, she won't. She still denies it saying that the night he came home and caught us was the only time he hit her; she denies and denies everything.

She won't open up and tell me even when the evidence is staring at us both. I tell her please invite the children over, my apartment is her home too. They can visit any day or evening. They can come for dinner any time she wants.

She thanks me but it never happens. I guess she is afraid of them finding out about us, that I am not just a friend.

So she meets them for lunch or coffees in the city. She doesn't want me involved.

She is even down to play Tosca, a role she once told me she would never play. The rehearsals start a few days after *Turandot* finishes. I am playing Charlotte in *Werther*. *Don Carlo* finishes and *Werther* rehearsals continue in an unbroken line. I actually think I should be saving my voice. This role was hugely demanding and intense when I played in Italy. But as usual, when the directors tentatively ask am I okay to do it and then go straight into *Carmen* with a week off I see no reason not to. Well it is still a week off, I am not going from the final performance of *Werther* straight into rehearsals the next day. They are reluctant to let anyone else play the role; they know of my success with Roma Opera and how much media attention I got.

Kriszta tells me I should not do it. I tell her she is now getting jealous of my success since she is getting the roles she always wanted. We shout one night as I tell her she is turning into a diva. There is only space for one diva in this place. Turandot and now Tosca. I am happy for her. I would love to play Tosca if I were a soprano but I do not resent it. I think she is finally committing herself to what she really should have done years ago.

She says if there is only one space for a diva, fine she will leave. I block the doorway and we wrestle to the floor. "Let me out!" she shouts at me.

"No! Stop walking away from me, Kriszta. Where are you going to go now anyway?"

"You don't want me here," she says. "What do you care?"

"Don't be crazy. I want you here. Why do you think you are here? It's not charity, Kriszta. I am not kind like that."

"You only liked me when I was in supporting roles! You resent my success, it was all about you, Natalija! You are the worst diva I ever met in my career! You stab everyone in the back and are so ruthless, you would kill for a role. You are arrogant and rude to everyone you work with!" Kriszta shouts.

I am shocked by her outburst. She never said any of this before, if anything she liked the fact I was ruthless. She liked my success.

"Is that what you really see? Is that what they all see?" I say feeling suddenly so empty.

"Yes!" she yells. "You are renowned for it. God knows what you will be like if your voice continues and you carry on with success. By the time you are 40 you will be vile. You will be the most demanding diva in the whole world!"

"Oh," is all I say. I sit down. "Oh." I can't cry, I can't shout, I don't know how to respond. Because she sounds like she hates me.

I go into the bedroom and just lie down curled up holding the pillows and not knowing who I am any more.

Kriszta sits on the bed and says she is sorry. She is under so much pressure and she knows she will never match me. She is sorry if she hurt me with her words. She says maybe she is a bit jealous at times because I will be the best and most famous opera singer in the world one day. No kidding. I have an amazing talent and I will be a superstar.

"I don't want you playing Charlotte because of your health, Natalija. I know how it damaged your physical and mental health before. I think you need to get well. I am not jealous of your roles. You know I am not. And I am playing Tosca, I am playing roles that to be honest I never thought they would consider me for and that is thanks to you. Remember when I first met you and I was Liù? You freed me from my slave girl shackles, you set me free to become who I should have been all along." She sounds so broken and exhausted by this outburst.

"Takes it out of you, doesn't it?" I ask sitting up, recognising the signs.

I put my arm round her. She nods. She is not used to feeling the pressure like this. Not used to the demands of being the lead soloist. Supporting roles always seem so easy in comparison. The stress of being the lead with everything that goes with it and the pressure to sing to absolute perfection is so demanding and this is the first time Kriszta has experienced all this. But there is something else troubling me and I need her to be honest with me, she has denied and denied that her bruises were anything other than drunken falls. I know she will not like it. I have asked her before but in a less direct way, when I saw marks on her neck, sometimes her arms. She had brushed it aside and said she had liked it rough, shrugged it off, not wanting to discuss it. I need her to say it. I need her to finally admit it all to break free from the violence.

"Your husband, I know he was violent towards you and it wasn't just that night was it?"

She looks at me angrily. "No, why do you say that? Who have you talked to?"

"No one."

"Well, why say it? He was mad at us that night he found us in his house, yes, but he was never violent before then."

"But he didn't like you to have success, did he Kriszta? That's why you never pushed further than you did. Why you are doing it now."

"Natalija, will you shut up," she says her voice full of hidden anger.

"He never wanted you to be successful, did he? He would want you at home. He even overlooked your affairs but he never wanted you to be a star," I say.

"Stop it," she says with tears in her voice.

"He wanted a wife not a diva. That was what he couldn't stand. *Turandot* must have pushed him over the edge," I carry on.

"Shut up, just shut up!" Kriszta is fighting me now, pulling my hair and wrestling with me on the bed like an angry child.

"I saw the bruises, Kriszta. I saw the marks on your back, your neck, your wrists where he held you down and took what he wanted from you because you were his wife. What he always did because he owned you."

"Shut up, Natalija, shut up!" she screams.

Kriszta collapses into heap on the bed, her long dark hair covering her face, the tears now flowing.

"He hurt you, Kriszta and you never ever told me. How long had he been doing that? You had bruises and scratches the whole time I knew you. I saw the marks. He never hit your face because he wouldn't spoil that beauty and he never wanted anyone to know. And you acted so confident, so tough to cover it all up. All those lies, the bravado, the comments about liking it rough. You couldn't ever admit to anyone, even me. Only I saw more since you began *Turandot*. That bite mark on your chest, those marks on your neck during *Turandot* rehearsals. Kriszta, what would you have said if a man had done that to me?"

"I'd fucking kill him," she says. She cries into her hands.

"Kriszta, no one is ever going to hurt you again. Remember when I was stalked and attacked in my dressing room, remember how you were and that was one time? Why don't you feel you deserve more? Why do you feel you don't matter?"

"Damn you for not noticing before," she says as I hold her tight. "Damn you."

"I did. You just brushed it away, like the carefree Kriszta I always knew. Or you got mad at me. I knew all along, Kriszta. I knew."

"Don't leave me, Natalija. I am not so strong. Please never leave me, I don't want to hurt any more," she says.

I stroke back her hair and wipe her tears. I never ever

tell her about what her husband did to me.

"I promise you, and you are strong. You just needed rescuing that's all and no one will ever, ever touch you again, I promise," I say. I take her face in my hands. "I promise you, it is over. No more beatings, no more pain, no more lying about the bruises. You don't need to do that any longer."

"I never wanted you to see me like this. I never wanted you to see me weak. I was always the carefree girl, not the sort of woman who fears her husband. I stayed out all night so many times and he would go mad but mainly he would shout. If I got back late, he didn't care. But every time I got a good role, he got worse. When I didn't perform much, he left me alone. He just worked. But he took what he wanted when he wanted when I was in his bed like I was his property and I kidded myself it was okay because we were rich, we had a beautiful place to live and mostly he was out of the house."

"I know, I know."

"I don't think I ever loved him," she says. "I don't think I ever did even at 20 years old. And the children never knew what he was like towards me, I never want them to know. I kept quiet to protect them. I kept quiet because I was too ashamed to admit it to anyone because everyone sees me as fun-loving, carefree, don't give a damn about anyone Kriszta. Only she's only half of me, the rest of me is bruised and I was always thinking if I left everyone would say I should have left earlier so I didn't leave, and he kept hurting me and hurting me again."

"It's okay, it's going to be okay now," I tell her. "I promise, no one will ever hurt you again and I don't think any less of you because you didn't leave. You are so strong, Kriszta. You just needed someone to set you free, like you said from your slave girl shackles. I did. You are free now. You will always be free."

She cries and cries and I just hold her and keep telling her that she is safe now, she will never ever be hurt again. Wherever I am performing in the world, I will make sure she is safe. I can't always be there but I promise her that I will have someone make sure she is safe whenever I am away.

I don't tell her that I actually want to kill him. I want to kill her husband for putting her through this for all those years. Crushing her spirit. Beautiful, lively Kriszta. He is a bastard and I hope he burns in Hell. She doesn't talk to me about it any more. I tell her the apartment is hers, she doesn't have to worry. It belongs to my father and she can stay here as long as she wants. It is a lovely place, ideal for downtown and the Opera, she has everything she needs here. It is also very safe. Two double locks and a big bolt and the neighbours are elderly, they are always there if there is any trouble but she must never ever let her husband in, she must take taxis home and make sure the driver waits until she enters the main door. I won't be here much because of my new schedule from April onwards.

My father comes over to see I am okay, which is touching given his poor health. He meets Kriszta and says he has seen her on the stage, she is stunning. He is more than happy that she can stay in my apartment when I go to Italy, look after it, just pay the bills to him, no need for the rent. He bought me the apartment and he doesn't take rent.

She thanks him profusely but as we three sit in silence on the sofa over coffee after the Opera conversation has dried up. I know the reality is so dark and harsh. It has gone from fun and laughter to serious and painful.

I show my father out and he tells me with clarity, for

once his mind not fogged up from the pills, that he is glad I am happy, I have found someone to make me happy. A pity I have to go to Italy but a plane ride is not so far, and there are cheap direct flights between Budapest and Roma.

This Kriszta, she sent you flowers in hospital I remember and she called me to tell me how bad your eating disorder was and we got you into that clinic in Vienna. She even drove you and picked you up. She seems so kind. She is older than you, she has a good heart, she will make sure you take care of yourself, Natalija. I can rest knowing you will be okay. He smiles as he kisses me goodbye. He is so pleased that someone will be looking out for me that I haven't the heart to tell him what a mess it all is. It is just nice to see him smile and look like the István I knew before his illness robbed him of his soul.

He doesn't know about Fiamma. He thinks it is over between me and Fiamma.

Fiamma calls me every few days and when I speak to her in Italian, Kriszta is silent and sad. She understands most of what I say although she only uses the language for Opera. She is behaving like Fiamma does, unlike the carefree Kriszta I always knew. But I don't think she is weak or pathetic. I just feel so sorry that I just hurt everyone around me with my selfishness, with my huge ego.

But I never say *I love you.* To either of them. Because I don't. They are better than any of the men I have been with. I trust them, I let myself be taken care of, but I don't know if my heart can truly love anyone.

I wondered early into my career if I would end up in Italy and it is looking dead set after all. I have talked to the Opera in Roma, to Napoli and La Scala and now I have opportunities in so many opera houses with occasional returns to Budapest. I might be able to get well, I might be able to work everything out.

Fiamma is still wanting me to stay with her full-time in Napoli and I say no, absolutely not. For one thing my schedules are split and I have more in Roma than the other two places. Besides Roma is in the middle of the two cities. I prefer it to Napoli which is always so tense and edgy, and I definitely prefer Roma over Milano which is just industrial and cold. To me, Milano only exists for La Scala.

Fiamma looked so sad those last days I saw her after I ruined her marriage, but she seems to have settled for the fact my transfer to Italy is enough.

She will put up with my cheating and lies and unfaithfulness just to keep me.

Who says Giuseppe would have been any better? I had asked her when she had called off the engagement and we were in her apartment how could she deal with it.

"I don't know, Natalija, I don't know if I would have done to be honest. To be like that with a man, is something I don't know if I could do. Especially after, after....you know."

You idiot, I want to say. *You think you could suddenly turn straight? You want to please your family by being the dutiful little wife they wanted? Fiamma, you need to accept your real needs.*

But I remind myself she is damaged, she has been hurt so badly and she has the small town Sicilian mentality of wanting to make her parents happy, to make them proud of her, as they always asked why she never talked about her boyfriends. *Surely she had all the men in Napoli chasing her?* They had asked.

But she still will not return to *Carmen* for the fourth run despite being invited once again; she says Budapest holds such bad memories. She will wait in Italy. In any case, Napoli has her down to play Liù in *Turandot.* I know I will cheat on her. I hope she can take whatever is thrown at her because I know I am not going to change.

But there is also Kriszta who has had to disappear when Fiamma comes to visit me for a weekend and I had to hide everything in the apartment belonging to her. Difficult as she has so much stuff so it goes in the spare room, bursting out of the closets and drawers. She watches me put it all away without offering to help. She stays with a friend, reluctantly. Angrily slamming the door. "Enjoy your love nest," is her parting remark. "Enjoy your fucking wedding dress too."

I open the closet and find Kriszta has taken a knife to Fiamma's wedding dress and slashed it to pieces. It lies on the floor, beads and sequins everywhere.

Goddamn jealous woman, I need to hide this mess before Fiamma gets here. What is wrong with Kristza these days? She is so ungrateful.

I have to stuff thoughts to the back of my mind, thinking I could have done something earlier. I could have saved her from one more bruise, one more night. I feel guilty as though I am responsible.

But after Kriszta returns to the apartment I mention the dress, that she shouldn't have cut it up as it wasn't really mine. She just glares at me and then sees the box of heart-shaped chocolates Fiamma brought me on the coffee table. In a moment of jealous rage, she hurls them out of the window, hitting a dog walker four floors below who yells up, 'What the fuck?' This could be funny except it isn't as Kriszta slams the window shut, angry and hurting. "Goddamn dog owners. It's a sad state of life when people run around after animals picking up their shit."

Then she sits down on the sofa without a word, arms folded, eyes blazing full of jealous fire looking with hatred at me. Then I get mad too, as she is living rent free and this is a lovely apartment. We are hardly in a dosshouse in the VIII. And she is out of her abusive controlling marriage. The one that killed her career, that only now is she finding her real voice, not the seductive wild Kriszta but the real voice, the talented soprano she should have always been since her early twenties.

And it was a goddamn chocolate box that started this sulky, silent argument.

"Kriszta……" I begin.

She holds up her hand and I stop. I go into the kitchen and open the fridge. I pick up the Nutella jar and I am mad as I told her not to buy that trigger food stuff. I slam the door and sit at the table boiling the kettle for a distraction.

Kriszta smoulders in the doorway. "You're a bulimic and the stupid bitch buys you chocolates. You might as well give a self harmer razor blades. Like Fiamma, with her wrist slashing," she says nastily and bangs the cups on the table to make some honey and lemon.

"Kriszta that is cruel. I told you about Fiamma in confidence and you say that. That's horrible of you even if you do hate her. And you've got Nutella in the fridge," I say. "I asked you not to. I told you it is the worst trigger food for me, I told you a thousand times, Kriszta. It's way worse than a chocolate box."

Without a word Kriszta opens the fridge and hurls the jar at the wall.

"Are you satisfied now, Natalija? Are you happy?" she yells. "Happy you got what you want?"

"Yes," I say looking at my scabbed hand. "But you shouldn't have hacked up my dress, the wedding dress that wasn't even mine. It wasn't right, Kriszta. You should have told me and I could have left it in my father's house. You don't talk, you just act and lash out all the time."

"Yeah, Natalija. You want that bitch's wedding dress??? For what?" she screams in my face.

"What for? You want to get married? Who to?"

"No," I say. "Look what it did to you."

She is cursing as she pours out the drinks and crying angry tears. I try to put my arm round her but she shakes me away. "I didn't mean that in an accusatory way, I just hate to see you hurting, Kriszta. No one deserves that, especially not you."

I sit back down again.

She silently makes the honey and lemon then pulls up the chair next to me and takes my hand, the scarred one. She looks at all the scrapes, fresh and old where my knuckles keep hitting my teeth as I throw up.

"You're right, I was wrong to do that to your dress and I am sorry Fiamma cut her wrists, I shouldn't have mentioned it again. I was jealous. I am jealous. Jealous of that girl who has your heart." She says rubbing her eyes, smudging the kohl liner.

"Fiamma doesn't have my heart," I say. "I have to work in Italy, I need to stay with her sometimes but you know I will have my own apartment. I even showed you the photos."

I don't tell her it belongs to Marina's family, the senior soprano who gave me Tosca's crucifix as I think Kriszta will assume I also am involved with Marina. Marina is married and it was her apartment when she was younger, it is near the Opera and it is small but bright. I trust Marina.

"You need to stop, you need to stop locking yourself in that shower for half an hour and thinking I don't hear you. I want you to stop locking that door. I know you have relapsed Natalija. I know, before I even hear you showering for all that time, before I even see your hand. You have gone back to it, haven't you?"

"Can't I have privacy in my own apartment?" I say like a child, trying to pull my hand away.

She holds it tighter and looks at it closer, a testimony to my horrible habit. More horrible now as my father's money went into that clinic. All the staff thought I was the model patient; the inspiration for all the other girls. The beautiful opera star who also suffered just like they did, those teenage kids who looked up to me. They thought that if I had problems, they were not so weak. That if I could kick my bulimia so could they. I have let everyone down. And I let Kriszta down, I promised I was cured.

"No you will have no privacy, not when you do what you do," she says quietly. "I am going to sit in that bathroom when the water is running and you shower until you stop hurting yourself. Your career, Natalija. Everything you ever wanted, everything you sacrificed to get here and you are fucking it up for yourself. I really thought you were better after Vienna. I thought you were cured."

We sit in silence and stare at the Nutella where it hit the wall. The lemon paint is streaked with chocolate and the glass jar has dented it and shattered on the floor.

"I will have to clean up that wall," I say, getting up. Kriszta pulls me back down again.

"Soon you won't be able to sing and you are only 28. Is that what you want? We're talking your whole career over at 28? I can hear your voice is different when you speak, it is lower and huskier than when I first knew you. You told me what the throat specialist told you and warned you of," she tells me. She still grips my hand, not letting me get up to clean the wall and end this conversation.

"I know," I say.

"Everything, everything you worked for, all the pain and sacrifice and fighting and sore throats, La Scala waiting for you and you still keep doing it," she says angrily. "You think if I had a quarter of your talent I would do what you're doing?"

"I'm sorry," I say.

"Tell that to yourself. Tell that to the mirror. Tell that to La Scala when you can't sing anymore at 28, don't tell me," she says.

My tears fall into the cup of honey and lemon and I sip away and it eases my throat.

She doesn't comfort me. She just sits there, silent and still resentful, burning with rage and other mixed up emotions.

In the end she unscrews the lock from the bathroom door. I just look at the door and think, *But I can still do it when she is out. She can't watch me 24 hours a day.*

I am angry with her at times for just not discussing anything and then angry when we do. I am also anxious that I have to leave Kriszta to spend time alone in an apartment in Roma and also in Milano. The only help I will have is when I stay with Fiamma in Napoli. But I don't think she can help. Fiamma has so many of her own problems. I will have very few guesting occasions in Budapest. All at once I am dependent on this fiery, beautiful Kriszta and despite all the arguments and chaos I wouldn't change her for the world. Fiamma will not do things like sit when I shower and unscrew the bathroom lock and drive me to the clinic and hurl chocolates out of the window to save me. And I am terrified of being alone now.

I have also grown to realise that Kriszta has way more depth than I ever thought imaginable. She drives me mad but I know she is trying to help me. But she absolutely hates Fiamma. She is so jealous of Fiamma I can actually feel it as tangible as an emotion can be when my phone rings, or a text comes through. I have to password lock my phone or Kriszta starts reading the texts and saying, "The stupid, sad cow."

All her venom is directed against this poor girl.

And even one night when my phone chimes late she puts the pillow over her head and says, "God, why doesn't she just commit suicide properly and cut us all a break."

I am so mad that I get up and go and sleep in the spare room and Kriszta just falls asleep, not caring I am angry with her. I knew I shouldn't have told Kriszta about the suicide attempt, I knew she would throw it back heartlessly. She doesn't even say sorry for the remark. Not then, not the next day either. She just wakes me up with some juice and says, "Sleep well, Miss Perfect?" before flouncing off to the shower.

She is cruel, underneath it all. Cruel and careless.

She also doesn't know I had to tell Fiamma that she was staying in my apartment. There were just too many of Kriszta's clothes, books, millions of shoes to hide. So I stuffed them all into the spare room and ruffled the bed and made the room into Kriszta's. I told Fiamma the truth and instead of crying and saying I was betraying her, which is what I expected, Fiamma had just looked at me sadly when I told her that Kriszta's husband beat her, that he choked her and he has been getting more violent since she got bigger roles. I had to take her in, he was hurting her so badly I was worried what he would do. And no one else knew. Not even her mother.

I expected tears and sulking and accusations but all Fiamma said was, "How terrible. Poor, poor Kriszta. You are so kind-hearted, Natalija. You hide it, but you really are kind underneath it all. Of course it is right she stays here. And when you are in Italy she will have a place to live. It is right, Natalija. Thank you for telling me," she says squeezing my hand. "I know you're honest with me and it is good. You are not hiding anything. You are such a good person underneath all that glitz and ambition. You have a good heart."

Which made me feel such a liar. I was a cheat and no, my heart is not good. I am a heartbreaker.

So I am madder at Kriszta's reaction which is so heartless compared to Fiamma's generosity which was so full of concern for someone she didn't like, a bitter rival for her affections. How she bought the spare room lie I don't know. I had made the spare room so full of Kriszta's junk maybe she really did buy it.

Kriszta is so untidy she hardly notices that I have now put all of her clothes and possessions in the spare room. She leaves things everywhere. I am forever picking up her stuff. It moves itself back into my room, the living room, the kitchen as if it has a life of its own. I tidy up and a few days later, everything has morphed back into the rest of my apartment which I have always kept so tidy. So I just leave it and let it be. I am too tired to argue. Maybe she is having her teenage rebellion because her husband's place in Buda was immaculate. He probably beat her for leaving a cup out of place.

Every week Fiamma sends me a postcard to say she is waiting for me. Kriszta just looks at them and mutters, "Pathetic."

"How much longer are you going to do this, Kriszta? What about when you are in the theatre and I am not? What about when I am in Italy?" I say soaping my hair. She is sitting supervising me in the bathroom.

"Then your devoted little girl Fiamma is going to have to help you, because I can't watch you 24 hours a day. I actually think you need to check into an eating disorders clinic for a month, Natalija, I really do. I think you need intensive help. You will also be alone when you are in Roma. You will need a lot of help there. You really need to take a month out, however long it takes and kick this bulimia."

I don't answer. The company doctor told me the same thing. He handed me a leaflet for a private expensive eating disorders clinic in Vienna. He said I should consider a month or two. I had to tell him ashamed, that is the very clinic I spent a month in only last summer.

Then you need longer, Natalija. You need 2 or 3 months. Not next summer, not when you have time. Now.

I know he is right, Kriszta is right. I turn off the shower. She hands me a towel without looking up from her magazine.

"What happened to your throwing up then, Kriszta? You always did it and said it was okay. When I first met you, you used to throw up in work," I say nastily.

"Because I care about you so much, I don't do it any more. I don't even do it in work to spare you. I have stopped full stop because I can't be a hypocrite and tell you to stop if I do it. Because I will not let you do this to yourself, Natalija."

She rubs my hair roughly with a towel. The tears in my eyes stay there and I swallow hard to stop them falling. Why does someone care so much for me? Or more like two people care so much and I don't feel I am worth their care and devotion. Despite my arrogance, I feel like I am starting to splinter, that I am liking myself less and less. The illness doesn't help. It has made me much weaker and my immune system is a wreck.

"I got you something," she says and her voice has the magic sensuality and mischievous sparkle of the old Kriszta.

I am sitting in bed exhausted. "What?" I say.

She hands me a book. *Death by Chocolate.*

I open it and it is full of recipes including the infamous *Death by Chocolate* cake. It is in English.

"Why are you giving me this?" I say.

"I bought it for my grandmother when she was starting to lose her mind. She always loved cakes. When I gave her the book one Christmas she looked like I shot her and said, 'Death by Chocolate? Fancy scaring people like that!' Especially as her English wasn't good, she took it literally. She kept forgetting the title and then looking at the recipes and asking what the book was. Each time she said the same thing about the title. Don't you think it's funny, Natalija?"

I don't because chocolate is my worst enemy. I sigh and put the book down.

"I didn't cheer you up, did I?" Kriszta asks sadly.

"No," I say. "You didn't. I really will die by chocolate the way I am going. What is that cake anyway?"

"I had some in London once, it's so rich and calorific that's why it's got that name," says Kriszta. She sits down and tells me she will help me as much as she can but I need to want help. I have to work with her to get better.

I know. I know. I have to get better. Not next month, not after this or that. But starting now. I have to try to change.

At least I still have Kriszta to help me through since we will be working together on *Carmen* in February where she will play Frasquita. It helps to have the same schedule. It means if I need to throw up, I will really have to get creative.

I wish this could work. I wish Fiamma and Kriszta could accept each other. In a crazy idea, I have the three of us living in one apartment but in a heartbeat I see Kriszta strangling Fiamma on the kitchen floor while Fiamma tries to tear Kriszta's hair out to break free. It has turned from having one jealous lover into two. I would only have to leave the room to get a drink and they would be physically fighting each other.

In late January, Kriszta makes me return to the clinic for a weekend. She won't let me pay. She does and she tells them I am worse than ever, and they try to sign me in for a month but I can't. I say I can give a week in between *Werther* finishing and *Carmen* rehearsals starting, which is end of February. I am already taking this weekend off to see the doctors again when I should be preparing for the dress rehearsal of *Werther* on Monday. Kriszta tells me I have played Charlotte before and we are going to stay in Vienna until Sunday then we will drive back. She is also taking time off she can't afford. She needs to be concentrating on *Tosca*.

"I can't get it through to her," Kriszta tells the nurse. "She needs help so badly."

At the end of *Werther* there is no celebration. Kriszta is in *Tosca* the next night and she puts me on the train to Vienna and I am left there for a week. And collected at the end of it. I am told to rest my voice, to not even speak unless I am rehearsing. To save it from greater damage.

The atmosphere at home is tense. Me wanting to rehearse, to talk but I feel Kriszta would sew my lips together to stop me. I have to write everything down on paper and she talks on and on to me.

I hate the feeling of being mute. I write this.

She says, "Well, can you see what your future holds if you don't get yourself well? It could well be like this for the rest of your life, only you will be able to talk just not sing."

I can't imagine a life without singing. I can't let that happen. I am about to speak and she presses her hands on my mouth and tells me, *No! Can't you listen to me. No speaking unless you are singing. Just do it.*

I cry and cry in the dress circle box, as I am alone, because I love *Tosca,* because Kriszta appears wonderful and fragile and beautiful and demanding all at once. In 'Vissi d'arte' as she crumples to the floor I think of her in her domestic life, beaten and hurting for a lifetime. All her pain is concentrated into this aria and it is tangible. At the end of the aria, with tears on her face and her eyes closed, the audience applaud and shout, *Brava!*

They can feel it too. She has put everything into her role and it shows. I am so proud of her this makes me cry too. And I cry for me, for my damaged voice. I cry for what I could lose which is so precious; the diva in the silver dress and diamond crucifix on the stage, and also for my voice, my talent which could fail on me any day soon. Fiamma would probably not want me either. She only knows Natalija the diva, the jewel of the Hungarian stage snapping and spitting and smouldering and hypnotising the audience as *Carmen.* She doesn't know anything else.

I could be left with nothing.

I want 'Vissi d'arte' played at my funeral. I feel death is close or maybe I am just visited by Puccini's ghost. I should not have sat on dress circle left. It is supposed to be haunted. The right hand side is not as the doors lead backstage but on the left the corridor leads nowhere and is said to be haunted, everyone knows that.

CARMEN 4

It is one of those days in March when everything seems warm and beautiful. The spring is floating in the air and I am well into my third year with the opera company and I am popping painkillers and vitamins masking anything bad which is going on in my body. My concession to health is to eat more bananas to bring up my potassium levels which were dangerously low. I have been better than ever on stage despite my health. Every night of *Carmen* has been more magnificent than the last and I feel stronger. But I still do not look very healthy, I still have heart palpitations. I put it down to the coffee. But Kriszta knows it is the purging my body of potassium by drinking salt water after bingeing, she knows too well and despite her best efforts I still cannot stop completely.

The performances are going so well; my Don José is a passionate Italian who keeps trying to stick his tongue down my throat when we kiss. I think he is attractive but I am not really up to this. I tell him to stop dragging me around the stage so much. He seems to think that his jealousy has to be wild; at the end of Act 3 he is pulling me around by my hair as his character is getting more jealous and possessive. I feel like a rag doll. I keep telling him to cool it a bit; yes the acting has to be believable but he is taking it one step too far. I have bruises from his grip on my arm after one show. He is very sorry, he is Italian and passionate. To be fair he is a quiet and gentle man off the stage, but seems to lose it once he is on it. He grows in stature and puts his whole soul into the role. His finale 'C'est toi, c'est moi' is the best I have ever performed thanks to him.

And yet, off stage I don't even think about having any kind of physical relationship with him whereas last year or two years ago I would. Some strange kind of shift in me. I don't know whether it is loyalty to Kriszta or the fact I am becoming so driven, I will not become involved with anyone I am performing with. I want everything to be totally professional.

Kriszta is back to her old self. She sparkles and is getting more roles after her success as Turandot. She goes to to see her children at her mother's house and the marriage is well and truly dead. They do not know about me, I said it is better left unsaid and she agreed. She stays over to see them once or twice in her mother's house and I even miss her then. I feel lost without her around.

I am still sorry about the fact I didn't save her earlier. She throws her arms up and says, "You know what, Natalija, if I had never met you I would still be in that loveless and violent marriage, taking on supporting roles until my career ended, having affairs with people, never satisfied, hiding my bruises under my bitchy, flirty exterior. You did me so much good in all ways. I think you saved my life because that was no life, no life at all until you came along."

She tries to make light of it, but the darkness is there, threatening to swallow us both up because I know that she loves me, that she always did. I know it is hurting her that in a couple of weeks I will be gone.

She also tells me after one of her weekends away she has a surprise. I feel ill thinking she will announce she is moving out, that she loves someone else. She hands me a rehearsal schedule.

"Well?" she says.

I look closer and it is in Italian. *Madama Butterfly* and the stamp on the top is Roma Opera.

Her name is next to *Cio-Cio San* for May rehearsals and June performances.

"You really have the role? You went over to Roma without telling me? When? Is that why you were so secretive, staying over at your mother's so you said? I was beginning to worry you found someone else."

"Yes, I had to fly over to Roma and I wanted to surprise you so much," she says. "And yes, okay I did want you to be jealous and worry I was with someone else, I wanted to see some emotion from my Natalija. I hope you can get the chance to watch me, just for one night. And I hope you would let me stay in your apartment when I am there," she says this last bit cautiously as though I will not want her.

"You can stay as long as you want, Kriszta. Here and in Roma. I promise you. My apartments are yours too."

She sings 'Un bel dì,' in the middle of my apartment right there and then. And the haunting sound rips into my heart. The one fine day which will never come, where Butterfly is holding a shred of hope even she knows is unreal. The one fine day is just a dream. Kriszta stretches out her arms into nothingness, her eyes far away, reaching for the moment and the day which is unreachable.

I cry for many reasons and Kriszta is lost in the aria, the feeling for the role, she doesn't notice.

One fine day we will be together again. Oh, Kriszta. What am I doing? How can I leave?

It is on my mind so much. I know that leaving her will be hell as we have both been together so much really since I first started in Budapest because she was always here and I guested only occasionally during the last few years. However much I have going for me in Italy, it is hurting to break up what I have here.

I think she wants me to say what she always wanted to hear. But she also knows that for my career I can't. She is selfish and wouldn't care about Fiamma. But she won't let me mess up my career for her. If I sat down and told her I would stay for her, she wouldn't allow me to.

I wouldn't stay, I can't tell her the dark secrets of my heart and she knows that too.

At times I have almost wanted to, to sit her down and say, "Kriszta, I want to stay for you. I want to tell you what I thought I could never say to anyone."

But I couldn't stand myself for that. At times I look at Kriszta sleeping and want to tell her secrets I am holding so close to my heart I don't know if I could even put them into words.

If only........*Un bel dì, vedremo*..........

So I don't try.

I hand Kriszta a box. Christmas is something we don't really bother about. Is is work after all, but birthdays are something special. And I hope it says what I can't put into words. "What's this?" she says in delight.

"Early birthday present and for getting the role of Madama Butterfly. If you don't like it, I can get you something else," I say dismissively.

She tears off the wrapper and ribbon impatiently and opens the box. Inside, made out of silver is a necklace, heart shaped. Maybe too obvious so I didn't engrave anything like ***Forever.***

It simply says ***Krisztyna, Un bel dì ......***

Maybe as much as I could say.

Kriszta says, "It's beautiful, it means so much, Natalija, but you called me Krisztyna, people only call me that if....." She doesn't finish the sentence, she knows what I mean and

I know what she was about to say. Her dark eyes are moist and I am afraid I will cry as she hugs me.

I want her to tell me not to go. I want her to tell me to stay with her. But I can't.

I also now couldn't stand to be at the mercy of The Royal Hungarian Opera for everything. The deeper I have become embroiled in the company the more vicious I realise it is. I am in favour now, but I know as others have done in the past, it doesn't take much to fall out of favour. Someone could come along more backstabbing than me and really stitch me up. No, better to have four opera houses to work for. Three in Italy and one in Budapest and just be a guest of Hungary. I am trying to be positive. Kriszta now has her first role in Italy for Roma Opera. She might get some others and she can stay with me. The flights are cheap and frequent to Napoli, to Roma and to Milano. This isn't the end but it feels like it. *Un bel dì, vedremo,* I whisper into her hair. Maybe Kriszta will get more roles in other Italian theatres too. She is feeling the pressure of Budapest. She is becoming successful and hated and the country is holding so many bad memories for her, of years of pain and lies.

The new life is waiting but I am fearful. I have already booked to see an eating disorder specialist in Roma and in Napoli and I have details of a clinic in Milano. I will see a doctor in whichever city I am in every week even if it kills me. All the glitter, the diamonds, the glory will be gone and I will just be Natalija. I know I really need 2 months in that Vienna specialist clinic which was good but I just didn't stay long enough to change my way of thinking and I just can't take a month off, not now. I am 28 and I have made it, I have made the big time. But there is no joy to be had. It means more and more work, more stress. There is a feeling I am only as good as my last performance. I can never rest in this theatre world. I can never sit back and relax and feel I have done well. There is no margin for error in La Scala. The audiences are brutal if the singers are not 100% there in the performance, if the standard slips just a fraction it is all lost. I have heard many stories of experienced singers reduced to tears after catcalls from the loggionisti who sit in the gallery and shout abuse. Having never performed in La Scala I can only imagine what that would feel like.

Only in the early days, such as when I first performed in *Aida* in the open air festival at the start of my time with the The Royal Hungarian Opera did I feel a sense of achievement, that I could take a breath and enjoy the moment. Now, I have to work harder than ever to keep up. I can't relax, I can't let anything slide. And the competition for the few leading mezzo roles is making it worse. Not for the first time do I wish I had a soprano voice. It isn't just my love of Puccini; I would have so many more roles to choose from.

Kriszta has taken Fiamma's role of Frasquita. It is nice to have someone on the stage who is on my side for once. Especially her. When we raise our glasses on stage in *Carmen,* I know Kriszta isn't acting like the others. She is there for me. The last replacement back in the spring, a pretty yet cold Russian called Elena was okay. She sang and then went back to Moscow. She didn't get involved in anything, there was nothing to like or dislike about her. Kriszta referred to her as a dry sponge cake. "Plain sponge that girl. Nothing passionate, dangerous or exciting there. She must be like a corpse in bed." Typical Kriszta, she always thinks of how a person will be in the bedroom department. Mercédès is always played by someone who hates me as they want my role, as I did when I first performed in *Carmen* in the very same role; I wanted the lead so badly it hurt.

"I am the best, none of you will be as good as me. Why do you think I get all the leading roles? And Carmen is mine for life. I am her, I look like her, I live the role," I say partly to myself in the mirror and partly to Anna whose face is so full of anger in the glass, it looks as distorted as a funhouse mirror. She is hanging around my dressing room door wanting to talk to me, God knows why; it is before the performance and I just want her to leave me in peace. We have had our vocal warm up and I need to focus alone. It is ironic she is playing Micaela, my enemy in the opera, so gentle and loving on stage, a pure woman and yet in real life Anna is horrible. She is generally not a popular woman. I think this Anna is overrated and should stick to the chorus and at the back too. The fat ugly. She could stop stuffing her face or better still, start throwing up afterwards. Ugly okay, she could cover that up with make up but no one needs to be fat. I think back to the first and second times we put on *Carmen* and Frasquita was played by Fiamma, the beautiful devoted Sicilian girl, the one I hurt so much. She was asked to return to play the role for the third time, but she declined, so they said. I know why. She couldn't have her heart broken every day by me. And now it is the fourth *Carmen,* the second without Fiamma. I am the biggest selling point. La Scala have me down for their version of *Carmen* in May and in other operas in between Roma and Napoli. I am reaching the gold at the end of the rainbow.

I wish Fiamma had come back for *Carmen* but I knew this time she never would. After missing the third *Carmen,* she could easily be replaced and now Kriszta has replaced her. And Kriszta says we will work something out; I will be in Italy and she will be here in my apartment but we will work something out, she promises.

She will be in Roma soon enough, in May, although I will be performing in La Scala then but in early June I am in Roma; our schedules overlap for a few weeks and I will see Kriszta perform Butterfly as I start rehearsals for *Aida*. Marina, the soprano I will rent the Roma apartment from, knows about Kriszta. She is more than happy for her to stay. *Better than those dark apartments they shove the poor guesting singers in*, she says. I say 'friend' to Marina, but she is not fooled.

"She is special to you, Natalija, I know," she had told me. "You don't have to explain."

We will be able to see each other, we will work everything out, Kriszta tells me again and again.

I don't know what she means by that. I don't know how I can ever work anything out.

I just envisage Fiamma leaping off a bridge if she ever found out what a traitor I really am.

I close my eyes and Fiamma disappears along with my guilt and I step back into the role. The here and now of *Carmen* and that bitch Anna is waiting for me to continue with my lecture, as she is still standing in the doorframe of my dressing room. So I do. I tell her straight what the directors don't. She needs to hear it from someone.

"Besides, you couldn't play Carmen. It's a mezzo role. Your voice hasn't got the range. Soprano voices are too glass cutting high. You all sound like you want to bring the whole chandelier crashing down with those notes. A mezzo-soprano has such richness, such depth and power to the voice," I say powdering up my face with the heavy sticky stage make-up. My skin is also suffering from my bulimia and I am having to cover up its pallor. Without it, I look like the sickly girl I am, not the golden skinned glow of the once healthy Natalija. Gypsy girl of the ice. More like the Snow

Queen now. I am pale in the way junkies and anorexics are. My hair is dry and brittle too. My long black ringlets, once shiny and swinging with health are looking damaged and dull, a dusty coal black instead of shining raven.

Anna is standing there as I am trying to get ready and the stage manager has just announced the half hour call. She is still standing there but I am not looking at her now as I am lost in my own thoughts. "Too bad your girlfriend is a soprano too, does she know what you think of us?" says Anna nastily.

"Kriszta has depth and vocal range and above all beauty and sensuality on the stage. Everything you don't, and yes Kriszta knows my feelings about everything. But Kriszta has played major roles. Turandot, Tosca and she will play Butterfly too. Roles you could never get even in provincial theatres in Hungary. Kriszta knows my feelings about sopranos, especially bad ones like you. She is my friend after all."

"She's a lot more than that, everyone knows about you, Natalija. They know about you and Fiamma, and you and Kriszta and you and half the men in this company. You are just hiding under the behaviour of a slut and you are too afraid to admit to your relationship with your beloved Kriszta. Kriszta too, with her showcase family and husband. Long before you arrived Kriszta was the biggest whore in this company. And her family never attend premières with her, you do! I even heard someone say she left her husband for you and was living at your apartment. At least Fiamma had a heart and was not afraid to show it and you just used her, exploited her weakness."

"Yeah, yeah, just gossip about our lives, you know nothing, nothing about any of us, Kriszta never left her husband for me, we are friends," I say.

No she didn't leave her husband. He threw her out. And how the hell does anyone know Kriszta is in my place? We have made sure we kept that quiet. Her address for work is given as her mother's address in Buda, not my apartment and we never said a word to anyone. Some bitchy spy no doubt. I am right not to trust anyone. There are spies and backstabbers everywhere.

Like I give a damn what Anna says anyway. She's wrong. I am not this or that or anything. I just love beauty and people seem to love gossip especially if it involves someone of the same gender. My conquests contain way more men than women. Although I do wonder about Kriszta. Fiamma is just obsessed with me, but I always reflect on Kriszta and think that the currents run so much deeper. Even from our first meeting on the stage of the open air theatre, running away into the woods like two magical creatures, the summer heat still in the starry night sky, the world a beautiful place as Kriszta said herself.

"Please just go, Anna. I need to get ready," I say applying the red lipstick and looking at my jet coloured hair, admiring my beauty now it is blemish free. But my throat feels sore from throwing up earlier. I hid it from Kriszta in the theatre toilets backstage. She has managed to stop me in the apartment and won't allow any trigger foods in the kitchen. But I am crafty, I will always find a way.

And Kriszta knows when she sees my hand. She has taken to examining it every day calling me a liar when I say I didn't throw up. She knows I am still at it. She shouts at me and tells me she will drag me to the eating disorder clinic herself. She will personally call the theatres in Italy and tell them my schedule is on hold for a month if I do not stop. And I know she actually might.

"As soon as you arrive in Roma, you must see that

psychiatrist. And Milano and Napoli. You must go every week and you must not lie to me on the phone. I will be there soon after and I will be so mad at you if you have lied. I know you will be alone and under stress and that is when it is dangerous. If you can't stop now, with all the support around you, how are going to be when you have a bad day or bad night in Italy? What if you get cat-called on the stage in La Scala? I know exactly what you will do. You won't go home and lie in the bath and think the audience are bitchy tonight, you will go home and hurt yourself. I want you to call me if that happens. Even if it is 3am, just call me, I don't care how late it is. I will tell the opera company you are sick and can't sing if you do not take the help you need so badly, Natalija," she told me only the night before at home.

I promise to do as she says. I promise and promise I will not hurt myself.

I desperately need to stop as my voice will be ruined. It will turn from mezzo-soprano into tuneless scratchings if I do not cut out this terrible habit. I will be done for in a year. Maybe even less. I promise myself as soon as I get on that plane, I will change. I will be honest with the doctors, and I will stop. I will stop before it stops me and kills everything I worked for. Because without Opera, I will be dead. I cannot live without singing.

I pour out my honey and lemon from the thermos flask next to me. I look at the dressing room which is empty apart from one bouquet of flowers, from my younger brother Levente always thoughtful even though he is busy in Munich. I am a star and this is what I get. To hell with them all. I keep getting tonsillitis. I sing on top of my illness despite the company doctor telling me to cut back.

If I delay going to Italy I could lose all my work. I could

mess up my career even if my health depends on taking time out. If I tell Fiamma I am not coming, even if it is just a delay, I think I really will burn in Hell forever. If she finds out about Kriszta she will do more than cut her wrists. I am actually afraid she would kill herself. She never threatens this but after her marriage didn't happen just because of me, I know she is as fragile as a paper flower. She tried to make her life work without me and once I stepped back into it, she fell apart like crystal. She is Madama Butterfly, she once said. She understood Butterfly so well when she sang the role. I couldn't forgive myself if she did something fatal because of me. How ironic that Kriszta is to perform Butterfly, how she always had it in her. Beneath her smoking, sensual exterior was a voice so full of pain and heartbreak and such power.

I put my head in my hands and wish for a minute that I could stay with Kriszta, that life didn't have to change, that I didn't have to push myself to work for three opera houses in Italy and return to Budapest as well. That Kriszta could stay with me in Roma, that ....

But I shake the thought away. No, my career comes before any happiness. I have already sacrificed everything for my whole lifetime to get to this point. I cannot stop now or step down, not even a tiny step as I might fall all the way.

Kriszta senses I am fragile. But she doesn't know how bad; and I am hurting her too, the once untouchable siren whose heart is softer and more tender than she ever let on. The cold carefree facade has crumbled and I see the delicate Butterfly beneath. No wonder she got the role. I never heard 'Un bel dì' sung like that, just in my living room but with such resonating feeling and yearning hope, yet sadness and longing fused. I know when I see her sing the role on stage I will cry. Puccini is made for crying to. The master of sadness, great puppeteer of emotions.

This is the final show of *Carmen* and my stage death is getting more perfect each time. I act better than anyone in the company and I know it. I feel everything and I live the part to the extent that I cannot let go of it. When I am in rehearsals and on stage, I am the role. I am strong tonight, I have been taking extra medication to boost my potassium and eaten a lot of bananas.

As we stand in the swirling stage smoke and the lighting state turns to arterial red, I am ready as I toss the ring from Don José to the floor with a laugh, rejecting him. I am ready for my death. This time it feels real as he whacks the blade in; it hurts and I think I have taken the acting too far and we slump to the floor as the sounds of Escamillo and the toreadors ring out from inside the bullring in the distance but something is wrong. I am struggling to breathe through the smoke but it is not the smoke that makes me struggle, my lungs are rasping and Luca has a look of horror in his eyes as the curtains close and the applause begins.

He is looking at his hands as I am collapsed into his arms, lying on the stage. There is blood, or is it just the light. My back is wet with sweat. Or something else.

"Help us!" he screams in English. "That knife is real, I stabbed her, help!"

The stage crew who are standing in the wings are dumbstruck for a moment until the stage manager rushes on.

I am losing consciousness. I can only hear the applause. The rest of the cast are waiting to come on for the curtain call. I feel the tension in the air as I am slipping away but I know exactly what has happened. The prop knife has been traded in for a real one and Luca has not checked, why would he? By his shouting and horror, I know it has nothing to do with him. He is an innocent victim, an Italian performing for the first time with our opera company. He has no reason to hurt anyone. But the women have many reasons. This is no accident. It has to be someone in the company, no one could get access backstage as our security is so strict. It is someone on the inside. It is one of our own.

I thought I was untouchable, thought I was ruthless and backstabbing. But it turns out someone else was more ruthless and literally ready with the dagger to my back. There is always someone hungrier than you in this world of poison and lies, this artifice of beauty hiding deep ugly undercurrents of jealousy and murderous hatred. The audience only see the beauty, the high art, the wonderful operas we immerse them in. They have no idea how much suffering and paranoia and ugliness hide bubbling just behind the curtains.

Those same curtains which are threatening to open again now and show the whole auditorium the reality.

“Hold the curtains, hold those curtains and get a goddamn ambulance!” someone is shouting, but it is far away, stretching like bubble gum as I sink under.

Kriszta has rushed onto the stage, breaking free from the stage manager who tries to hold her back, as Kriszta is screaming at her and telling her to get the doctor, get help, do anything. The stage manager had tried to stop Kriszta, saying *not to touch anything, help is coming*. It is basically a crime scene now. Although this is not said I can figure it out in my head and they don’t want anyone else touching the stage but Kriszta won’t leave me to lie there with only Luca desperately trying to help. The stage manager is asking me, *To stay awake, stay with us, Natalija.* I see her face swimming in front of me and I don’t know if I can stay awake, I am feeling weaker. I can hear the doctor running along the corridor, with his shoes slap-slapping on the wooden floor and Kriszta is kneeling next to me, saying, "Natalija, my Natalija, what have they done to you?"

I can feel her arms reaching for me, pulling me close but I am already limp and flopped over as Luca is trying to stem the bleeding with his jacket, telling me in Italian, *It will be okay, help is coming, keep strong.*

I am travelling away from the person I have become, the one I do not like much underneath the facade. I do not have to pretend now. I give in. The unbreakable Natalija is growing weaker. Am I dying for real in Kriszta's arms instead of playing dead in Luca's? Is this what God intended for me all along? Is this the end? I lived for art, I lived for passion and this is how God repays me? I reached the stars with my voice, I aimed for the Heavens, I gave so much beauty. I gave so much to everyone.

And I hope the visions flashing before me are not the end; don't they say that if everything flashes before your eyes like a cinema reel then you are dying? I don't regret so many things I did, I don't regret hurting so many people but I have visions of Fiamma, her face beautiful and pure and I want to tell her so much. I want to tell her how sorry I am for hurting her, for treating her so mean, that I won't hurt her again but then nothing matters now, only Kriszta who is holding me so tight, her tears falling on my face as I feel myself drifting away. I never ever told her how much she means to me but I can't get the words out. *Krisztyna*....I think but it doesn't even reach my throat.

As I bleed out from the knife wound, I desperately need to tell Kriszta what I should have told her all along; that my heart is not so cold after all but it is beating and maybe it could love but with this realisation every pulse is draining the life out of me.

Also by Kiára Árgenta

Infinity

"You will end up killing each other. It will be disastrous. Stop this relationship now with this volatile man and find someone who is normal and nice, Kiára. Find a stable rock of a man who is not a volcano. Listen to my advice, for God's sake."

I should follow this advice as the shrink knows what he is talking about. But damn the rock. I rip up the guidebook and the map and plunge into the forest of thorns for pleasure and pain. Obsessive love and hate know no limits and the spikes of their extremes propel me into eternity.

I want to flat-line but I can't. Not now I have met István, the first king of Hungary.

I want to stop the bright colours and sharp edges that make us Kiára and István. I want to trade in the swirling dizzy vortex of Italian Futurist art for the softness of a Monet. Just for one day I want to live without this bipolar illness which has dragged me into the Heaven and Hell which is my Hungary.

Maybe you waited a thousand years for me as you said, István. Maybe it is all a myth. I only know there is no end for us, no rest and no escape.

There is only infinity.

Also by Kiára Árgenta

Fragments

'She is a true ice princess. Beautiful and delicate, but her heart doesn't seem to be warm. I have visions that it is not even beating, that I have imagined she is real and she is just a figment of my distressed imagination. It is the first unravelling I have experienced. Sure, I fell apart after Kiára's death and I existed in a mist until I met Lilla but this is a splintering feeling. As though I am cracking like a mirror and shards of my personality are starting to fall to the ground.'

Two years after the death of the love of his life, István cannot move on. He is ill with bipolar disorder and is convinced the answer is to find the image of his dead love in someone else. He meets Lilla on a Budapest street; young, fragile and impressionable and he is desperate to possess her. However, Lilla has her own darkness and over time, István's jealousy, his anger, and his violent obsession turn her into someone who carelessly smashes his heart into fragments.

www.ingramcontent.com/pod-product-compliance
Lightning Source LLC
Chambersburg PA
CBHW050734180626
46814CB00002B/748

* 9 7 8 1 9 0 4 9 5 8 6 5 9 *